COPPER SUN

SHARON M. DRAPER

COPPER SUN

ATHENEUM BOOKS FOR YOUNG READERS

NEW YORK · LONDON · TORONTO · SYDNEY

Atheneum Books for Young Readers • An imprint of Simon & Schuster Children's Publishing Division • 1230 Avenue of the Americas, New York, New York 10020 • This book is a work of fiction. Any references to historical events, real people, or real locales are used fictitiously. Other names, characters, places, and incidents are products of the author's imagination, and any resemblance to actual events or locales or persons, living or dead, is entirely coincidental. • Copyright © 2006 by Sharon M. Draper • Excerpt of the poem "Heritage" by Countee Cullen on page vii used by permission. • All rights reserved, including the right of reproduction in whole or in part in any form. • Book design by Sonia Chaghatzbanian • The text for this book is set in Life. • Manufactured in the United States of America • • 10 9 8 7 6 5 • Library of Congress Cataloging-in-Publication Data • Draper, Sharon M. (Sharon Mills) • Copper sun / Sharon M. Draper.—1st ed. • p. cm. • Summary: Two fifteen-year-old girls—one a slave and the other an indentured servant—escape their Carolina plantation and try to make their way to Fort Mose, Florida, a Spanish colony that gives sanctuary to slaves. • ISBN-13: 978-0-689-82181-3 • ISBN-10: 0-689-82181-6 • [1. Slavery—Fiction. 2. Indentured servants—Fiction. 3. South Carolina—History—Colonial period, ca. 1600–1775—Fiction. 4. Florida—History—Spanish colony, 1565–1763—Fiction. 5. African Americans—History—18th century—Fiction.] I. Title. • PZ7.D78325Cop 2006 • [Fic]—dc22 • 2005005540

AUTHOR'S NOTE

I am the granddaughter of a slave.

My grandfather—not my great-great-grandfather or some long-distant relative—was born a slave in the year 1860 on a farm in North Carolina. He did not become free until the end of the Civil War, when he was five years old.

Hugh Mills lived a very long life, married four times, and fathered twenty-one children. The last child to be born was my father. Hugh was sixty-four years old when my father was born in 1924.

I dedicate this book to him, and to my grandmother Estelle, who, even though she was not allowed to finish school, kept a written journal of her life. It is one of my greatest treasures. One day I hope to write her story.

I also dedicate this to all those who came before me—the untold multitudes who were taken as slaves and brought to this country, the millions who died during that process, as well as those who lived, suffered, and endured.

Amari carries their spirit. She carries mine as well.

HERITAGE

BY COUNTEE CULLEN

What is Africa to me:

Copper sun or scarlet sea,

Jungle star or jungle track,

Strong bronzed men, or regal black

Women from whose loins I sprang

When the birds of Eden sang?

One three centuries removed

From the scenes his fathers loved,

Spicy grove, cinnamon tree,

What is Africa to me?

COPPER SUN

IN SPITE OF THE HEAT, AMARI TREMBLED.
The buyers of slaves had arrived. She and the other women were stripped naked. Amari bit her lip, determined not to cry. But she couldn't stop herself from screaming out as her arms were wrenched behind her back and tied. A searing pain shot up through her shoulders. A white man clamped shackles on her ankles, rubbing his hands up her legs as he did. Amari tensed and tried to jerk away, but the chains were too tight. She could not hold back the tears. It was the summer of her fifteenth year, and this day she wanted to die.

Amari shuffled in the dirt as she was led into the yard and up onto a raised wooden table, which she realized gave the people in the yard a perfect view of the women who were to be sold. She looked at the faces in the sea of pink-skinned people who stood around pointing at the captives and jabbering in their language as each of the slaves was described. She looked for pity or even understanding but found nothing except cool stares. They looked at her as if she were a cow for sale. She saw a few white women fanning themselves and whispering in the ears of well-dressed men—their husbands, she supposed. Most of the people in the crowd were men; however, she did see a poorly dressed white girl about her own age standing near a wagon. The girl had a sullen look on her face, and she seemed to be the only person not interested in what was going on at the slave sale.

Amari looked up at a seabird flying above and remembered her little brother. I wish he could have flown that night, *Amari thought sadly.* I wish I could have flown away as well.

PART ONE

AMARI

I. AMARI AND BESA

"WHAT ARE YOU DOING UP THERE, KWASI?"
Amari asked her eight-year-old brother with a laugh. He had his
legs wrapped around the trunk of the top of a coconut tree.

"For once I want to look a giraffe in the eye!" he shouted. "I
wish to ask her what she has seen in her travels."

"What kind of warrior speaks to giraffes?" Amari teased. She
loved listening to her brother's tales—everything was an adventure
to him.

"A wise one," he replied mysteriously, "one who can see who is
coming down the path to our village."

"Well, you look like a little monkey. Since you're up there, grab
a coconut for Mother, but come down before you hurt yourself."

Kwasi scrambled down and tossed the coconut at his sister.
"You should thank me, Amari, for my treetop adventure!" He
grinned mischievously.

"Why?" she asked.

"I saw Besa walking through the forest, heading this way! I
have seen how you tremble like a dove when he is near."

"You are the one who will be trembling if you do not get that
coconut to Mother right away! And take her a few papayas and a

pineapple as well. It will please her, and we shall have a delicious treat tonight." Amari could still smell the sweetness of the pineapple her mother had cut from its rough skin and sliced for the breakfast meal that morning.

Kwasi snatched back the coconut and ran off then, laughing and making kissing noises as he chanted, "Besa my love, Besa my love, Besa my love!" Amari pretended to chase him, but as soon as he was out of sight, she reached down into the small stream that flowed near Kwasi's tree and splashed water on her face.

Her village, Ziavi, lay just beyond the red dirt path down which Kwasi had disappeared. She headed there, walking leisurely, with just the slightest awareness of a certain new roundness to her hips and smoothness to her gait as she waited for Besa to catch up with her.

Amari loved the rusty brown dirt of Ziavi. The path, hard-packed from thousands of bare feet that had trod on it for decades, was flanked on both sides by fat, fruit-laden mango trees, the sweet smell of which always seemed to welcome her home. Ahead she could see the thatched roofs of the homes of her people, smoky cooking fires, and a chicken or two, scratching in the dirt.

She chuckled as she watched Tirza, a young woman about her own age, chasing one of her family's goats once again. That goat hated to be milked and always found a way to run off right at milking time. Tirza's mother had threatened several times to make stew of the hardheaded animal. Tirza waved at Amari, then dove after the goat, who had galloped into the undergrowth. Several of the old women, sitting in front of their huts soaking up sunshine, cackled with amusement.

To the left and apart from the other shelters in the village stood the home of the chief elder. It was larger than most, made of sturdy wood and bamboo, with thick thatch made from palm leaves making up the roof. The chief elder's two wives chattered cheerfully together as they pounded cassava fufu for his evening meal. Amari called out to them as she passed and bowed with respect.

She knew that she and her mother would soon be preparing the fufu for their own meal. She looked forward to the task—they would take turns pounding the vegetable into a wooden bowl with a stick almost as tall as Amari. Most of the time they got into such a good rhythm that her mother started tapping her feet and doing little dance steps as they worked. That always made Amari laugh.

Although Amari knew Besa was approaching, she pretended not to see him until he touched her shoulder. She turned quickly and, acting surprised, called out his name. "Besa!" Just seeing his face made her grin. He was much taller than she was, and she had to stand on tiptoe to look into his face. He had an odd little birthmark on his cheek—right at the place where his face dimpled into a smile. She thought it looked a little like a pineapple, but it disappeared as he smiled widely at the sight of her. He took her small brown hands into his large ones, and she felt as delicate as one of the little birds that Kwasi liked to catch and release.

"My lovely Amari," he greeted her. "How goes your day?" His deep voice made her tremble.

"Better, now that you are here," she replied. Amari and Besa had been formally betrothed to each other last year. They would be allowed to marry in another year. For now they simply enjoyed the mystery and pleasure of stolen moments such as this.

"I cannot stay and talk with you right now," Besa told her. "I have seen strangers in the forest, and I must tell the council of elders right away."

Amari looked intently at his face and realized he was worried. "What tribe are they from?" she asked with concern.

"I do not think the Creator made a tribe such as these creatures. They have skin the color of goat's milk." Besa frowned and ran to find the chief.

As she watched Besa rush off, an uncomfortable feeling filled Amari. The sunny pleasantness of the afternoon had suddenly turned dark. She hurried home to tell her family what she had learned. Her mother and Esi, a recently married friend, sat on the ground, spinning cotton threads for yarn. Their fingers flew as they chatted together, the pale fibers stretching and uncurling into threads for what would become kente cloth. Amari loved her tribe's design of animal figures and bold shapes. Tomorrow the women would dye the yarn, and when it was ready, her father, a master weaver, would create the strips of treasured fabric on his loom. Amari never tired of watching the magical rhythm of movement and color. Amari's mother looked up at her daughter warmly.

"You should be helping us make this yarn, my daughter," her mother chided gently.

"I'm sorry, Mother, it's just that I'd so much rather weave like father. Spinning makes my fingertips hurt." Amari had often imagined new patterns for the cloth, and longed to join the men at the long looms, but girls were forbidden to do so.

Her mother looked aghast. "Be content with woman's work, child. It is enough."

"I will help you with the dyes tomorrow," Amari promised halfheartedly. She avoided her mother's look of mild disapproval. "Besides, I was helping Kwasi gather fruit," Amari said, changing the subject.

Kwasi, sitting in the dirt trying to catch a grasshopper, looked up and said with a smirk, "I think she was more interested in making love-dove faces with Besa than making yarn with you!" When Amari reached out to grab him, he darted out of her reach, giggling.

"Your sister, even though she avoids the work, is a skilled spinner and will be a skilled wife. She needs practice in learning both, my son," their mother said with a smile. "Now disappear into the dust for a moment!" Kwasi ran off then, laughing as he chased the grasshopper, his bare feet barely skimming the dusty ground.

Amari knew her mother could tell by just the tilt of her smile or a fraction of a frown how she was feeling. "And how goes it with young Besa?" her mother asked quietly.

"Besa said that a band of unusual-looking strangers are coming this way, Mother," Amari informed her. "He seemed uneasy and went to tell the village elders."

"We must welcome our guests, then, Amari. We would never judge people simply by how they looked—that would be uncivilized," her mother told her. "Let us prepare for a celebration." Esi picked up her basket of cotton and, with a quick wave, headed home to make her own preparations.

Amari knew her mother was right and began to help her make

plans for the arrival of the guests. They pounded fufu, made garden egg stew from eggplant and dried fish, and gathered more bananas, mangoes, and papayas.

"Will we have a dance and celebration for the guests, Mother?" she asked hopefully. "And Father's storytelling?"

"Your father and the rest of the elders will decide, but I'm sure the visit of such strangers will be cause for much festivity." Amari smiled with anticipation, for her mother was known as one of the most talented dancers in the Ewe tribe. Her mother continued, "Your father loves to have tales to tell and new stories to gather—this night will provide both."

Amari and her mother scurried around their small dwelling, rolling up the sleeping mats and sweeping the dirt floor with a broom made of branches. Throughout the village, the pungent smells of goat stew and peanut soup, along with waves of papaya and honeysuckle that wafted through the air, made Amari feel hungry as well as excited. The air was fragrant with hope and possibility.

2. STRANGERS AND DEATH

THE STRANGERS WHOM BESA HAD SPOKEN OF arrived about an hour later. Everyone in the village came out of their houses to see the astonishing sight—pale, unhealthy-looking men who carried large bundles and unusual-looking sticks as they marched into the center of the village. In spite of the welcoming greetings and looks of excitement on the faces of the villagers, the strangers did not smile. They smelled of danger, Amari thought as one of them looked at her. He had eyes the color of the sky. She shuddered.

However, the unusual-looking men were accompanied by warriors from the Ashanti tribe, men of her own land, men her people had known and traded with, so even if the village elders were concerned, it would be unacceptable not to show hospitality. Surely the Ashanti would explain. But good manners came first.

Any occasion for visitors was a cause for excitement, so after the initial amazement and curiosity at the strange men, the village bubbled with anticipation as preparations were made for a formal welcoming ceremony. Amari stayed in the shadows, watching it all, uneasy, but not sure why.

Their chief, or *Awoamefia,* who could be spoken to only

through a member of the council of elders, invited the guests to sit, and they were formally welcomed with wine and prayers. The chief and the council of elders, made up of both men and women, were always chosen for their wisdom and made all the important decisions. Amari was proud that her father, Komla, was one of the elders. He was also the village storyteller, and she loved to watch the expressions on his face as he acted out the stories she had heard since childhood.

"We welcome you," the chief began. "Let your yes be yes and your no be no. May you be protected from evil, and may you live to a ripe old age. If you come in peace, we receive you in peace. Heroism is the dignity of our ancestors, and, in their name, we welcome you." He passed the wine, made from palm tree leaves, to Amari's father, then to the other elders, and finally to the strangers.

The men with skin like the milk of goats and their Ashanti companions drank the palm wine from hand-carved gourds that had been decorated with ceremonial tribal designs. The newcomers then offered gifts to the chief: small ropes of sparkling beads unlike anything Amari had ever seen, casks of wine, and lengths of fine cloth—so shiny and smooth that Amari marveled. She knew no human could have woven it.

No real explanations for their presence had been given yet, but with the exchange of gifts, the feeling of unease began to lessen and everyone knew that the dancing and drumming would soon begin. Ceremony was important. Business matters always followed proper celebration. It was not yet the time for questions. First came the stories, Amari reminded herself, starting to feel excited.

As chief storyteller, Amari's father was highly respected. Komla knew every story, every proverb, every bit of tribal history ever told or sung or drummed by her people. He spoke at each birth, funeral, and wedding, as well as at unexpected special occasions like this. The villagers crowded around him in anticipation, although even the youngest child knew by heart every story he would tell. The strangers sat politely and waited.

"Let me tell you of the wickedness of Chief Agokoli," her father began. "He was a wicked, wicked man."

"Wicked," the people responded with enthusiasm.

"He would give the Ewe people impossible jobs—like weaving baskets out of sand."

"Impossible!" the villagers responded almost in unison.

"The Ewe people finally found a means to escape from the wicked ruler," Komla recounted. "The people crept out through a hole in the wall and fooled the soldiers of Chief Agokoli. And how did they do that?" he asked the crowd, who, of course, knew the question was coming, as well as the answer.

"They walked backward in the dirt!" the people responded enthusiastically.

"And so they did," Komla said, ending his tale with a tapping on his drum. "They walked backward on the dirt path so their footprints looked like the prints of someone arriving into the village, not departing!" He looked over at Amari as he finished the tale with a wink he saved for her alone.

Everyone in the small community, including Amari, laughed and clapped their hands at the familiar story. Amari loved her father's stories, and the sound of his deep, gravelly voice had always made her feel safe, whether he was whispering silly noises in her ear, speaking formally in a meeting of the elders, or chatting with affection with her mother.

To the family's great amusement, Komla would sometimes sing to them in their small hut after the evening meal. "You sound like a monkey in pain," Amari's mother would tell her husband fondly. But when he was telling stories, his voice was magical; Amari could listen to him all night.

The feeling of tension faded. The drumming would come next, and, after the storytelling, this was Amari's favorite part of her village's celebrations.

Amari looked around for Besa. He was the assistant to the village master arts man, the one responsible for the creation of all the dances and drum rhythms. She knew Besa would be anxious to show off his skill on the drum he had carved and painted himself. Amari was proud of how devoted Besa was to learning the rhythms. He'd told her once, "You know, Amari, the drums are not just noise—they are language; they are the pattern of the rhythm of our lives."

He had no need to look at his hands to produce the drum sounds that lived within him. She loved to watch Besa stare into space, smiling as he drummed, lost in the rhythms he created.

As soon as the master drummers started playing, everyone in her village felt the call. The younger boys, whose fingers itched to show their skills, grabbed their own small drums and joined the beat. Villagers began to get up and move to the rhythms. Besa played with the confidence and skill he always did. Amari's eyes were on only him; her heart beat faster as Besa's fingers caressed the sounds out of his skin-covered drum.

Drumbeats echoed in the approaching darkness. The fire in the center of the assembly area glowed on the faces of the dancers, mostly younger children and women at first, but soon nearly everyone in the village joined in, even the old ones whose toothless grins spoke their happiness. All spoke to the spirits with their joyous movements. Their bodies swayed, their hands clapped, their feet stomped in a glorious frenzy, all to the rhythm of the drums.

> *Ba ba   la ba do   ga we do*
> *the words are sounds are words from deep within*
> *from a place that was lost now found*
> *sobo hee   we do so ma   da ma da so so*
> *sound is self is you is we   sound is past is now is so*
> *sobo hee   we do so ma   da ma da so so*
> *from remembered past to forgotten tomorrow*
> *drum talk throbs breathes life   speaks song   sings words*
> *Ba ba   la ba do   ga we do*
> *warriors pulse   maidens sway   elders children rejoice*
> *thrum to the heartbeat thrum to the heartbeat*
> *ba ba la ba   ba ba la ba   ga we do*

Kwasi, as round and brown as a Kola nut, danced with the rest of the children, gleefully spinning in the dust. Amari watched him and remembered how he once had captured a small bird and copied its movements, flapping his arms like wings, telling her, with much laughter, that he intended to learn how to fly. And as Kwasi stomped and glided through the dust that evening, it seemed to Amari that he really *was* flying.

He ran over to Amari then, breathing hard with excitement. "Come," he said, grasping her arm and trying to pull her into the dancing. "Why do you hide in the shadows? Come dance for the strangers!"

She pushed Kwasi away gently, reminding him she was no longer a child. She was to be married soon, and she preferred peeking at Besa, who stood behind his waist-high drum on the other side of the fire, watching her as well.

The drumbeats rippled in the darkness, the dancers swayed and stomped on the hard-packed earth, and Amari's people clapped and laughed as the firelight glimmered in the night.

The first explosion came from the end of one of the unusual weapon sticks the strangers carried. Louder than any beat of even the largest drum, it was followed by a cry of horror. The chief had fallen off his seat, a huge red bleeding hole in the center of his chest. More explosions followed in rapid succession, then everyone was screaming. Confusion and dust swirled throughout the village. Amari watched, aghast, as a mother with her baby wrapped on her back tried to flee, but both mother and child were clubbed down into the dirt by one of the Ashanti warriors. An Ashanti! How could this be? Villagers ran blindly into the fire, trying to escape and screaming for mercy, only to be felled by the terrible fire weapons of the strangely pale men.

Amari knew she should run; she knew she should try to escape into the forest, but her feet would not move. She could only stare in horror. She gasped as she watched an Ashanti grab her mother and try to put thick iron cuffs on her mother's wrists. She turned her head and followed, in slow motion it seemed, her father's bellows of rage as he leaped toward her mother to rescue her. But before he even reached her, one of the milk-faced men thrust a knife into his stomach, and Komla fell silently to the earth. Amari's mother screamed in anguish and bit her captor's hand. Enraged, he hurled her to the ground. Amari watched, unable to breathe or move, as her mother's head smashed upon a rock. Amari wanted to scream, *Mother, get up, oh, please, get up,* but she was unable to say a word. Her mother did not move. Amari needed her parents to come get her, to tell her not to be afraid, to run with her into the underbrush for safety. But they just lay there, their blood beginning to stain the dust. Amari doubled over in agony. Her parents were dead.

She looked frantically for Besa and Kwasi, but all was smoke and screams and death. Finally, she saw Kwasi running toward her, screaming, "Run, Amari, run!" Her feet loosened then as he reached her. She grabbed his hand, and they ran wildly out of the village into what they hoped was the safety of the darkness. Sharp branches cut Amari's face as she plunged through a thick tangle of trees. The smell of sharp, acrid smoke, not of gentle hearth fires, but of the flames of destruction, followed them. Birds and monkeys above them cried out in alarm, but their noise could not cover the screams of the slaughter of her people.

Suddenly, Amari heard fast-moving, thudding footsteps behind them and the whirr of a spear. Kwasi held her hand tighter and they ran even faster, Amari trying in vain to be as invisible and swift as the wind. *Fly, my baby brother,* she thought desperately. *Fly away!* One moment they were leaping over a fallen log, and the next moment she heard Kwasi moan softly, then his hand slipped slowly from hers. He slumped to the ground, a look of soft surprise on his small face. A spear had sliced though his whole little body. Amari sank down beside him and held him to her. He died in her arms.

She lay there in the darkness, cuddling his small, lifeless body, unable to weep, unable to run any longer. She hardly cared when she was grabbed by one of the strangers. Her arms were wrenched behind her, and iron shackles with heavy, rusty chains between them were snapped onto her wrists, holding them there. Amari was marched back to where the burning village had once stood so happily, grabbed by her hair, and shoved into a pile of other survivors from the village.

No one spoke. No one wept. They were defeated.

3. SORROW AND SHACKLES

WHEN THE SUN ROSE THE NEXT MORNING, Amari looked with horror at what was once her tribe's village. All of the homes had been burned, their roofs of thatch and walls of reeds consumed by the fire. The charred and bloodied bodies of relatives remained where they had fallen, with no one to perform proper rites for burials, no one to say the prayers for the dead. Amari knew that the pale strangers probably did not know their customs, could not understand the seriousness of the proper burial procedures, but the Ashanti were people of her own land, supposedly brothers in spirit with Amari's people. *How could they do this and face their own future?* she wondered in horrible confusion. It was just one of many questions for which she had no answer. *Where did these strangers come from? Why do they want to hurt us? How can I continue to live without my family?* It took all of her strength not to look at the bodies of her parents. Amari's heart hurt in a way she could never have imagined.

Twenty-four of the villagers had survived the slaughter. She glanced around the group and realized that most of them were around her age—young and fairly healthy. None of the elders had been spared, none of the children. Esi and her new husband, Makafui, huddled together, even though they had been shackled apart. Amari knew that Esi was carrying her first child, for she had announced it with joy just two days before. Amari also had seen that the parents of both Makafui and Esi were included among the dead. Kwadzo, a young man known in the village as a fierce hunter, pulled angrily at his shackles, his wrists already bleeding as he fought their restraint. A huge gash on his head had stopped bleeding but was open and untreated. He needed the medicine woman to wrap it in healing leaves, but no one seemed concerned about his injury. All of the young male captives had sustained some type of injury.

Finally, at the far end of the huddled circle of captives, Amari spotted Besa. He looked at her with glazed, saddened eyes. In the distance, where such a short time ago he had played with such power and joy, she spotted his beloved drum, crushed and in splinters in the dirt. Amari wished she could smile at Besa to give him hope, but she had no hope to offer. He looked away.

Suddenly, one of the pale-faced men with the death sticks came over to them, shouting in a language she did not understand. He made it clear, however, that they were to get up from the ground immediately. Most of their captors, both black and white, carried both whips and fire sticks. Amari looked around in fear and tried to ask what was happening, but all she received in response was a vicious slice of a whip across her arms and neck. She cried out as she arched her back in pain, but she hurried to her feet and asked no more questions. She glanced at Besa. His face was distorted with anger.

One of the pale men then brought out objects that she would

not have used even on animals. They were similar to the iron bands on her wrists, except these fit around their necks! A length of iron chain connected each neck band, so each was linked to the next in a single file of chains and captivity.

As the iron band was placed around her neck, Amari felt as if she would choke. It was cold and heavy and cut into her shoulders. The chain was then pulled sharply as the next person in line was shackled behind her. Amari could not turn and see who it was. She could see only the back of the person in front of her. It was Tirza, the young woman who just hours before had been chasing that runaway goat. Tirza could not stop shaking with fright.

The pale-faced men fastened similar irons on their ankles, with a short length of chain between them, and a longer chain linking each person in the coffle together, thus making it impossible for them to run away or even walk very fast. Fastened together in groups of six, the wrists, ankles, and necks of each captive were painfully connected to the person on either side. Once the villagers were all linked, a white face pulled the first person with a rope, and those linked to him lurched forward as well. Amari stumbled, but the neck iron stopped her fall. She choked and tried to grab her throat, but her arms were shackled as well. Gasping, she fell into step with the others, who, with heads bowed, shuffled together toward they knew not what.

Besa, Amari noticed, was in the front of his coffle of captives. He would not look at her, glancing away whenever she tried to catch his eye. She realized he must be feeling terrible shame—shame that he could not rescue himself, or Amari, or change any of what was happening to them.

If one in their group stumbled, all of them stumbled or sometimes even fell, choking as the chains pulled them down together. Beaten with whips if they fell, beaten if they failed to keep the pace, they headed slowly away from everything they had once known. The bright red pain across Amari's back and on her wrists and ankles made her whole body tremble. She felt as if she might pass out. The heat of the sun showed no mercy, and she couldn't even wipe away the sweat that burned her eyes as it ran down her face.

Her tongue felt thick—she was so thirsty, and she couldn't remember the last time she had eaten. As she walked, she tried but couldn't comprehend the incredible cruelty of the men who had done this. Nothing made any sense. Her stomach knotted up every time she thought of her last glimpse of her mother and father—dead, unburied, and covered with flies. And little Kwasi—he was just a small boy who had never even hurt a grasshopper. How could he be dead? Amari felt dizzy, but she dared not stop or stumble.

The first path they traveled was the long road that led from their village to the big river several miles away. It seemed as if even the trees bowed their heads as they passed. The birds, normally full of chatter, were silent as the group marched past them for the last time.

Day after day the captives walked, saying very little to one another or to their captors. One afternoon Amari heard Kwadzo try to speak to one of the Ashanti who guarded them.

"Why do you do this, my brother?" he whispered when out of earshot of the white soldiers.

"Our tribes have been at war before," the Ashanti responded, a defensiveness in his guarded tone. "This time, however, I shall be greatly rewarded." He strode ahead then and said no more. Amari wondered what he meant.

The wound on Kwadzo's head grew swollen and purple, and Amari could tell he was in pain, but he continued on, as they all did, one foot after the other, mile after mile. His face was one of anger and hatred. Besa's face, when she got a chance to glimpse it, had become a mask.

The captives were never unshackled. Each set of six ate together, slept together, and had to urinate and defecate together. They were given just a little food each morning and very little water. Each group was forced into a rhythm, keeping a pace that was difficult for the slowest and weakest of them as they marched. In Amari's group it was Tirza who seemed to have given up. She walked slowly and stumbled often. Her back was soon a patchwork of welts from being whipped when she could not keep up with the rest. One night she whispered, "I cannot live like this, Amari. My parents, my sisters—all whom I love—are dead. I would rather die than be enslaved like this."

"Tirza, stop talking like that!" Amari whispered back. "We must live!"

"Why?" she asked dully.

"Because as long as we have life, we have hope!" Amari said fervently.

"Hope of what?"

"Escape, perhaps."

"You are a dreamer, Amari," Tirza told her quietly. "I have no dreams left."

And the next morning Tirza was dead. She had simply ceased

breathing during the night. The leader of their captors looked at her lifeless body and cursed. He unshackled her, tossed her body to the side of the road, and spat upon it. The rest of them were told to get up and move on. Amari was surprised and saddened to realize that the travel in their chained coffle, now five instead of six, was lighter and easier without Tirza. Her heart, however, seemed to beat more slowly and heavily. None of them wept for Tirza or even looked her way as they passed.

4. DEATH MARCH TO CAPE COAST 〰️〰️〰️〰️

AMARI LOST COUNT OF THE DAYS THEY WALKED.
Her neck, bruised and scarred from the iron brace around it,
could barely hold her head up any longer. Her wrists and ankles
were raw where the skin had been worn away, and insects
swarmed around the oozing wounds. Her bare feet left bloody
footprints upon the path—sliced by every stone and sharp stick
she stumbled over. At first these difficulties bothered her. But
gradually, she simply felt numb.

Kwadzo died one morning, probably from his untreated
wound, Amari thought, or maybe from his untreated sorrow, but
she could not mourn his loss. She actually envied him. Seven
others died during their long journey. Esi, the young wife of
Makafui, first lost her baby, then her own life. Amari was sure
she bled to death. Unable to control his grief, Makafui grabbed
one of the leaders of the march and tried to strangle him with his
wrist chains. How he managed to get his hands in front of him,
Amari did not know, but before Makafui had a chance to succeed
in killing the man, one of the others calmly picked up his fire
stick and shot him. He was left on the side of the road for the
hyenas, as the others had been.

Amari had no idea where they were being taken or why. They just marched, prisoners in a land so full of beauty and harmony that Amari could not bear to watch the golden sun rising in the east or the freely running giraffes and elephants in the distance.

Occasionally, other coffles of slaves would join their group. They looked with dead eyes at Amari and her sad little procession. No one spoke. Eventually, all of the prisoners were herded together, moving slowly down a path that was becoming increasingly wider and more well traveled. The dirt was packed hard by the feet of those who had passed that way before. Amari wondered if they, too, had been coffled and shackled.

Finally one day they arrived in a city—so much larger than what Amari had ever known that she stared in wonder at the huge buildings made of stone. The variety of noises—screeching monkeys in cages and vendors loudly proclaiming their goods from the side of the road—made her head throb. She marveled at the people who lived there—people with dark and pale and even honey-colored skins. Black men and women who walked freely and laughed loudly, speaking in languages she did not know. White men walking arm in arm with black men, with no chains on either of them. Amari was amazed and understood none of it. Some of the people looked at the group of enslaved captives with pity as they were marched through the center of town, but no one made any move to help them. In fact, Amari noticed that most turned away as if the miserable group were invisible.

The air smelled salty and felt wet upon her skin. The little river in Amari's village had smelled of mud and of the animals that used it as a gathering place to drink the water. But here she could smell a larger body of water—something huge and foreign and frightening.

Although Amari could not understand the language of the white men, she soon began to recognize words they repeated often, such as "slave" and "price." Once they entered the city, she kept hearing them say, "Cape Coast, Cape Coast," with great excitement. *What is this place?* she thought to herself. *Why are we here? And how will we ever find our way back home?* Then she gasped. There *was* no more home. She had no more family. And, for the first time, she began to weep.

Amari and the rest of the captives were guided to a huge white building made of bricks and stone, larger than any Amari had ever seen or even imagined. The leader of the pale warriors barked orders to someone in a colorful uniform at a gate. Huge doors opened and they were led inside. The bright sunlight was suddenly gone, and she had to adjust her eyes to the gloom inside the structure. It smelled of blood and death. She could hear terrifying wails that seemed to be coming from the walls of the place. Amari was filled with dread.

The men were then separated from the women, and Amari's neck irons and leg irons were finally removed. She rubbed her wrists and couldn't help but breathe with relief. Nothing could be worse than what they'd already gone through, she thought.

She was wrong. A huge stone door with iron bars slid open, and Amari was shoved inside a room with the rest of the women who had survived their journey. She thought she was blinded at first because the darkness was so total and sudden. The smell engulfed her next—the odor of sweat and fear, of body wastes and hopelessness. As her eyes slowly adjusted, she could see women—dozens of them—lying on the floor, huddled against the walls, curled into balls. Some of them looked up when the newcomers were tossed into the cell, but most did not bother to acknowledge their presence. Amari trembled with fear and disgust, afraid she would become like they were, afraid she already was.

Amari found an unoccupied place by the wall and sat down on the floor, which was wet and slimy. The room had no window, just a large hole near the ceiling for a little bit of air to circulate. No one spoke to her. Those who were talking among themselves spoke in dialects she could not understand. Only a few could she decipher. Amari surmised that women from many different tribes and countries were imprisoned here—Ibo, Ga, and Mandinka. She was amazed at the thoroughness of their captors, how they had managed to capture so many of them. Had they murdered the families and destroyed the villages of everyone here as well? The thought of so many dead seemed to crush her. She covered her head with her arms and barely stifled a scream. No one listened.

Amari gradually grew accustomed to the dim light and looked around the room. She spotted a woman in a corner who was rocking a child who was not there. She sang to it and caressed it gently, but her arms were empty. The woman's sorrow was raw and palpable, like spoiled meat.

Amari's stomach growled. She could not remember the last time she had eaten, so when the guards tossed some chunks of bread through the opening, she was grateful. But by the time she got up to get some of the food off the floor, the previously quiet women had already rushed past her and savagely fought over every scrap of bread. She ended up with nothing. Amari dropped to the cold wet floor, bowed her head, and wept.

A large woman came and sat down next to her and offered her a small piece of her own portion. Amari took it gratefully.

"Crying won't help, child," she told her. "This place is slimy with tears."

Amari was surprised to hear the woman speak in her own Ewe language. She wiped her eyes and said in barely a whisper, "I feel like a broken drum—hollow, crushed, unable to make a sound."

"You must learn to make music once more."

Amari was miserable. "I don't understand," she told her.

"In time, you will."

Amari pondered this for a moment while she nibbled at the bread to make it last longer.

"Where is this place?" Amari asked her.

"Cape Coast Castle. It is a prison for our people. We will be held here until they have captured enough of us, then we will be sold and sent into the sea." She breathed deeply.

"Sold? I do not understand."

"You were chosen because you are young and strong. You survived the long journey here. You will fetch a great price."

"From whom? For what?" Amari asked in confusion. "Who

would want to sell me or buy me? I am just a girl who has seen barely fifteen summers. I have no skills."

"There are white men who will buy you to work for them by day and amuse them by night."

Amari looked up, her eyes wide with disbelief. "How do you know this?"

"I have been sold before," she replied quietly. "My master, a fat white man from this city, grew tired of me and sold me to buyers who brought me here."

"Have you been here long?" Amari asked.

"Long enough to see one group sold and sent away. We were marched into the courtyard, and white men bargained for us. One by one they were taken through a small door. I could see the white sand and the blue of the sea beyond it, but no more. All I know is they never returned."

"Do you think they were killed?"

"No. They had value. They did not die. At least not physically," she added.

"Why were you not sold?" Amari asked her.

"I caught the attention of the leader of the guards." She paused. "He sends for me to come to him at night."

At first Amari didn't understand, but suddenly she realized what the woman meant. Amari looked at her in horror. "You mean he . . . ?"

"Yes, child. It is terrible. But I am allowed to bathe. I get extra food rations. I do not allow myself to think while I am with him. I hate him. But I will live. My spirit is too strong to die in a place like this."

Amari looked at this woman, at her strong body and kindly face, and began to cry once more, huge racking sobs of despair. The woman took Amari in her arms and let her cry, the only comfort she had known since that horrible night in the village.

5. THE DOOR OF NO RETURN

ONCE A DAY AMARI AND THE OTHER WOMEN were taken from the cell in small groups. Cold water from large wooden buckets was tossed upon them. Their clothes, what little that remained, were torn and barely covered their bodies. The soldiers who guarded them liked to rip the tops of the women's garments so their breasts were exposed. Amari learned to swallow her shame.

The woman who had befriended her was called Afi. She made sure Amari had food each day and protected her from some of the other women who had grown fierce and violent from their captivity. She showed Amari how to walk with a limp and look with a vacant, stupid stare to make sure the soldiers would pass her by when they looked for women to come to their rooms. She also showed Amari how to exercise inside the cell, to stay strong and ready for whatever may come next. At night she crooned soft songs similar to the ones Amari's mother had once sang to her as a child. Afi told Amari that her husband and a daughter about Amari's age had died two years before. Amari figured that Afi needed her as much as she needed Afi.

"Do you think the ancestors can speak to us in this place?" Amari asked Afi one hot night. The air was thick with the stench of excrement.

"I don't know, child," she replied, trying to cool Amari by fanning her with her hand. "I know they see us, however. And they weep for us. I can feel it."

"We need more than weeping, Afi," Amari said quietly. "We need an army of warriors to come and unfasten the locks, kill our captors, return us to our homes, and bring our families and friends back to us, alive and smiling."

"You know that is not to be, my child," Afi replied gently. "We are caught in a place where there is no hope, no escape from the misery of the present or the memories of the past." They were silent then, for there was nothing more to say.

One day, without warning, Amari and the rest of the women were brought into the center of the prison by the white soldiers, who chained their hands behind them and shackled their feet as well. Then strange white men, one of them so tall and thin that he seemed to sway when he walked, looked over each of the women as if inspecting goats for slaughter.

The thin man came up to Amari and lifted her upper lip, pinching the flesh with his long, bony fingers. He smelled unwashed. Amari whipped her head away from him, her eyes dark with anger. Glaring at her, he slapped her face so hard, she almost fell to the ground. Then he yanked her back up, grabbed her chin, and held it tightly while he pulled at her lip again.

"Open your mouth!" Afi hissed at her.

Terrified, Amari did so. The tall man took his time inspecting the inside of her mouth. He ran his fingers along her teeth and gums, mumbling to himself as he did so. When he was satisfied with his inspection of her, he moved on to the next woman.

Amari stood close to Afi, shivering with fear and disgust as the rough hands of each of the white men examined and prodded her arms, thighs, calves, and breasts.

The men yelled and spoke very fast in their strange language. Amari heard the word "price" many times. Finally, they seemed to come to a settlement. Cowrie shells were counted and passed from the trader with the willowy body to the men who had captured them. Amari saw cloth also being exchanged and jewelry and gold. They had very little need for gold in her village, but she knew what it was. She knew it held the value of her life.

One by one the women were taken through the door that Afi had spoken of earlier. Some screamed; some fought back and had to be pushed. The door was narrow and very low to the ground. No one could stand upright and pass through it; the only way to go through that passageway was to crawl.

A soldier grabbed Amari roughly and pushed her toward that door. He forced her to the ground and then kicked her in the direction of the passageway. She had no choice but to proceed. It was difficult with the chains on, but she managed to crawl, painfully and slowly. The walls were smooth and worn, as if many bodies had passed through that narrow, low tunnel.

At the end of the passage a pair of hands pulled her up, and she had to close her eyes to the brightness of the sun. When she could finally open them, she saw that beautiful white sand lay in front of her. The salty smell that she had grown accustomed to was now overwhelming. As her eyes adjusted to the light, Amari cast her eyes for the first time upon the ocean. Travelers had occasionally come to her village, so she had heard tales of the blueness and vastness of the ocean. But nothing could have prepared her for water so blue, so beautiful, so never ending.

After so many days of the darkness of her cell, the glory of that view was powerful—and very, very frightening. Would she be thrown into the sea? And what was that strange house in the distance that seemed to rest on the surface of the water? It could not be a boat—boats were small and held one or two people. Boats were used for fishing or visiting family members downriver. This was huge, with white fabric dancing from it. That could not be a boat, Amari decided. It must be a place of the dead.

Before she had a chance to absorb it all, a man dragged her to what looked like a goat pen. A fire burned brightly in the center of it, even though the day was very warm, and the man was steering her toward it, Amari realized with fear. *Am I going to be cooked and eaten now? Why couldn't I have died with my family?* she thought wildly. Panicked, she tried to pull away from the man, but his grip only tightened.

A black man who spoke the language of the white men pushed her roughly down into the sand and held her firmly so she could not move. Amari could see only the feet of the second man, but he moved toward the fire, leaned down to pick something up, then walked purposefully toward her.

Intense, fiery pain pierced the sweaty softness of the skin above her left shoulder. Amari could hear her flesh sizzle, and she nearly fainted as she realized she was being branded. Like a wounded animal, Amari screamed and screamed. *Why?* was the only thought in her head. Someone then pulled her away from the fire, smeared a horrible-smelling salve on her wound, and yanked her over to another holding pen full of prisoners like her, all dazed from the pain of the hot branding iron. Many of them sat hunched over, trying to nurse their wounds. A few stared at the pale blue sky, the deep blue of the unbelievable expanse of water, and the death house that tossed on the waves in the distance.

The salve must have been effective, for the intense pain gradually subsided and was replaced by a duller throbbing that would not go away. Amari saw then that Afi had emerged from the prison as well. When she was branded, she did not cry out. Amari could see the pain on her face and the tears roll down her cheeks, but Afi did not utter a sound.

Afi was thrown into the holding pen soon after that, and they hugged each other gently, avoiding the fiery sores on their shoulders. "What happens now?" Amari whispered.

"Child, I've heard stories, but I've never seen the ocean before. I have heard that the water spills over the edge of the world and that only death is found there."

"There has to be something on the other side of the great water," Amari reasoned. "The white soldiers had to come from whatever that place is."

"It must be a place of death, for sure," Afi replied, agreeing with Amari. "For only such a horrible place could create such creatures who could burn a person with a flaming hot iron."

Amari started to remind her that they had been held down by

people of their own land—people who looked just like them. But at that moment several men were shoved into the holding cell. Three of them were some of the very same Ashanti warriors who had helped to capture the people from her village. They looked stunned at their sudden change in status. Another new captive, who looked positively irate, was the black man who had just held Amari down on the sand while she was branded. He held his freshly branded shoulder and called out in the language of the whites, but they ignored him. The last man to be tossed into the pen was Besa.

The men had been kept from the women, housed in a separate section of the prison. Amari had not seen Besa since they had arrived. He was thin and filthy and looked absolutely beautiful to her. She wanted to call out his name, run to him, and hug him, but she found she could say nothing as he was taken to the far corner of the holding pen and chained there.

Besa looked up and gazed directly at Amari for just a moment. His face, once so proud and happy, showed only defeat. She understood.

The pen offered no shelter from the intense heat of the day. No water was offered to them. Men in uniform and men with obvious power and authority strode across the sand all afternoon, clearly preparing for something. *But what?* Amari wondered.

Then several of them climbed into a small boat that rocked and tossed in the waves of the large water, and they rowed out to the floating house in the distance. The boat returned with more men in uniform and a load of heavy chains. Amari knew they were for them.

The sunset that evening was unlike any Amari had ever seen.

The spirit of the copper sun seemed to bleed for them as it glowed bright red against the deepening blue of the great water. It sank slowly, as if saying farewell. The shadows deepened and darkness covered the beach.

As night fell, the leader of the captors ordered small fires to be made on the beach, and Amari soon smelled the welcome odor of food cooking. It had been a long time since they had been given anything to eat, and she was amazed when the holding pen was opened and generous portions of water and food—fresh fruit, boiled cassava, and some kind of fish stew—were distributed to them. Nobody questioned the offering, and the food was consumed greedily and quickly.

Licking her fingers, she asked Afi, "Why do they feed us so well tonight?"

"To prepare us for the journey, I believe."

"What journey?"

Afi hesitated.

"Tell me," Amari urged.

"We will be taken to the boat of death on the horizon, and we will never see this place again." Her voice chilled Amari even more than the brisk wind that blew off the ocean.

"I do not understand."

"We are slaves, Amari. Slaves."

"I know this." Amari knew, of course, what slaves were— some of the wealthier elders in her own village had a few slaves. They had been won in battle or traded in negotiations between villages and tribes. They were usually respected and sometimes even adopted as extended members of a family.

"But this is not like anything we've ever known, is it?" Amari asked her. She braced herself for Afi's answer.

"No, child. Horrors unimagined, I feel, will assault us."

Amari thought back to the night she was captured and the journey to this place. Her mind could not imagine worse. She shivered in the night air, the brand on her shoulder throbbing. She thought of Kwasi, the little bird who would never fly again, but, in a way, she was glad he would not have to endure any of these horrors. Finally, leaning against the pole she was tied to, she managed to fall asleep.

6. fROM SAND TO SHIP

AMARI AWOKE STIFF, SORE, AND VERY COLD the next morning. Small, beach-living insects had feasted on her skin overnight, and she scratched at the red bites that covered her legs and arms. She looked around in alarm, because the dark wall of Cape Coast Castle, which had surrounded her every night since coming to this place, had disappeared. Then she remembered the small door, the bright sand, the blue water, and the fiery burn on her shoulder.

Afi, already awake, looked at her without smiling. "Today is the day, Amari." Amari did not need to ask her for what.

They were all fed generously once again, and more salve was applied to their wounds. The men were then kicked and yelled at, shackled back together, and marched out of the pen. Besa was the last in line. He turned and glanced back at Amari with a look that said, *I would have been a good husband, Amari. I would have loved you more with every sunrise and sunset.* Then he was gone. Amari pulled her shackled hands up to her face. The chains rattled in rhythm to her sobs.

"You knew him?" Afi asked her.

"Yes, he is from my village. We were captured on the same day."

"He is special to you, am I right?"

"Oh, yes!" Amari told her, a small smile breaking through her tears. "We were to be married." Her smiled faded then.

"You must forget him," Afi told her harshly.

"But—," Amari protested.

"He is dead to you now. Just as your parents and your brother and my family are dead—gone to be with the ancestors."

"But why, Afi? Why must I let go of the only link to who I truly am?"

"What you are is a slave," Afi told her, her voice cold and firm. "You have been bought by men who will sell your body and will do with it what they want. You can be beaten and raped and killed, and your young man can do nothing about it."

"You are cruel!" Amari cried, shaking with anger.

"I am honest," she replied sadly.

"So why should I endure this? Why did you not let me just die in there?" Amari cried out.

"Because I see a power in you." Afi lifted her shackled wrist and reached over to touch Amari. "You know, certain people are chosen to survive. I don't know why, but you are one of those who must remember the past and tell those yet unborn. You must live."

"But why?"

"Because your mother would want you to. Because the sun continues to shine. I don't know, but you must." She said nothing else, just sat down and began tracing pictures in the sand with her finger.

Amari had little time to mourn Besa's removal or her own past or future, however. The soldiers came for the women next. They were herded together, then lined up and shackled, two by two. Afi was chained to Amari, to her great relief.

She tried to stay calm, but it was impossible. It was terrifying, not to be able to understand what was happening and not to know what was to come. She saw she wasn't the only one—some of the other women screamed and tried to grab handfuls of sand as they were forced out of the holding pen.

Led across the sand, Amari found it surprisingly hard to walk. Her feet sank with every step. As they got closer to the edge of the beach, Amari noticed that the water never stopped moving, sending huge waves of itself against the sand—first blue, then white, then blue again. Bubbling, churning, even leaping onto the land, it seemed to Amari that the ocean was reaching out to grab and devour her. Many of the women backed away from the surf and were promptly lashed. Amari was frightened, but she knew the water would not kill her. Not today.

She watched as the last of the men were loaded into small rowboats, which rocked wildly on the waves. Some of the men cried out in terror. The boats became smaller as they got closer to the death house in the distance. Then Amari could see them no more.

A set of empty rowboats, much larger than Amari had first thought, awaited the next group of captives. The women were pushed from the soft warmth of the sand to the water-soaked beach, and Amari very quickly found herself standing in water up to her knees. She screamed in spite of herself at the sudden coldness of the water and its constant movement against her legs. It crashed against her as if it were angry and seemed to be trying to pull Amari away from the land. Her feet could not find a safe place—the sand beneath the water kept shifting. The water splashed onto her face, and she discovered with surprise that it was salty—like tears.

Afi, sloshing in the shallows just ahead of Amari, was knocked sideways by a wave and fell, taking Amari with her. They both struggled to raise their heads above the water, but the weight of their leg and neck irons pulled them down. Water seeped into Amari's mouth and nose. She could not even scream.

Their captors cursed and hauled Afi and Amari up, then shoved them into the small rowboat. Afi breathed hard and tried not to show how frightened she was. Amari felt no need to hide her fear. She gripped the side of the boat fiercely and shrieked with every swell of the water, with every spray of water in her face. As the captives were loaded into the boat, it rocked and tilted as if it were about to toss them into the water once more.

And then the boat left the shore. Forty terrified women and girls howled as the boat began to float upon the sea. The soldiers on shore laughed at their fright, and the sailors on board beat them with their whips. Amari's arms and face were lashed and sliced as she huddled with Afi in the bottom of the boat, trying to get away from the sailors' ferocity. *Why do they beat us?* Amari thought wildly. *To silence us? To stop our fear?* Nothing made sense.

The screaming gradually subsided into deep, burning groans, which no salve could soften. Amari lifted her head and looked around. The land was quickly disappearing, the soldiers looking like miniatures of themselves as they dragged another coffle of slaves into another small boat. She could hear the cries of the seabirds above and the rhythmic splash of the oars as the rowers carried them away from her land and closer to the huge ship waiting for them. She looked back with longing at the land of her birth.

Amari knew that she would never see this place again.

THE WATER, WHICH NEVER STOPPED ROCKING the small boat, carried them swiftly to the side of the huge ship. As they got closer, she knew she had been right: It was a place of death. Amari could not see the top of it. It rested upon the great water like a beast, ready to swallow them all up, she felt. Two of the captives who had been yoked together grew hysterical as they approached the looming structure and leaped without warning into the sea. The slave women gasped as one. Amari did not know the language of her captors, but she could tell they cursed as nets were cast overboard for the escaped slaves.

Amari and the other prisoners in her boat watched, however, in horrid fascination as the two women—a mother and daughter— tried in vain to swim back to shore. The mother struggled to keep her daughter afloat, but the chains were heavy and they were weak from hunger and captivity. Suddenly, the mother disappeared from sight for a moment, only to reemerge screaming in agony. The ocean bled bright red. Two huge gray fish with fins of silver surfaced for just a moment, their backs gleaming in the sunlight. One of them clenched a brown arm in its teeth. Then both mother and daughter disappeared. Amari stared at the spot, waiting for them to reappear. They didn't. She had held her breath through the whole thing. She was so stunned, she could not even pray.

The sailors were now even angrier than before. The whips slashed across the backs of the remaining slaves once more, as if those still alive had to pay for the loss of the two who had died. No one else tried to jump.

A rough plank had been rigged for them to climb from the small boat to the ship. It was narrow and shaky, but the sailors made sure the women had no opportunity to escape into the sea, should they dare. When she got to the deck, Amari stood amazed—it was like a small city made of wood. Poles taller than any tree reached to the sky. Loud, flapping pieces of cloth, larger than a hut, were attached to the poles by ropes, some of which were thicker than her whole body. Barrels and boxes littered the area, and dozens of men ran around shouting at one another and clapping one another on the back. They were laughing and cheerful, but Amari noticed that everyone seemed to carry a weapon—a gun, a sword, a knife. Confused and frightened, she didn't know what to think.

Amari had very little time to think, anyway. A whip lashed across her shoulder as she gazed around the ship, and she was quickly jolted back to reality. She jumped and yelped at the sudden pain. She and the other women were herded to one side of the deck, where a hole in the floor awaited. They were pushed into that hole and slid down into what Amari knew just had to be the underworld.

She wished that she had breathed more of the fresh air on the deck and in the boat, for the air in this place seemed to have been sucked out and replaced with the smells of sweat and vomit and urine. The male slaves had all been loaded before them, and she looked in disbelief at the sight before her. On narrow shelves made of wood, hundreds of naked men and boys lay chained together, wrists, necks, and legs held tightly by iron shackles. Only a few inches separated one man from another.

Each man had about six inches of headroom, not even enough to sit up. Under the upper level of boards a second level had been constructed, and under that, a third. Each row of shelves held men—human beings—chained like animals and stacked like logs for the fire, row after row, shelf after shelf.

The first row seemed to have more headroom and breathing area, but the second and third rows beneath them were already slimy with waste. The men on the bottom were splattered with the blood of the men who had been beaten, as well as the vomit and urine and feces that the men chained above them had no choice but to eliminate where they lay.

A large rat ran across Amari's feet as they were marched past the men. She felt faint—surely this could not be real. Some of the women cried out as they found a man they knew. Amari did not want to see Besa tied like an animal. She turned her head and moved on.

The area for the women was in a separate location. Their feet were locked in leg irons and they had only the rough boards to lie upon, but Amari noticed that they had more room and that the air was a bit fresher. Nor were they stacked the way the men were. Amari was surprised to notice a number of children in their area. The men who had captured her group had killed all of the children—she had supposed because they were too much trouble to take care of. But the captives on this ship, as she found out later on the journey, came from all over Africa and by many different ways. Amari saw a small boy who huddled near his mother; he was about the same age as Kwasi had been. She wished for a moment that he had lived so that she could hold him and comfort him. Then she shook that thought free; she would never want him to know these horrors.

The ship of death was surprisingly very much alive. It inhaled and exhaled the foul air of where they lay chained, and it rolled with the rhythm of the water. Loud noises echoed down to them—pounding, clanging, and screeching. And it seemed the white men were always shouting. She also heard laughter above. No one in the hidden, dark area beneath the ship laughed. All were silent with fear.

Eventually, the activity above seemed to slow down. Amari felt a sense of anticipation, as if something was about to happen. Perhaps it was night. She could not tell. Afi, still chained next to her, quietly began to hum an old Ewe song. It was the lament sung at a funeral—a death song. She sang to the ancestors and to the other slaves. Gradually, even those not of that tribe joined in. Close to a hundred women softly sang with her. It was the saddest sound Amari had ever heard.

8. TOWARD THE EDGE
OF THE WORLD

HOURS PASSED—IT WAS IMPOSSIBLE TO TELL IF it was day or night. Amari was unbelievably hungry and had to relieve herself. She was still chained and had no idea what she should do. She nudged Afi, who, as usual, was watchful and awake.

"Feel the motion of this ship of death," Afi whispered.

Amari could feel a gentle rocking, rhythmic and constant. "It feels different somehow," she told her.

"We float on the face of the sea," Afi murmured. "And we travel toward the edge of the world."

Amari started to ask her how she knew, but then she decided to trust Afi's instincts. "There is no escape?" Amari asked, even though she was certain of the answer.

"Not only is there no escape, there is no land to escape to. They have stolen that as well."

Amari did not understand. She had no time to ask her, for at that moment several sailors, with cloths tied around their faces, came down, unchained the feet of the women, and led them up out of the hold. After climbing the ladder up to the deck, Amari gasped with astonishment. Afi was right.

The land had indeed disappeared. Bright blue water surrounded them. The beach, the fort, the small boats—everything had vanished. One woman lurched at the sight, grabbed Amari's arm, and squeezed it so tightly that she left marks. She mumbled words in a language Amari did not understand. Another woman fainted. Some covered their eyes from the sudden brightness; others cried out fearfully. Afi said nothing. She had known.

The sailors began throwing salt water on the women from buckets on the deck. The water stung Amari's wounds and coated her with brine. Other women twitched and howled as the water hit them, and the sailors laughed at their discomfort. A barrel had been set on one side of the deck for the women to relieve themselves, and they were given food—some kind of beans mixed with an oily substance that Amari could not identify. It was horrible, and she gagged as she swallowed it, but she ate it all.

A sailor spoke sharply to the women, and they all stared at him blankly. He repeated himself again and again. "Now you dance! Dance! Dance, you monkeys, dance!" None of them had any idea what he meant. Finally, a young white man who looked to be about Amari's age brought out a small drum and began pounding a beat. It was just a simple, basic rhythm—*DRUM-dum, RUM-dum, DRUM-bop-bop; DRUM-dum, RUM-dum, DRUM-bop-bop*—over and over again. The women looked around in confusion. The dull beat made by that foreign drum carried no message and certainly offered no cause for celebration. *It has none of the life and voice our drummers were able to coax from a drum,* Amari thought.

A whiplash stung Amari's face and she jumped. The sailor holding the whip nodded, pointed to her, and jabbered some words as he hopped up and down. Amari then realized what the men wanted them to do. *They expect us to dance, or at least jump, to this horrible rhythm!* Amari thought incredulously. Slowly, reluctantly, the women began to jump.

Amari supposed it was for exercise. But it was also for another purpose, she noticed with a sickening realization. Most of the female captives had on very little clothing. Their clothes had been ripped and torn and stripped from them since they had been taken from their homes. The sailors, all carrying knives or guns, walked among the women as they danced. They watched the women closely, sometimes touching their bodies. The women knew what the men were looking for.

One of them, a huge man with bright orange hair, kept watching Amari. She had never seen a person with hair that color before, and he frightened as well as fascinated her. He never touched her, but while the women danced, she noticed he kept his eyes on her face rather than on the rest of her body.

At the end of the dance, instead of being taken back down to the hold where they had been chained all night, the women were tied to the sides of the deck. The children were untied and allowed to run free.

"Keep your child close to you," Afi told one mother. "Who knows what these strange men like to eat!" The mother nodded and grabbed the boy.

It wasn't exactly pleasant on the deck of the ship—it was dreadfully hot, and the constant salty wind on her face only increased her thirst. They had been given no fresh water to drink since that first meal of the morning—but Amari was glad to be away from the stench of the bottom of the ship.

"They will come for us tonight," Afi whispered to Amari, jarring her thoughts back to a harsh reality. "They treat us like animals, but tonight we will be forced to be their women."

"But, but . . . I do not know what to do!" Amari wailed, thinking with embarrassment of her dreams of lying in Besa's arms after they were married.

"Submit in silence. If you fight back, it will go worse for you," Afi said sadly.

"Perhaps it is better to die," Amari told her sharply.

Afi sighed. "If you die, they win. We cannot let that happen."

"They have already taken everyone I loved," Amari replied, ashamed to look at Afi in the face. "And tonight they take the only thing I have left that is truly mine. Death would be a relief."

"You will live because you must," Afi said sternly. "I should welcome death, but I cannot—not yet. And neither can you." She turned away from Amari and looked out at the sea.

Amari did not know how to reply. She trembled violently at the thought of one of these strange, smelly, milk-faced men taking her against her will. *Shall I throw myself overboard?* she thought. *It would be so much easier to give up and die.* Yet she could not do that. And she didn't know why.

The male captives were brought to the deck next, a few at a time. They also screamed as the salt water was thrown on them, and then they were forced to perform the same horrible dance.

Amari listened to the thunder that their feet made and thought ruefully, *The feet of my people bring forth rhythm even when the noise of the white men can produce none.*

Afi nudged Amari and whispered, "Death has come for some of us."

Amari stared as several bodies, stiff and lifeless, were pulled from the decks below. The sailors, again with cloths tied around their mouths and noses, unceremoniously tossed the dead men overboard. Amari was too numb to even remember the words of a prayer.

The male slaves, unlike the women, were not allowed to stay on the deck after they had been fed and made to dance. They were whipped and chained and led back to the fetid dungeon where they had been all night. Every hour a few more were brought up and put through the same routine, until at last there were no more.

The sailors cleaned up the deck and whistled cheerfully. Night was approaching. Amari looked at the sun as it disappeared into the sea; it burned coppery bright and beautiful. She tried to sear that beautiful sight on her memory as a shield to the ugliness that she now knew was about to happen.

9. LESSONS — PAINFUL AND OTHERWISE

WHEN NIGHT FINALLY ENVELOPED THE SHIP and only a wisp of the moon shone dimly, the deck was dark except for the light from the torches the sailors used. Like pigs in heat, they came for the women. One by one the women were unchained and dragged, screaming and kicking, to a distant area of the ship or a corner of the deck. Amari heard them plead for mercy, for under- standing, but no one listened. Two men grabbed Afi and led her away. She lowered her head and did not cry out or try to fight them.

Amari huddled in a corner, trying to make herself look like one of the children, trying to look lame or stupid or unappealing. But then someone grabbed her arm. She looked up. It was the sailor with bright reddish hair. She moaned.

He pulled Amari to a small room that held nothing but a box made of wood and a sleeping area that seemed to be elevated off the floor somehow. *These men don't even sleep on mats on the ground?* she thought briefly, but then the horror of what was about to happen overwhelmed her and she looked around wildly for a means of escape.

The man closed the door, and the room was suddenly very

small. His large body took up most of the area and completely blocked the door. He pushed Amari roughly onto the floor. She could hear the cries and screams of other women as they were being attacked.

"Scream!" he yelled at her harshly.

Amari did not know what he meant, so she just sat there, about to faint from fright.

"Scream!" the redheaded sailor yelled again, and this time he raised his huge, hairy arm as if to hit her.

Amari screamed.

He mumbled some words and seemed to be pleased. Then he put his finger to his lips and whispered, "Shhh." It was the same sound Amari used to make for Kwasi when she wanted him to be quiet. Her whole body shook with dread and fear. The sailor spoke more words, but to Amari they sounded like wooden buckets clattering together. She could make no sense of any of it.

His voice sank to just above a whisper, and he put his huge hand across Amari's mouth so she could not make a sound. She could barely breathe.

He's going to kill me! she thought with terror.

But he removed his hand and signaled for her to remain silent. She did.

He spoke more words that she could not understand, rattling on as if she understood. Amari had no idea what he was talking about, but he did not seem to be in a hurry to rape her, so she relaxed a little.

He grabbed a pouch around his neck, and Amari tensed, ready to cry out again. Slowly, he pulled an object from the pouch and handed it to Amari. At first she was afraid to take it, fearing it might be a means to poison her or put a spell on her. But he smiled as he handed it to her, so she took it hesitantly.

It was small, not much bigger than the palm of her hand, and made of wood. It was a carving of a child, a white child with long strands of hair. Amari looked at it in wonder, thinking it must be some kind of talisman. The sailor pointed to the carving and then pointed to himself several times. Then he took the small carving away from Amari, kissed it gently, and pretended to rock it. *Either this is a madman or that is a likeness of his child,* Amari thought.

"Child," the sailor said.

Amari said nothing.

"My child," the sailor repeated.

Confused, Amari had no idea what he was saying. She coughed a little.

He pointed to a bucket of water on the floor and made sipping motions as he lifted a dipper.

She nodded slightly, and very gently, considering the size of the man, he gave her a dipper of water. It was cool and fresh, and she drank it thirstily.

"Water," he said, pointing to it.

Amari wasn't sure what he meant.

"Water," he said again. "Water, water, water, water." He kept repeating the word and pointing to the liquid.

"Wa-ta," she said slowly.

The large sailor slapped his thigh and laughed.

Amari looked at him cautiously, not sure what to say or do next.

"Water," he said once more.

"Wa-ta," Amari repeated.

"Bucket!" he said, kicking the bucket with his foot.

Amari thought once more that surely this man must be mad. Why would he do such a thing?

"Bucket!" he repeated, pointing to the wooden object now lying on its side.

"Buh-ka," Amari repeated quickly, suddenly understanding. He was teaching her the language of the white skins! "Buh-ka," she said again, more clearly this time. If he was going to teach her, she fully intended to learn it. She hated not knowing what the sailors were saying.

Amari thought briefly of her father, who loved meeting men of other tribes and learning their languages. Then she inhaled sharply and squeezed her arms around her body, the painful reality hitting her that her father would never again discover a new word or idea to share with her.

The sailor looked at her with what looked like concern and jumbled out words that seemed to be a question, but Amari just shook her head. She felt that her father's spirit was there with her and that somehow he had protected her this night from the certainty of rape.

Hesitantly, Amari pointed to the door of the small cabin. He told her the word was "door." She repeated it over and over until she could remember it.

The strange, redheaded sailor taught Amari the words "ocean" and "ship" and "man" and "floor" and "wall," as well as many other simple words and phrases. She also asked him, through pointing and signs, to tell her the words for "chain" and "whip" and "shackle." He frowned, but he told her.

Knowledge of the language of the white men was a powerful weapon that she could possibly use one day to her advantage. Coldly and thoughtfully, she listened and learned. After a couple of hours, when most of the screams of anguish from the women had long since ceased, he opened the door of the small room and led Amari back to the deck.

He made sure she had fresh water, let her relieve herself, and tied her gently to the deck pole, which he told her was called a "mast." Then he disappeared.

Most of the women back on deck were curled into balls, shivering in the chill night air. Some rocked back and forth, trying to erase the terrible memories of the past few hours. Afi, wide awake as usual, waited for Amari. Her face was bruised, her upper lip bleeding.

"He did not take you?"

Amari shook her head no, almost ashamed that she had escaped the fate of most of the women.

"He was kind to you?"

Amari thought about it and realized that what had happened to her really was one drop of kindness in this huge sea of evil that surrounded them. She nodded her head yes. She was afraid to look Afi in the eye.

"Good. You were lucky . . . this night. But prepare yourself, child. One of them—probably many of them before this journey is over—will take you."

Amari gasped. "How much longer can this journey be?" she asked Afi, suddenly very frightened again. "Surely the next day will bring us to our destination—wherever that might be."

In spite of her injuries, Afi managed to twist her lips into a rueful laugh. "No, child. This is just the beginning of many nights of horrible humiliation. I feel that this journey will be very long."

Amari touched Afi gently.

"Many will die," Afi said quietly. "Some will live but will die inside. Others will pray for death and be forced to live. But we all will be changed forever." She did not cry or wail as some of the other women did, but Afi's face was covered in tears, which mixed with the blood on her face and lips.

"What shall we do?" Amari said finally, burrowing into Afi's arms—as much as their chains would allow.

"Find strength from within," Afi told her, stroking her head.

"How do I do that?" Amari whimpered.

"It is there. You will know when it is time to use that strength as your shield from what they will do to you."

Amari suddenly felt overwhelmed with powerlessness. "I want it to be like it was," she sobbed. "I want my mother."

"Oh, child," Afi whispered gently. "I know you do."

"It's not fair," Amari cried.

"Nobody promised us happiness or fairness, child. I have known much happiness in my life—the love of a good man, children, a village of friends and loved ones—and much sorrow as well. You have yet to find that, my child. Your destiny lies beyond."

"Beyond what?" Amari asked.

"I do not know. Some things the spirits keep secret." She chuckled, in spite of everything, and hugged Amari once more.

IO. THE MIDDLE PASSAGE

AFI WAS RIGHT. THE NEXT NIGHT THE KINDLY redheaded sailor was nowhere to be seen. Amari was taken to a filthy corner of the ship by a dark-haired, skinny sailor who used her, hurt her, and tossed her back on the deck, bruised and bleeding, all of her dreams finally and forever destroyed. Afi said nothing but held Amari and rocked her until her tears stopped flowing.

The following night Amari was taken by two sailors. They took turns. She wanted to die.

The morning after that brutal assault Amari spotted Besa in a group of men who were brought on deck. It was the first time she'd seen him since they had been on the ship. He had lost weight, as most of them had, and his body was covered with welts and sores. He made brief eye contact with Amari, a flicker of hope in his eyes for a moment. The pineapple birthmark looked distorted and shrunken. But she could not face him, for she was no longer the innocent girl he had once loved. She no longer felt worthy of his admiration or even his friendship. Amari turned away from him in shame.

The routine of the ship took on a horrible monotony. The

everlasting indigo blue of the ocean surrounded them day after day. The copper sun and the piercing paleness of the sky, which were so welcome in the captives' homeland, imprisoned them each hour. Every morning the women were fed, doused with salt water, and made to dance. Oh, how Amari hated that drum! The men were then pulled from the hold, squinting in the bright sunlight—filthy, weak, and almost crippled from being tied down for almost twenty hours each day. More and more bodies were tossed overboard, where the huge gray fish waited hungrily for their meal.

Every evening the sailors prepared greedily for their night of pleasure. Sometimes Amari was rescued by the redheaded sailor, but on most nights she was just another female body to be used by one of the forty or so sailors on board that awful ship. A couple of times she had seen the large redhead climbing up the mast to do the night watch, so she figured that perhaps he did not always have the opportunity to save her from a night of defilement. Or, she thought, perhaps he just did not care that much.

Amari no longer smiled—ever. She learned to harden herself from feelings and emotion, as well as from physical pain. She was, however, grateful for any evening of escape from the other men and for the large redheaded man's attempts to teach her their language.

She learned his name, which was Bill, and how to say "yes" and "no" and quite a few conversational phrases. He showed her how to count using the fingers of her hands. She learned the words "hungry" and "eat," even though hunger was a constant and the food she was given was barely life-sustaining, as well as verbs like "try" and "cry" and "die."

The language of the white skins was strange and fell heavily on her tongue, but she continued eagerly. She gathered words as weapons to be used later.

"What that?" she asked Bill one rainy night as she pointed to the rain slicker he wore. He told her the name for it, as well as the names of other articles of clothing. He taught her the names of the parts of the body, words for weather, and words for food. She pointed, he named it, she repeated it. He showed her how words connected into phrases. Verbs were difficult for her.

"I am Bill," he explained.

"You am Bill," she repeated.

"No, you say, 'You *are* Bill.'"

"I not Bill. I are Amari." She was often confused, but slowly, it made sense. Amari found that she could understand more than she could say, which she knew was an advantage. Sometimes she repeated words and phrases to herself as the men made her dance or while she was tied up for hours on the deck of the end-lessly rocking ship. It kept her from going mad.

When Amari awoke one morning, the sky was thick with dark, ominous clouds. Cold winds blasted the deck. The ship rocked violently as waves splashed high over the roping on the sides. The women, drenched and terrified, were flung wildly about, held only by the ropes that tied them to the masts.

One woman, whose name was Mosi, screamed with despera-tion as her daughter, who was about four years old, was torn from her arms. At that instant another huge, foaming wave washed over the deck, and the child disappeared with it as it fell back into the ocean. Mosi pulled at her ropes like a crazed animal, broke free, and ran across the deck to the place where her child had disappeared. She looked over the side of the boat and, pointing to a spot some distance away in the water, yelled to the women, "I see her! I see her. Oh, my baby!" Amari pulled at her ropes, but she could do nothing.

A sailor had spotted Mosi and headed toward her. She took one look at him, one final look at the women—as if to say farewell—and leaped gracefully into the sea. Amari watched frantically, waiting for someone to rescue them, but the sailors, too busy with the sudden storm, never even bothered to glance overboard to see the fate of the mother and child. They were simply two more dead slaves.

They did, however, untie the women then and lead them to the lower deck. It had been many days, perhaps weeks, since they had been in this area of the ship—Amari had lost all count of days and time. The stench, which had been unbearable at the beginning of the voyage, was now almost unbreathable. It seemed that no one had bothered to clean out the lower deck since the voyage began. The men, tied there for over twenty hours a day, had no choice but to lie in the filth.

Many of the bottom levels of the shelving were empty, Amari noticed. That was the result of the constant stream of stiff, dead bodies that were tossed overboard each morning, she realized.

Amari and the other women splashed slowly though the slime of urine and feces and vomit that covered the floor. Rats, now grown huge and healthy, chewed on the emaciated bodies of some of the men chained there. Too weak or too tightly chained to shake them off, the men suffered in silent agony.

The women were chained to what the sailors called the "tween" deck. The door of the hold was closed behind them. Amari vomited, unable to fight the nausea. So did many others.

Hour after hour the ship bucked through the storm. Children clutched their mothers, women moaned, everyone prayed. At first Amari prayed for the storm to stop. Soon she simply wished that the ship would be taken by the storm and sunk to the bottom of the ocean.

But no relief was to come that night, nor the next day. The winds kept roaring, the ship rolled, and the slaves chained beneath the decks suffered endlessly.

Finally, finally, Amari realized that the movement of the ship had slowed. She could no longer hear the wind. Too weak to move, she lay huddled in a ball, bemoaning the fact that she was still alive.

She heard the sound of a door opening. The sailors who entered began to curse at the sight before them. They unchained the women and led them to the deck. They did not bother to tie them, for they were too weak to even stand. Of the ninety women left on board, sixteen had died during that storm. Ten of the children had died as well. The women watched with empty eyes as the bodies were tossed overboard. Amari wished that she had been one of them.

MANY OF THE SAILS AND SEVERAL OF THE MAST poles had been damaged in the storm. Crew members scurried about making repairs. If she listened carefully, Amari could figure out bits and pieces of the conversation between the captain and his crew.

"Can you tell what they say?" Afi asked Amari.

"Not exactly," Amari whispered back. "But they seem to be worried that the ship is damaged."

"That I can see," Afi said with a chuckle. "Perhaps destruction is the only thing these barbarians understand."

"They are headed to something called Carolina," Amari told Afi later that day. "What do you think that means for us?"

"It means that place is where your destiny lies, my child," Afi said with assurance.

"And yours as well," Amari added, almost as a question.

Afi gazed out upon the ocean.

"Afi! Your destiny is with me, is it not?" Amari pleaded desperately.

Afi did not look at Amari. "When I have an answer for you, I will tell you," she said finally.

Amari stopped asking, but her heart was heavy.

For the next few days the slaves were treated a little differently. The men were brought up on deck more often and allowed to stay for longer periods. They all started receiving larger food portions and generous rations of water. The ship's doctor checked each one of them carefully, applying salves to their many wounds and giving medicine to those who appeared to be sickly. The sailors were no longer allowed to molest the women at night. All activity seemed to indicate the end of their journey—crates and cartons were packed, sails were sewn and repaired, and sailors whistled as they shaved their beards.

"Huh! The sailors seem to be excited to return to their own women," Afi said bitterly as she and Amari sat quietly on the deck watching the activity.

"What will happen when we arrive in their land?" Amari asked.

"We will be sold once more—perhaps many times. We no longer belong to ourselves, Amari."

"What do you think it is like there?"

"The same sun shines upon their land. The moon and the stars glow each night. Trees grow green and tall in the sunlight. But I have a feeling it will be as different from our land as life is from death."

"I'm afraid, Afi," Amari admitted.

"So am I, child. So am I."

Amari had very little time to worry about the future, however, for she heard Bill, the redheaded sailor, who was working on the tallest sail of the ship, suddenly shout, "Land ho!"

She wasn't sure what the words meant, but by the loud, boisterous reaction of the sailors, who whooped in celebration, she knew it could mean only one thing. This part of their journey was almost over.

Amari could see seabirds flying overhead, and she looked with the rest of the women at the faint hint of green in the distance. She did not share in the joy of the sailors, however. Amari was overcome by fear.

KA-BOOM! THE SHIP'S CANNON FIRED SUDDENLY, sending the slave women on deck scurrying for cover. Amari cowered close to Afi, sure that her life was about to end. The sailors, however, seemed unconcerned, even cheerful, as they steered the ship toward its destination. Some of them whistled, a sound that Amari found to be particularly distasteful. She peeked over the edge of the ship, and suddenly, green and golden beyond the blue of the sea, the land appeared from the distant mists. Amari had had no idea what to imagine, but the land she saw was surprisingly beautiful, with lush green trees growing quite close to a long, sandy beach.

"Afi," she whispered, "the land is lovely. I thought it must surely be an ugly place."

"Yes, it is beautiful to look at. Remember that when the ugliness overtakes you," Afi told her. "Find beauty wherever you can, child. It will keep you alive."

"I could not have survived without you, Afi," Amari told her, giving the older woman a clumsy hug.

"And you have been a gift to me as well, Amari. I'm glad we were together for this horrible journey."

"What happens now?" Amari asked.

Afi had no time to answer, for a small boat came up close to the ship, and a balding white man climbed on board. He wore a cloth tied across his face. The captain of their ship laughed and welcomed him aboard.

The first thing Amari noticed was that the newcomer was clean, smelling strongly of the scent of too many flowers. He coughed and choked as if the very air of the slave ship would infect him with illness. It was clear he was reacting to a terrible odor.

Amari could make out only a few of the words between them. She could figure out the words "stink" and "slave" and "cargo" and that the man who had come on board was some sort of official from the land they were heading toward. Amari realized as she listened intently to their conversation that she and her fellow slaves were the cargo. Then she saw the captain hand something to the man. It was a small leather pouch that bulged with silver objects. The man took it greedily and stuffed it into his shirt.

The captain then laughed again and pointed to Afi and Amari and the other women on the deck. The man walked over to the slave women and rubbed his hands together. With a look that seemed to Amari to combine disgust as well as desire, he proceeded to examine each of the women slaves very carefully.

Afi was called first. Like the rest of the women, she was just about naked. He checked every bone and muscle of her body by running his hands over her, noting flaws or bruises. Afi's back showed many scars, and he frowned with displeasure. He looked inside her mouth and checked her teeth. He checked her genitals.

She kept her eyes closed. Amari knew that Afi's mind was in another place.

"Good breeder," she heard the man say as he smacked Afi on the buttocks. Amari did not know what that meant.

Afi was sent back to her place on the deck, and Amari was called next. Using Afi's strength as an example, Amari stood quietly as she was touched and examined and fondled. Her impulse was to jerk away from him, but she forced herself to stand silently.

The rest of the women were checked next, then the men, who had been brought up on deck, were examined as well. The man scribbled some marks on a flat sheet he carried and gave it to the captain. Amari listened carefully to his words, and even though she did not fully understand their meaning, she knew that her life was about to change again. "Your cargo is approved to land, Captain. Welcome to Sullivan's Island."

13. THE SLAVE AUCTION

THE NEXT DAY THE SLAVES WERE TAKEN IN GROUPS
from the ship. The women were placed in small boats similar to
the ones that had taken them away from their homeland; fewer
boats were needed to unload the surviving slaves than when they
had started out.

As he helped her from the ship into one of the small boats, Bill
refused to look at Amari directly. He mumbled into her ear, "Be
brave, child. God have mercy on you." Amari glanced back to see
him, but he was gone.

The rowers were swift and the journey was short. It took only a
few minutes to reach the beach on the place they called Sullivan's
Island. Chained and pushed, Amari was unloaded with the others.
She tried to walk, but she kept falling onto the sand. Her legs felt
like they were made of mashed fufu. She glanced around and saw
that most of the slaves, and some of the sailors as well, had difficulty
adjusting to land after such a long time journeying on the ocean.

A long, well-trodden path lay in front of them. Tall grasses
grew in abundance on either side of it. Three solemn seabirds
flew overhead. All was unusually silent.

When most of the slaves were able to walk, they were led to a large building about half a mile from the beach. It was made of wood and stone—a smaller version of the prison at Cape Coast. None of their captors spoke to them, except to yell or curse, nor did they try to explain what was happening. Talk surrounded them, however, as one slave was pointed to with great interest or another was laughed at.

The slaves were fed, given water, and even supplied with extra water in small basins with which to bathe. Their wounds were patched or covered, and they were oiled and prepared for whatever was to come next. The whole area was full of nervous tension.

A tall black man entered the room. He limped noticeably, and he was dressed in a ragged version of the clothing of the whites. He looked at them, shook his head sadly, then addressed the slaves in the white language, seemingly giving instructions. They gazed at him blankly.

Finally, as soon as all of the white men had stepped outside of the building, the black man switched to the Ashanti language, speaking quickly and softly. "Listen, my brothers. I know not all of you can understand me, but I can see that some of you are Ashanti and Ewe. I will be whipped if they catch me 'talking African,' as they call it, but I must tell you some things. You must learn their language quickly—it is called English—but try not to forget your own. Submit and obey if you want to live. You are at a place called Sullivan's Island, where you will be kept for ten days, until they are sure you have no disease. Smallpox is the worst. Then you will be taken to a place called Charles Town, where you will be sold to the highest bidder." A white soldier reentered the building, and the black man smoothly switched back to the language of the whites.

The black man, whom the soldiers called Tybee, passed out some rough garments for them to wear—a simple smock for the women, a shirt and trousers for the men. He told them the names of each item in English as he gave it to them—"shirt," "shift," "apron"—then pointed out other words they would need, like "massa," "yes'm," and "yessir." Amari was surprised and pleased that she was able to understand quite a few of the words he said.

They stayed there on the island for several days, waiting for the unknown. During the day the slaves were fed and their wounds were treated, but at night fear was the blanket that covered each of them.

Amari lay on the ground one particularly hot night, trying to escape into sleep. She curled herself into a ball, but as she closed her eyes, memories assaulted her, so she sat back up, leaning against the rough wooden wall. She looked over and was surprised to see Besa, who had worked his way as close to her as he could in spite of his chains. She quickly lowered her head.

"My lovely Amari," he greeted her quietly in their language, as if hope still shone in their sky. "How goes your day?"

"Better, now that you are here," she said, remembering sadly that day that seemed so long ago. "But I am no longer lovely, and my days will never be happy again." She tried not to cry.

"When you look at the sun and the stars," he whispered, "I want you to remember me and smile. I want you to know that you will always be my lovely Amari."

One of the guards noticed them talking then and slashed at Besa with his whip. Besa glared at him, but he understood the danger of retaliation. He allowed himself to be led back to the far side of the men's area, where the guard kicked him fiercely. Amari had to look away.

Early the next morning the slaves were once again shackled and packed into boats. Looking healthier and feeling stronger than they had in a very long time, they were ready for sale.

The shoreline, Amari noticed as they were unloaded at the place her captors called Charles Town, was rocky and harsh rather than soft beach.

Amari looked then at an amazing sight. Tall buildings and people, seemingly everywhere, crowded the area. *What has happened to the trees?* she thought. *And what are all these structures? Surely these white people must have great magic to make such buildings! And there are so many of them!*

"Afi," Amari whispered. "The faces of brown and black that I see—are they slaves?"

"I cannot tell for sure, but I think so," Afi whispered back. "Most of them do not seem to walk with authority."

"I think we have arrived in a backward world—where black skins are few and not respected and pale skins seem to rule," Amari commented quietly.

They were taken to a place that Amari heard them call the "customhouse." It was a big drafty building with a large door. Pushed into a small shed next to it, the slaves waited in silence on the dirt floor. The sun rose, the room began to get unbearably hot, the hours passed, and the sun set again. They were given food and water at the end of the day, then locked back in the shed for the night.

Amari, hot and sweaty, whispered to Afi, "What are they waiting for?"

"Buyers," Afi declared. Amari's stomach clenched with fear.

Early the next morning white men lined up the slaves, sloshed cold water on them, and had other slaves rub oil all over their bodies. The oil stank, and Amari coughed at the odor.

"Now it begins," Afi said sadly.

By the time the sun had begun to shine brightly, the sale had started. Besa and a coffle of men were taken as the first to be auctioned off. As he and the others were led from the holding area, a great cry of enthusiasm could be heard from the crowd outside. Amari could hear loud, excited words tossed back and forth, much like the tones of bargaining her mother had used on market days. She heard someone say the word "Sold!" and she knew she would never see Besa again.

The rest of the men, some in sets of two or three, some singly, were sold as the morning went on. By midday it was time for the women.

In spite of the heat, Amari trembled. She gazed out of the shed's single window at the sun, which glistened bright and harsh. No warmth. No soft shadows to hide her embarrassment. No hope. She wondered how the sun could shine so brightly on this land of evil people. Nothing made sense to her any longer— not days or nights, not past or present.

This was the summer of her fifteenth year, and this day she wanted to die.

More buyers had arrived. Afi and Amari and the other women were stripped naked. Amari bit her lip, determined not to cry. But she couldn't stop herself from screaming out as her arms were wrenched behind her back and tied. A searing pain shot up through her shoulders. A white man clamped shackles on her ankles, rubbing his hands up and down her legs as he did. Amari tensed and tried to jerk away, but the chains were too tight. She could not hold back the tears.

Amari shuffled in the dirt as she was led into the yard and up onto a raised wooden table, which she realized gave the people in the yard a perfect view of the women who were to be sold. She looked at the faces in the sea of pink-skinned people who stood around pointing at the captives and jabbering in their language as each of the slaves was described. She looked for pity or even understanding but found nothing except cool stares. They looked at her as if she were a cow for sale. She saw a few white women fanning themselves and whispering in the ears of well-dressed men—their husbands, she supposed. Most of the people in the crowd were men; however, she did see a poorly dressed white girl about her own age standing near a wagon. The girl had a sullen look on her face, and she seemed to be the only person not interested in what was going on at the slave sale.

Amari looked up at a seabird flying above and remembered her little brother. *I wish he could have flown that night,* Amari thought sadly. *I wish I could have flown away as well.*

PART TWO

POLLY

POLLY REALLY DIDN'T LIKE NEGROES. AS FAR AS she was concerned, they should all get shipped back to Africa or wherever it was they came from. They talked funny, they smelled bad, and they were ugly. *How could the good Lord have made such creatures?* Polly wondered as she glanced with boredom at the slave sale. Dark skin, big lips, and hair the texture of a briar bush—they were just plain unpleasant to deal with. Besides, Negroes made it difficult for regular folks like herself to get work. Who could compete with somebody who worked for free?

She scratched an insect bite on her arm, unrolled a sheaf of paper, and leaned against the wooden wagon of Mr. Percival Derby, owner of Derbyshire Farms. Proud of the fact that she could read, Polly looked over her certificate of indenture one more time.

She mumbled and moved her lips as she read, "'His Majesty King George the Second, in the Year of Our Lord One Thousand Seven Hundred and Thirty-Eight, on this, the second day of June, in the city of Charles Town, colony of South Carolina, hereby sets the indenture of one Polly Elizabeth Pritchard, age fifteen years, to Mr. Percival Derby, for a period not to exceed fourteen years.'"

Polly frowned. She'd not been able to shorten the fourteen-year term. A normal indenture was seven years, but she had to pay off the debts of her parents, and the only way she was allowed to do that was to sign up for a double indenture. She'd have to work for Mr. Derby until she was an old woman—almost twenty-nine—but she was determined that long before that time she would have figured out a way to get out of the contract.

She looked back at the slave sale. The women were wailing and acting as if something terrible was happening to them. Polly snorted and turned away. Living here in the colonies had to be better than living like a savage in the jungle. *They ought to be grateful,* she thought. She thought of the Negroes she'd known as a child—well-fed and happy slaves, with no worries about finding employment. No, she had no sympathy.

The sale was getting boisterous. Polly looked up. "Fresh from Africa," the auctioneer told the crowd. "Mold 'em into what you want 'em to be. Look at 'em! All of them healthy and ready for childbearin'! Come on up and take a look! Feel free to inspect the merchandise."

An unbelievably large white man who smelled of strong wine and an even stronger body odor waddled past Polly and up to the auction area. She covered her nose and laughed behind her hand. He seemed to have difficulty breathing. He climbed onto the riser where the Negro women stood and headed directly to the youngest one there—a girl about her own age. He opened the girl's mouth and put his fingers inside.

Polly grimaced, not because she felt sorry for the girl, but because the man was so repulsive. Then the fat man touched the girl's breasts and ran his hands down her legs. "Nice," Polly heard him rasp. "I'll give ten pounds for the girl," he said to the auctioneer, wheezing between his words. He ignored the woman standing next to the girl.

"Do I hear more than ten pounds for this fine example of African womanhood? Hardly a scratch on her. Bright enough to be taught simple commands, like 'Come here' and 'Lie down'!" The crowd laughed at that, but Polly didn't.

"Twenty pounds!" called a voice from the back of the crowd.

The fat man looked up in astonishment. "Thirty!" he responded loudly. He sat down on the edge of the wooden platform and pulled out a filthy handkerchief. He wiped his face, which was sweating profusely.

"Forty pounds!" called the voice from the back again. People turned to see who was outbidding the large man in the front.

"She's not worth forty-five!" the big man yelled to the crowd.

"Is that your bid?" the auctioneer asked.

The fat man hesitated. "Yes," he said then. "I want her!"

"I hear forty-five. Do I hear fifty?" The crowd waited in anticipation.

"Sixty pounds for the African girl," the voice cried out at last. "I want her for my son. Today is his sixteenth birthday!" The crowd cheered. No one seemed to want the large man to win this one.

The auctioneer looked at the large man, who was still wiping his brow. "He can have her," the big man said finally. "I'll get me a young gal another day."

"Sold," the auctioneer said loudly, "for sixty pounds to Mr. Percival Derby of Derbyshire Farms." Polly looked up with surprise. She hadn't known who was doing the bidding. Then she shrugged. She just hoped Mr. Derby's new purchase would get put out in the fields where she belonged.

"Will you be wantin' her mama, sir?" the auctioneer said to Mr. Derby. "I offer her to you first, out of respect, you see."

Polly watched as Mr. Derby, who had walked up to the stage to claim his property, glanced at the older woman standing next to the slave girl, then said, "No, Horace, but thanks for the offer. Family ties only confuse the poor creatures. They'll forget each other as soon as the sun sets. Trust me."

Mr. Derby grabbed the arm of his new slave and attempted to lead her off the stage, but for some reason she just went wild. Polly watched, fascinated, as the girl squirmed and screeched and babbled incoherently. Polly wondered if Negroes from Africa had feelings and intelligent thoughts or if that gibberish they spoke was more like the screaming of monkeys or the barking of dogs.

When she was five or six years old, back in Beaufort, where she'd been born, she'd played with Negro children sometimes, running through the tobacco fields, playing hide-and-seek. But her father had frowned on such and would call Polly inside their small house. He'd say, "The company you keep will rub off on you, Polly-girl. Don't get your hands dirty by dealin' with darkies."

Her mother would shake her head at her husband, then pull Polly close to her. "I want you to grow up to be a fine lady, my pretty Polly. I don't want you to have to do laundry like I do. So let the slave children tend to their work in the field, and I will read to you from the Bible." Polly would snuggle on her mother's lap and fall asleep listening to the rhythm of her voice as she read.

Turning her attention back to the sale, Polly realized that the girl they were dragging off the auction block now was weeping real tears and seemed to be genuinely attached to that older female African whose shackled hand she wouldn't let go of.

Mr. Derby slapped the girl across the face, but she continued to pull and buck on the chains. She lurched toward the woman, but her leg chains got twisted and she stumbled. She fell hard, landing at the woman's chained feet. The older woman, who was also crying, leaned down and quickly whispered something in the girl's ear.

The girl was then pulled with difficulty from the stage, dragged across the dirt courtyard, and forced into the back of the wagon that Polly leaned on. The people in the crowd cheered at the spectacle, but Mr. Derby did not seem to be amused. He glared at Polly, who stepped quickly out of his way. He turned on his heel then and went to pay for his purchase.

Polly watched him coolly as he strode away, his shiny black boots getting dusty as he walked. She knew he wouldn't leave right away. His son, who he had sent to pick up supplies from the wharf, had not yet returned. The bidding continued as the last of the women were sold. It seemed to Polly that the slave girl curled in a corner of the wagon would never stop crying.

15. POLLY AND CLAY

POLLY, WITH HAIR THE COLOR OF DRIED GRASS and eyes the color of a stormy sky, understood tears. She also knew that tears fixed nothing. As far as she was concerned, crying showed weakness and was simply a waste of time. Tears had not kept her father out of prison, nor had crying made a difference when he'd died of smallpox. She'd wept bitterly when her mother had died of the disease as well, but not one tear had given her a bite to eat or a place to stay. So she did her best to ignore the slave girl who hiccuped and shook with sobs.

Mr. Derby's son, presumably the young man with the birthday and the tearful gift in the back of the wagon, arrived then with a smartly dressed black man who struggled under the weight of several bags of supplies. "Hurry up, Noah. Get these loaded," the boy yelled to the black man. The young Master Derby carried a small whip, and he used it liberally to make Noah work faster. Polly noticed that the slave breathed slowly and loudly, as if he was tense, but he made no attempt to stop the young man from hitting him. She was always amazed at how much abuse slaves took without it seeming to bother them.

Perhaps they didn't feel pain the way others did—she wasn't sure.

"Yassuh, Massa." Noah, dressed in clothing almost as elegant as a white slave owner's, bowed, then continued to load the wagon.

"Do you dress all your slaves as fine as King George?" Polly asked.

Clay turned slowly. "How dare you speak to me!" he responded furiously. "If you're the gal whose indenture my father just bought, you best learn your place around here."

Unintimidated, Polly gazed directly into his angry gray eyes and replied, "The slave owners I've encountered seem to clothe their slaves in just enough to allow for decency—certainly never in finery. Do you dress them all like that one?"

Clay burst into laughter. "They could all run around naked as far as I'm concerned, but when Daddy comes to market, he likes to arrive with his driver dressed with style," he explained.

"So why do you hit him?" Polly asked. She didn't like Negroes particularly, but she saw no reason why they should always be beaten.

"They expect to be disciplined," Clay explained. "It shows them that I care enough to make sure they do their tasks correctly. That's what my father always taught me. And what business is it of yours, anyway?"

"Just curious."

"Curiosity can get a gal like you in a heap of trouble. You best learn to keep your mouth shut," Clay warned.

"I've seen a heap of trouble," Polly replied. "I'm not afraid of you." But her heart fluttered under her smock.

Clay raised his arm as if to strike her, then lowered it as the anger on his face eased into a smile. "You're a saucy young thing," he said finally. He spat into the dirt.

Polly just looked at him with a cool stare.

"Was that your indenture I saw you looking at?" he asked. "You can read?"

Polly was not sure how to answer him, but she nodded as she quickly folded the paper and tucked it into a pocket of her apron.

"Let me warn you, girl. Women don't need to be reading, so just keep that ability to yourself. And don't ever get it in your mind to teach a slave to read! My father would have you whipped for such."

Polly inhaled sharply but did not answer him. She thought only slaves could be whipped. She noticed that Noah was gently picking up the trembling slave girl, moving her to the other side of the wagon and placing her on a blanket that lay wrinkled on the rough floorboard. The slave girl never opened her eyes; she just curled herself into a ball and huddled in that corner of the wagon.

Clay Derby mirrored his father in looks: dark, thick eyebrows that left his eyes in shadow, long fingers, and broad shoulders. His father, walking with swift authority, approached the wagon. People moved out of his way as he walked.

Clay seemed a little less sure of himself in the presence of his father, Polly thought. He pulled on his doublet, flicked some dirt from his boots, and smoothed his stockings. "Come," Clay said to Polly, taking her arm roughly, "I can see that Father has paid for my gift and is about ready to go. Whenever you speak to him, be sure to show proper respect. He hates women who don't know their place."

"Yes, sir," Polly mumbled sullenly.

"Did you enjoy the slave auction?" Mr. Derby asked Polly as he returned to the wagon and began to check on his goods.

Evading the question, Polly replied, "It was like nothing I have ever seen, sir." She looked at the ground.

"Speak up, girl," Mr. Derby commanded. "Look at me when you address me!"

Polly looked up at him, her blue eyes bright with a bit of defiance. "Yes, sir!" she said clearly. Mr. Derby opened his mouth as if to respond, then seemed to think better of it, for he turned to his duties instead.

The African girl, her hands tied in front of her with a rope, was still sniffling quietly. She was dressed in a thin shift made of a burlap seed bag. Her slender brown shoulders heaved.

"Quit that sniveling!" Mr. Derby yelled at her suddenly. He leaned over the side of the wagon and slapped her sharply across her face.

The girl, seemingly surprised, looked up and gulped back her tears. Polly noticed a brief smoldering anger on the girl's face, then it dissolved into a look of resigned submission.

"Noah, hurry and finish loading," Mr. Derby commanded the slave. "We have a long journey ahead of us." He did not use the whip as his son had. Noah packed up the rest of the supplies— farm tools, several bags of seed, and some rolls of cloth—and tied them down carefully. There would be barely enough room for Polly to squeeze in.

"Polly, you get in the back there," Mr. Derby ordered when Noah finished.

"Yes, sir," Polly muttered as she climbed into the wagon. She sat as far away as she could from the African slave girl, making sure the bundles separated them. The girl had covered her head with her hands.

"Polly Pritchard, my indentured girl, meet my new little savage. From my inspection of her, I figure the two of you are about the same age." Mr. Derby choked out a laugh.

Polly didn't see what was funny.

"And I know you have met my son, Clay," Mr. Derby said. Mr. Derby looked at his son with pride, but the young man had his dark eyes on the terrified African girl.

Mr. Derby climbed onto the seat of the wagon, indicated to Clay to join him, then gave the signal to Noah to begin the journey. Noah made a chucking sound to the horse, and the wagon lurched onto the dirt road.

Polly could feel each bump and jolt of the road beneath her as the wooden wheels lurched over each uneven place in the dirt or gouged hole left by other wagons. After one particularly deep dip in the road Polly was tossed across the bags of seed, landing hard against the slave girl, who opened her eyes and looked around frantically. Polly scrambled quickly back to the other side of the wagon.

The two girls eyed each other carefully. Polly had always prided herself on her looks. When she got the chance to glance in a mirror, she was always pleased at the peachy paleness of her face, which bore, thankfully, no scars from smallpox like many women she knew, and the blue-green clarity of her eyes. Unconsciously, she touched her hair, which her mother had loved to brush. It grew thick and straight—she remembered her father used to call it "golden flax." She knew the African girl was probably admiring her. Polly looked at the large brown eyes, the short-cropped hair, and the ebony-colored skin of the slave and saw nothing worthy of admiration. She sniffed. The girl even smelled bad.

The journey seemed to last forever as the wagon rumbled down the road. The sun, wickedly hot, seared Polly's fair skin. She longed for just a dipper of water.

Polly turned her attention to Clay. Sitting in a slouch, he kept spitting off the side of the wagon at regular intervals. Mr. Derby sat next to the driver, continually checking his fingernails and picking specks of dirt off his boots.

They had been traveling for almost two hours when Mr. Derby announced, "Well, Clay, what shall we call our latest acquisition? Since the new slave is to be yours, I shall let you name her."

Before Clay could speak, however, Polly spoke up quietly, "She probably already has a name, sir." Clay spun around and glared at Polly, as if to remind her of his warning about women staying in their place.

"Nonsense!" Mr. Derby replied, irritation in his voice. "Those jungle words have no meaning to civilized humans. I suggest you keep your opinions to yourself!" Polly said nothing more, but she looked long and hard at the slave girl's face.

Clay did the same thing. Finally, he said to his father. "I shall name her Myna, because she is mine!" He cleared his throat and spat once more.

Polly thought she had never met anyone with such an enlarged impression of himself.

Mr. Derby snorted. "It will do as well as any other."

"She is a most excellent birthday present, Father," Clay said as he glanced once more at the girl who huddled in the corner. He grinned and rubbed his hands together.

Mr. Derby looked at his son indulgently. "A boy turns sixteen only once! So I decided that just as my father provided a slave girl for me when I got old enough, I would do the same for you. I imagine one day you'll do the same for your son," he added.

Polly listened in amazement. She'd had very little experience with wealthy people, but she had never met anyone with attitudes like the Derby men seemed to have. She glanced at the African girl, who surely had no idea what her future held. She found herself feeling sorry for this new slave who huddled in the wagon, glistening with sweat.

"Black women are different, you know, Clay," Mr. Derby continued. "They like it when you pick them out for special favors at night. It keeps them happy, and . . ." He paused to flick a speck off his waistcoat. "And it reminds them in a very special way who is the master and who is the slave." He took a deep breath of the summer air.

"I will take good care of her, Father," Clay replied, pleasant anticipation in his voice. The wagon suddenly lurched to one side, the horse snorting and neighing as it pulled at the reins. Mr. Derby and Clay were tossed on the wagon seat.

"Can't you handle that animal?" Clay shouted at Noah.

"Yassuh," Noah replied, pulling the animal into a more controlled gait. "Musta been a bug or a 'skeeter that spooked him, suh."

Polly had a feeling Noah knew exactly what that horse was doing every moment. She also decided she didn't like this young man with the dark eyebrows, the sneering smile, and the repulsive need to spit so often.

Clay and his father continued their conversation as if Polly and the slave sitting next to her did not exist. "White women, like my Isabelle and your mother before her, are to be respected and treated like fine china," Mr. Derby told his son. "It's not often a man finds true love twice in his lifetime," he said with a lilt in his voice. "I wish you'd try harder to warm up to your stepmother, Clay."

"You should never have married her," Clay replied sullenly. "She's far too young for you, and she wears that vacant smile all the time. She reminds me of a sheep." He spat off the side of the coach once more, then shifted on his seat. "Why did you decide to purchase the girl's indenture?" he asked, glancing back at Polly.

"The little white girl comes to us with an indenture as long as my arm—there's no way she can pay it off in less than fourteen years. I figure she will be a good investment. She's from Beaufort, south of here. Both her parents are dead."

Clay turned to look at her. "Don't worry, Polly-girl. You'll like it at Derbyshire Farms. Lots of sheep, slaves, and chickens. And rice. Lots of work to do." He gave a small laugh.

Polly bristled. "Polly-girl" had been her father's pet name for her, and it angered her to hear it pour so carelessly from the mouth of this unpleasant young man.

A faint breeze moved the hot air as they traveled. No other wagons or people were to be seen. Huge live oak trees lined each side of the road, with dangling beards of Spanish moss hanging from each branch. Polly thought the trees looked like old men,

d exhausted from the heat. Perhaps they watched
lived here, she thought briefly. It had been a long
meone had cared for her.

After the deaths of her parents she'd lived almost like a pris-
oner in the rat-infested attic of a dirt farmer named Jeremy
Carton. He rarely spoke to her except to give her orders. He had
a wife and a daughter, both of them thick of mind and body,
who'd ignored her as well, except when the pigsty had to be
cleaned or the manure from the horses needed to be collected for
fertilizer. Polly longed for a kind word, a loving touch, but she
kept a stony distance from everyone. The Carton family never
saw her cry, not even when her parents died, never heard a word
of complaint from her. She knew they thought her to be cold and
unfeeling.

This is going to be my chance to make something of myself, she
vowed. *I shall not let anything or anyone get in my way. I intend
to make myself necessary to the Derby family, while learning how
the upper class lives.* It pleased her to imagine her grand goals,
but she was deadly serious about working her way up to be the
fine lady her mother had dreamed she would be.

The oppressive heat and constant rhythm of the wagon wheels
finally made Polly sleepy, and she dozed uncomfortably for a
couple of hours. When she was startled awake by a deep rut in
the road, she could see the fiery redness of the sun above the
trees in the distance.

The wagon pulled into a narrow lane then, and Polly could see
the two-story brick manor house ahead. It was almost blindingly
white in the late afternoon sun; it looked as if it had been white-

washed several times for the brick to be so completely covered, Polly surmised. Its red-gabled roof, nestled between two huge stone chimneys, also carried an aura of perfection. It was surrounded by a carpet of lush grass, kept short, she found out later, by the many sheep that grazed upon it. On her far right were green fields, and behind them dark woods grew full and deep. Far to her left many black faces labored in a large field near a river. They seemed to be standing in water.

"Welcome to Derbyshire Farms, Miss Polly," Clay said, making a sweeping movement with his arm. "The river you see yonder is the Ashley."

Polly didn't know what to say. Everywhere she glanced, she saw perfection. Not a stone was out of place on the path they drove on, not a flower in the garden seemed to be wilted. *Oh, to own such a glorious property!* she thought with an intake of breath. She noticed Mr. Derby looking carefully at his domain, as if checking to make sure everything was as it should be. Several slaves rushed out to meet the wagon. One carried a broom and began sweeping the path behind them. Another carried a tray of cold drinks for Mr. Derby and Clay. No one spoke to the master or his son.

Mr. Derby ignored the slaves and ordered Noah to turn to the right. They continued down a rutted lane, then stopped in front of a small shack made of wood. Polly noticed several other similar huts in the area, but she had no time to wonder about them, because just then Mr. Derby ordered them out of the wagon.

Polly nodded and climbed stiffly down. She motioned to the African girl to do the same. Mr. Derby pointed to the shack.

"Here is where you will live. This slave is your responsibility for now. I can't spare any field hands to break in a new African, and I certainly won't have anyone of my household doing such a task."

"But . . ." Polly looked at him with a surprised frown on her face and started to object. Then she suddenly realized with dismay what he meant. She was not to be installed in his household, where she could observe and absorb fine living, but would be forced to live with this slave girl instead. How humiliating!

"I could be of great help to you, sir, as part of your household staff," she offered.

"This *is* how you will assist me," Mr. Derby replied, his face showing impatience. "I need for her to act like a human instead of a monkey. Do you think you can tame a savage?"

"Yes, sir. I can do anything I put my mind to," Polly replied haughtily. But she hated the thought that she would have to deal with the black girl on a regular basis.

Mr. Derby looked at Polly carefully. His voice was like a sharp stone. "Don't underestimate me, child. I will not tolerate insubordination. Do I make myself clear?"

What was clear to Polly was that Mr. Derby was used to having his way. "I'm grateful for the opportunity, sir," Polly said with as much meekness as she could muster. "I will serve you well."

Mr. Derby folded his arms across his chest, then continued. "Your job is to teach her a little of the King's English, to teach her how civilized people live and act, and most importantly, to teach her absolute obedience. She belongs to my son, and when he needs her, it is your job to make sure she is delivered to him. Understood?"

"Yes, sir," Polly said quietly. Clay stood behind his father, chewing on a blade of grass, grinning.

"Both of you are to assist Teenie and not get in her way. I demand perfection, and I expect my servants to be useful and occupied at every moment of the day. In addition, I will not tolerate the questioning of any orders I give—ever!"

"Teenie, sir?" Polly asked, a frightened question mark in her voice.

"Do you have a problem with any of this, young lady? Because I can take you right back to where I found you—working for common scum like Jeremy Carton as a scullery maid. I have given you a home, a job, and an opportunity to better your life—much more than you deserve! Now get on with you before I change my mind!"

Mr. Derby ordered Noah to take the wagon back up to the main house. He motioned to Clay, and the two walked away. Polly breathed a loud sigh of relief as they left. The slave girl did the same, almost at the same moment. They looked at each other tentatively, but neither girl smiled.

POLLY ENTERED THE SHACK, NOT KNOWING what to expect. The slave girl, who was about the same height as Polly, followed hesitantly behind her. As her eyes adjusted to the dim light, she looked around. It was just one room, barely large enough to turn around in, made of rough wooden planks. It held a small wooden table, a chair, one bed, and a straw mat on the dirt floor. It smelled faintly of sweat.

"I've lived in places much worse," Polly said to the slave girl, who had already sunk to the floor and curled her arms tightly around herself. She thought back to the damp and moldy shack she'd shared with her mother while her father was in prison, and the attic room at Jeremy Carton's place.

The slave girl whispered words that Polly could not decipher.

"You'd better quit talking that jungle talk," Polly admonished. "I'm pretty sure that would be frowned upon in this place." She scowled as she looked at the confused expression on the girl's dark face. "I don't know what Mr. Derby is thinking. How am I supposed to make you civilized?"

Polly looked closely at the slave. Her cheeks were sunken into her thin face, which made her eyes seem very large, like a deer's. When the two girls exchanged glances, Polly could see bitterness flash in the slave girl's eyes for a moment. Her lips were full, but her nose was tiny, almost like Polly's own. Polly was unaccustomed to being this close to a Negro, and she marveled at how dark and mysterious the girl's face looked. A thin sheen of sweat covered the slave's slim body. Her hair, thick and matted, obviously had not been brushed in a long time. Welts and bruises, some of them quite recent, covered her arms and legs.

Polly's stomach suddenly growled, and she pressed her hands against it. When had she last eaten?

The slave girl watched Polly carefully, then grabbed her own stomach.

"Well, I suppose you're hungry too," Polly said. "You have no idea what I'm saying, do you?"

The girl just stared at her.

"This is impossible!" Polly shouted, and the slave cringed. "What am I doing out here in a shack taking care of some . . . some . . . savage!" Furious with frustration, she pummeled the lumpy straw mattress with her fists until she was out of breath. "What am I supposed to do with you?"

The girl shrugged as if she understood.

Polly sat down heavily in the wobbly wooden chair and ran her fingers through her own uncombed hair. Her stomach growled again. "I suppose we must start somewhere," she said with a sigh. "Hungry," she said, rubbing her own stomach.

"Hungry." Polly put her fingers to her mouth and moved her lips as if she were eating. "Hungry. Eat," she said, not expecting a response.

The slave girl looked around cautiously, then, to Polly's utter surprise, said, quite clearly, "Hun-gree. Eeet."

Polly looked at her suspiciously. "Either I'm a very good teacher or you are not as stupid as you look. Eat food," Polly said, adding a new word. The slave girl repeated the phrase easily.

"Well," Polly said with a look of amazement on her face. "I'm just going to talk to you as if you understand and teach you new words as we get to them. I imagine the sooner I complete this task, the sooner I can be assigned some more respectable duties, like sewing or serving the lady of the house."

The slave girl stared up at her.

"From what Mr. Derby told me, this place is called Derbyshire Farms," Polly began. "It is a rice plantation. Can you say 'planta-tion'?" Polly repeated the last word slowly. "Plan-ta-shun."

"Plan-ta-shun," the girl repeated. Although she certainly hadn't expected this, Polly refused to show the girl any encouragement.

"I am Polly, and I work for Mr. Derby just like you." She hesi-tated, then added, "Well, not exactly just like you. You're a slave, which means you belong to him."

"Slave," the girl said clearly. Her eyes narrowed and her lips drew back fiercely over her teeth as she said the word. *She knows exactly what that word means,* Polly thought.

"Let's do something easier, like introductions," Polly said, trying to change the subject. "I am Polly," she said, pointing to herself. "Pol-lee."

"Pol-lee."

"Yes," Polly said, allowing herself a smile, "and you are Myna. Can you say Myna? It's your new name." She pointed to the girl on the floor. "Myna."

The slave girl shook her head. "Amari," she said with pride, pointing to herself.

"I warned you about talking those African words," Polly reminded the girl. "You are Myna. My-na." She said it clearly several times.

"No Myna." The slave girl frowned and shook her head forcefully. "Amari!" She said it again slowly. "Ah-mar-ee."

Polly sighed and said, "Ah-mar-ee."

Amari smiled at her for the first time. "Amari!" she said again.

"Well, Amari, the master and his son say your name is Myna, so you better learn that one since it looks as though there's not much chance you'll ever get back to Africa. Just like I'll probably never get back to Beaufort," she added, almost to herself, "not that I'd want to."

The door of the cabin burst open then, and the shortest, skinniest black woman Polly had ever seen pushed her way through the door. She barely came to Polly's shoulder, but she carried herself with the dignity of a giant. Hiding behind her skirts was a very small boy—about three or four years old—who clung to her leg like a little insect. "Well, ain't this the berries! What we got here?" she boomed, even though the two girls were sitting right in front of her.

Finally, Polly said timidly, "How do you do? I'm Polly, and this here is Myna."

"I knows who you is," the little woman said with a smile. "I knows everything. Hiding stuff from me is like tryin' to put socks on a rooster! You want to know the dirt goin' on roun' here, just ask old Teenie. Tiny little Teenie." Then she erupted into a full, hearty laugh that didn't seem possible to Polly, considering how small the woman was. "And this here is my boy, Tidbit." The child retreated farther behind his mother, but he peeked out to see the new faces.

"Pleased to meet you, Miss Teenie," Polly said with difficulty. She didn't think a Negro deserved the title of "Miss," but somehow this woman seemed to require it. Her father had taught her to disrespect Negroes, but her mother had taught her to respect her elders.

"Don't be callin' me Miss Teenie lessen you want to get us both in trouble, gal. Just Teenie be fine. Y'all hungry?" she asked with a broad grin that showed she had almost no teeth. "Y'all both 'bout as thin as a bat's ear."

"Hun-gree," Amari whispered.

"Well, butter my butt and call me a biscuit! The little African can speak a little English, huh? Don't let the massa know, gal. Play dumb as long as you can." With that, she turned and headed out of the door, her child right behind her. "Come on to the kitchen. I'll set you up with some vittles. Lordy me," she said, "now we's got a African and a 'dentured gal to keep track of."

She walked toward a small building just off the big white house so quickly that Amari and Polly had to trot to keep up with her. The child Tidbit scurried next to his mother, and a small brown dog scampered up to join them. Smoke snaked from the chimney of the cookhouse, and the smells of stewing pork and fresh bread wafted from its narrow door.

Enticed by the smells, Polly eagerly entered the room. A stone hearth made up the entire back wall. A huge pot hung over the fire, which held a delicious-smelling sauce bubbling within it. *How did this tiny little woman lift that heavy kettle?* Polly couldn't help but wonder. Cooking pans and long utensils that she had never seen before hung from spikes nailed into the wall. She saw jugs and pointed sticks and even some utensils made from gourds. The floor was hard-packed dirt.

In a matter of minutes Teenie had two steaming bowls prepared for the two girls. Polly took a seat at a bench and motioned to Amari to do the same. Polly picked up her spoon and noted with disgust that Amari put her hand into the bowl and greedily scooped the food into her mouth. *Table manners,* she mentally added to the long list of impossible tasks ahead of her.

Tidbit sat with them, eyes large with questions. His bare feet swung beneath him. The dog curled quietly under the table. Polly smelled the food, then tasted it. *Brown peas, flavored with salt pork, maybe? Mashed with onions into yellow rice,* Polly thought. *Looks bad, tastes wonderful.* "This is very good," Polly said to Teenie between mouthfuls. "What is it called?"

"What's that you say, gal? You never had no Hoppin' John? Ain't you got rice and peas and salt pork where you come from?"

"Not like this," Polly admitted. "My mother wasn't much of a cook."

"The old folks say that iffen you eat black-eyed peas on New

Year's, it s'posed to make you rich for the new year," Teenie said. Then she added ruefully, "Never worked for me, though!" She laughed and scooped more into Polly's bowl.

As Polly ate, she thought with a smile of her mother, who always managed to either undercook the spoonbread, burn the occasional rabbit or squirrel her father brought home, or forget to add spice to the stew. They ate lots of fried catfish—some of it quite raw and some of it crispy black. When her mother had fixed Hopping John, it was crunchy and gritty—obviously not cooked as long or as well as Teenie's meal. Polly glanced at the girl who insisted her name was Amari and saw that her thoughts were far from this warm kitchen as well.

Tidbit watched every move the girls made. He giggled every time Amari stuffed her fingers into the bowl.

"What's the dog's name?" Polly asked Tidbit.

"Hushpuppy," the boy replied cheerfully as he reached down to hand the dog a scrap of bread. "He know how to hush and hide," the boy said proudly.

"I'm gonna give you two gals a couple of days to learn your way round here 'fore I put you to work," Teenie told them as they finished eating. "And, Tidbit, I done told you to keep that raggedy old dog outta my kitchen!" The boy just laughed and disappeared under the table with the dog.

"Come by here tomorrow and watch me work," Teenie continued. "That's the best way to learn. Just stay outta my way, 'cause I be busier than a stump-tailed cow in fly time. I fixes all the meals round here."

Before Polly could respond, Teenie added, "Your job, Miz Polly, is to explain everything you see to this here African gal. Teach her the words, 'cause Massa ain't gonna wait no long time 'fore he be expectin' her to hold her own. And Miz Africa, learn what words you can, but learn to keep your mouf shut, 'cause Clay, that hellhound, got less patience than his daddy!" She grunted with distaste. "That boy got a thumpin' gizzard for a heart!"

"Yes'm," Polly mumbled.

"Gal, where you from? I done told you 'bout callin' me 'ma'am' and 'miss.' Your mama done raised you right," she said with a grin. Tidbit giggled from under the table.

"I'm from Beaufort, in the low country," Polly explained. "Nothing much there but bugs and gators and a few folks scraping the dirt to make do. My mother is dead. My father as well." She swallowed hard.

"Oh, chile, how they die?" Teenie's face grew tender.

Polly looked at her and saw that Teenie really wanted to know. "My father was born in England, and he was a good-looking man," she began. She smiled as she thought of his charming grin. "He told me ladies used to follow him home from the pubs every night. He would buy them fine wine and expensive gifts and tell them the lies they wanted to hear. He lived a grand life until he ran out of money." She paused. "He was thrown in jail like a common criminal just because he couldn't pay his debts."

Teenie sucked in her breath but made no comment.

"He had friends in the court system, however, and he was given the chance to start over in the colonies as an indentured servant. He came here on a prison ship—a frightful experience, he said. Eventually, his indenture was sold to a man named Jeremy Carton in Beaufort, right here in Carolina Colony. That's where he met my mother, who put an end to his fondness for other ladies, but not, however, his affection for ale and wine. I was born there."

The slave girl gently petted the dog under the table, looking as if she was trying to follow the conversation.

Polly continued, "My father worked like an ordinary slave on a tobacco farm." She looked up to see if Teenie had reacted to that, but Teenie simply continued to stir the food in the pot over the fire. She used a whisk that looked like it was made from the twig of a tree. "He worked hard, but he could never make enough to pay off his debt. My daddy was a good man but not real careful with what little money he got. He drank too much sometimes. . . ." Polly shifted on the bench a little.

"What about your mama?" Teenie asked gently.

"My mother came up rough—she was an orphan. She was shuffled from family to family most of her childhood. She learned to make do for herself most of her life. She worked as a maid when she could, as a beggar when she couldn't."

"Well, pick my peas! A white woman as a maid and a beggar! Must not be no slaves from where she come from," Teenie commented.

"Not all white people are rich landowners," Polly said, almost coldly. "Most white folks I know scuffle for every scrap of food they get."

"But they ain't slaves," Teenie reminded her quietly. "Go on, chile."

Polly thought for a moment and continued. "My father kept getting in trouble, spending months in jail, and was unable to pay back his indenture. My mother tried her best to keep us together as a family, even signing on with Mr. Carton as an indenture herself, but there was never enough work or money or food, even though she offered to do other people's laundry after her work was done for Carton. Nobody would hire a white woman because folks knew they could get slaves to do the work for free!" Polly tensed as she thought of the unfairness.

Teenie took that moment to cut each girl a large slice of pumpkin pie. She cut a tiny piece for Tidbit, who stuffed most of it into his mouth in one bite, then grinned a large orange smile. The rest he gave to the dog.

"Well, the sun don't shine on the same dog's tail all the time," Teenie said philosophically. "Everybody got hard times at one time or t'other."

"I suppose," Polly began again, this time speaking very slowly. "But then, three months ago, my parents came down with smallpox." Teenie stopped chopping the onions for a moment. "Daddy died first, then three days later, my mother. I nursed them both, and I never got as much as a pimple." She paused, stood up, and walked outside of the hot cookhouse, taking deep breaths. "I am *not* going to cry!" she sternly told herself. When she felt she could continue, she went back into the kitchen.

"So how you end up here, gal?" Teenie rattled a stack of tin plates.

"Mr. Jeremy Carton decided that I must sign on to pay back

what my parents owed him, and I had no choice but to do it. His is just a small dirt farm, so, I suppose to prevent me from running off—and I would have, too—he took me with him to Charles Town to get supplies yesterday. But then he met Mr. Derby in a tavern, and he somehow sold my indenture to him. I'm not sure how or why. So here I am."

"Seven years to pay back yo' indenture ain't bad," Teenie pointed out. "You is young and got plenty o' time to make you a place in this here world. White women with indentures got it easy—eventually, you can fit in." Polly glanced over at Teenie, surprised at the emotion in her voice. Teenie poked furiously at the coals in the hearth.

"I must pay back fourteen years," Polly told her. "I must pay my own plus what was left of my parents' indentures. Mr. Derby says I should be glad he was willing to take on all that debt. I suppose I should be thankful. But I'm fifteen years old. By the time I pay him back, I'll be almost thirty—a wrinkled, old woman." She stared for a long time at the blazing embers in Teenie's fireplace.

"Thirty ain't so old," Teenie said quietly. "That's close to how old I be, far as I can tell." She gazed out the door of the small kitchen house and looked dreamily down the path that led away from the plantation.

Polly watched as Amari moved close to Teenie and touched her hand. Something seemed to pass between them—a look of understanding, perhaps. Amari whispered a few words in her own language.

Teenie moved away abruptly and returned to her brisk command of the room. "Go on now, you two gals get outta here. It be almost dark, and I 'spect you both at dawn. Tidbit, go fetch me some wood for my fire! And take that dog with you," she yelled, although she didn't seem angry. The boy disappeared into the yard.

Amari and Polly headed slowly back to the little cabin. Polly watched, amazed, as Amari rushed to grab the mat on the floor, shook it out, then curled up on it quickly.

"Why are you laying on the floor?"

Amari covered her head with her arms.

"You don't want to sleep in the bed?"

Again the slave girl ignored her.

Polly shrugged and climbed onto the narrow cot. The straw-filled mattress was lumpy and smelled of moldy vegetables, but it was better than anything she had felt in a long time. She slept.

The knock on the door startled Polly awake. It was Tidbit, looking like a tiny night spirit. He was shivering, and so was his dog. "Massa Clay say he want his birthday present now. I'm to take her there."

Polly gasped with realization and reached over to shake Amari awake. Amari sat up and looked from Polly to the trembling child. Her face was a question. Polly said slowly and with genuine sorrow, "You must go with Tidbit. Master Clay is asking for you."

Amari looked at Polly, then the child, and suddenly seeming to understand, she groaned. "No! No! No!" she begged.

Polly touched her arm but couldn't think how to help her.

Tidbit stood silently, shifting from foot to foot, looking very uncomfortable.

Amari finally took a deep breath, stood up without a word, and followed the child out of the door. The night was very dark.

PART THREE

AMARI

17. AMARI AND ADJUSTMENTS

THE NEXT THREE MONTHS WERE HOT, CONFUSING, and miserable as Amari tried to assimilate into the culture of plantation life. Dawn always came too quickly, and she woke each morning with a start as she heard the roosters announce the day.

Amari and Polly chopped and gathered wood for Teenie's fire, learned to set it, stoke it, and keep it blazing, and were taught how to hang the heavy pots so food would cook as Teenie commanded. Teenie showed them the stones that had been dug into the side of the fireplace where bread was baked and the iron grills where food was fried.

Amari still wasn't sure of how she felt about Polly, who at first seemed to be indignant that she wasn't working in the big house. Amari snorted with disdain at Polly's resentment. The white girl, she gradually learned, had the chance to be free one day. Amari knew too well that *she* would never taste freedom again.

Gradually, as they fell into a daily routine, Polly seemed to relax, but Amari could see she still felt somewhat superior to the slaves around her. She wouldn't touch any of them, not even to give Tidbit a hug. And she looked with longing at the main house all the time. Amari figured she was waiting for her opportunity to work there instead of in the kitchen with the slaves. The two girls merely tolerated each other.

Tidbit scurried everywhere with Amari and Polly, showing them how to turn the meat on the spit, the secrets of gathering eggs from the chickens without getting pecked, and what ingredients were needed to make the dough for the bread. For such a small child, he knew as much about the running of the kitchen as his mother, Amari thought, impressed. She thought sadly of how she used to try to avoid chores. How she wished she could help her mother once more!

Amari slowly learned how to cook and eat foods she never could have imagined. Sometimes they had squirrel or venison, which Amari learned was the meat of one of the many deer she saw around the place. The animal would be skinned and gutted, then the flesh was cut into long strips and hung in the smokehouse to dry over hot, smoked wood. Hams, mutton, even wild turkey hung there in the darkness of the smokehouse, waiting to be used in the winter, when food was not so plentiful. Teenie told Amari that it was the only building on the plantation that was kept locked at all times. Not even Teenie had a key.

Fresh fish was brought in by slaves every day, and Teenie taught both Amari and Polly how to clean it and fry it. Amari also showed Teenie how to make fish stew like her mother had made. It was on those days that she closed her eyes and dreamily imagined herself back, just for a moment, in the smoky hut of her parents.

One day, when Teenie brought in a basket of yams from the

garden, Amari babbled in excitement—half in English, half in her native language—unable to make Teenie understand at first that Amari's mother had grown yams just like these in her own garden.

"You talkin' 'bout how yams grow in Africa?" Teenie finally asked when Amari had calmed down.

Amari took a deep breath and grabbed a yam from Teenie's basket. "My mama," she began, then tears filled her eyes and she gave up trying to explain. She closed her eyes and sniffed it. She could almost smell her mother's boiled chicken and yams.

"You know, my mama come from Africa too," Teenie told her. "She teached me what she knew 'bout Africa food. Long as you remember, chile, it ain't never gone."

Amari nodded in appreciation.

Tidbit's constant laughter made the long workdays seem a bit easier. He laughed when Amari dropped food in the fire and when the rooster chased Polly and pecked her arm. Hushpuppy shadowed the child's every move, running with Tidbit in the sunshine, and Amari knew the dog slept curled up with him at night.

Tidbit jabbered all the time, asking questions, making little jokes, playing tricks on his mother and the two girls. Amari learned quite a bit of English from the boy, who seemed to know intuitively what she needed to know. She also liked the way Polly talked to her constantly, making sure she knew the words for each food or task they encountered. Although she was proud that her command of the language was growing, it bothered Amari that she still spoke it so poorly. She knew she sounded stupid, and she didn't like it. She got mixed up on verbs like "come" and "came," as well as on plurals of words like "house" and "mouse."

Why would these people say "houses" but not "mouses"? Why "mice" and not "hice"?

Amari understood much more than she let anyone know, however. Most of what was said around her she could figure out, but she knew the value of keeping her mouth shut and acting ignorant. An occasional slight nod from Teenie told her she was doing the right thing.

In the evening both she and Polly fell asleep exhausted, with Amari praying that she would not be called to the big house. But at least twice a week Tidbit stole quietly through the darkness to fetch Amari to come to the bedroom of Clay Derby. Each time, she forced her mind to go back to the dust of her childhood, to soft rain showers, to warm sunshine over her village—anything to help her endure, to help her forget his smell, his greasy hair, his damp hands.

But the worst was when he felt like talking—these were times she really hated because she was forced to stay in his room much longer.

"You ever talk to that cow my father married?" Clay asked her one night.

"Oh, no, suh," Amari had replied quickly. "I have no call to speak to the missus."

"She doesn't belong here," Clay said angrily, almost to himself. "And now she's having a child, and my father acts as if it is the next Messiah!" He ground his fist into the sheet.

Amari had no answer; she just wanted him to say she could leave.

He lifted his head off his pillow then and spoke directly in her face. His breath smelled of spoiled food, and Amari had to force herself not to gag. "You like me, don't you?" The question was sudden and abrupt.

Shocked at the question, Amari swallowed hard. If she said no, he might get angry. If she said yes, he might manage to misunderstand her hatred of him. So she pretended she didn't know what he meant.

"I asked you a question. I know you understand much more than you let on. You *do* like me, don't you?" he implored quietly. To Amari, his voice sounded a little plaintive, almost as if he *needed* her to say she liked him.

"Yassuh," Amari whispered, cringing.

Amari was amazed to hear him breathe a sigh of relief. "I had a feeling you cared about me," Clay said, assurance creeping back into his voice. "Did Teenie give you the extra blanket I left for you?" he asked, sounding concerned.

"Yassuh. Thank you, suh." What she didn't tell him was that she couldn't bear to touch the thing, so she had given the blanket to Sara Jane, a slave who had recently given birth.

"I think I'll let you come back tomorrow night," Clay said to Amari through the darkness. "I'm looking forward to it. Go on back to your place now."

"Thank you, suh," Amari whispered miserably. She crept out of his bed, down the back steps, and over the path through the darkness back to her cabin. She shivered uncontrollably and could not sleep. Morning always came harshly.

18. ROOTS AND DIRT

ONE AFTERNOON WHILE POLLY AND TIDBIT HAD gone to pick berries for a pie, Amari and Teenie were in a small garden Teenie had planted behind the kitchen.

"If you dig this yellow root here—it be called fever grass—then boil it," Teenie was telling her, "you can get rid of stomach cramps. And tea made from the bark of that tree yonder will stop a headache."

Ordinarily, Amari enjoyed these sessions with Teenie. It reminded her of times her mother had tried to teach her about herbs and roots and teas, but she had been too full of herself to pay much attention. But this day Amari was unusually quiet, having been compelled to spend the previous night with Clay, and he had forced her to do things that made her shiver with shame.

"The old folks calls this purple blossom buzzard root—it be good for female problems," Teenie told Amari quietly. When Amari didn't answer, Teenie looked into her face. "You look as low as a toad in a dry well, chile."

"You got root that kill?" Amari asked glumly.

To Amari's surprise, Teenie replied quietly, "Yes, chile, I reckon

I do. But death is not for me to give." She continued to dig furiously, her head down.

"Show me!" Amari implored, her heart beating faster.

"Not today," Teenie answered with a firm shake of her head. "Ain't nothin' you can do right now, chile." Teenie paused, then said, "For me, it was the overseer, Willie Badgett. Eventually, they gets tired of you and moves on—but the terribleness of it just goes to another slave woman." She reached over and touched Amari on the shoulder. She left her hand there a long time.

Grateful for the touch, Amari told Teenie, "I want die." She blinked back tears.

"No, chile, you was brought here for some reason—Lawd knows what it is, though." Teenie's voice was so sympathetic, Amari pressed her head into Teenie's chest.

"How long you be this place?" Amari asked after a moment, pulling away from her.

"I was borned here, chile. I tolt you my mama was a African like you be, but they sold her off when I was 'bout your age."

"Oh no—so very, very bad." Amari knew how deeply that must hurt.

Teenie's facial expression softened. "My mama be a strong Africa lady—Ashanti, she told me. She tell me how the thunder of the drums be echoin' 'cross the valleys, how the sun look at sunset—like a big old copper pot hangin' in the sky—and stories 'bout the antelope and the giraffe, 'bout the monkey and the spider. I tells Tidbit all I can remember."

"You telled me once that long as you 'member, nothin' ain't really gone," Amari reminded Teenie.

"I remembers it all," Teenie said softly. She reached into a pocket of her apron then and pulled out a small, faded scrap of multicolored fabric. Amari put her hand to her mouth with wonder. It was a tiny piece of woven kente cloth.

"Oh!" Amari whispered. It took her back to her father's loom.

"My mama give me this," Teenie explained. "When they snatched her away screaming from her mother, she grabbed on to her mother's head wrap. It ripped, and this little piece of it came off in her hand. She clutched it all the way 'cross the big water, even kept it in her mouth when she had to. When she got to this place, she buried it not far from that tree yonder, just to keep it safe. Just before they sold her, she give it to me, and she whisper to me that I never forget." Teenie sighed. "This be my little piece of my mother, my little breath of Africa. It's all I got." She carefully tucked it back into her pocket.

The two said nothing for a few moments while they let the memories come in. Teenie cleared her throat then, looked up at the sky, and said, "Prob'ly be rain tomorrow."

"S'pose so," Amari muttered. Needing to change the subject, she asked, "How you get to be cook here?"

"'Fore she died, the first Miz Derby put me in charge of the kitchen. That was right after Daisy the cook got sold because she tried to poison Massa Derby. Not too many folks willin' to challenge what old Miz Derby say. I been cookin' ever since."

Amari looked up with surprise at the mention of a first wife of Mr. Derby. "Other Miz Derby be dead?"

"Yeah, chile, she died givin' birth to that suck-egg mule, Clay. Maybe that why he be so evil—he ain't never had no mama to love him."

Amari thought about that for a moment and wondered how his first wife's death had affected the master of the house. But she didn't have all the words she needed to express it. So she asked, "Massa Derby miss first wife?"

"I 'spect so. She was shapely, black-haired, and good-looking for a white woman, plus she kept his house perfect, and he loved that. He used to act all addlepated when he was round her, like she was honey and he was the buzzin' bee. But she had a sharp tongue and would beat a slave for next to nothin'."

"What Massa Derby do when she die?" Amari asked.

"Massa like to die hisself—couldn't eat nor sleep. He wouldn't even look at that baby. Paid no 'tention at all to that chile till he be 'bout six year old. Clay grewed up alone in that big house with a bunch of nannies from 'cross the water."

"Why Massa marry up with Miz Isabelle?" Amari ventured.

"Why do white folks do anything?" Teenie answered with a laugh, holding her arms up to the sky. "All's I know is she had to come here to a cold ol' fish like Massa Derby, put up with his awful son and paintings of the dead wife, and be cut off from all her friends and family."

Teenie went back to digging for roots and plucking tomatoes then, not willing to discuss it any further. Amari returned to the kitchen. She picked up a broom made of branches and began to sweep the dusty floor. The harder she swept, the thicker the dust became—dirt swirled everywhere. She saw nothing but dirt in her own future.

ONE DUSTY AFTERNOON ABOUT A WEEK LATER
Teenie called to Tidbit, "Go fetch me some peaches for my pie,
boy. And take these two gals with you. Y'all look like you could
use some fresh air."

Tidbit jumped at the opportunity to stop shelling peas and
motioned to the girls to hurry before Teenie changed her mind.
Apples, peaches, and plums grew abundantly on the plantation,
as well as dozens of vegetables that Amari had never seen. Amari
followed the boy down the path, looked up at the same coppery
hot sun that used to warm her in her homeland, and breathed in
the fresh air thankfully.

Tidbit climbed high into the branches of the first peach tree he
came to. It was thick with sweet fruit. His job was to toss the
fruit down to Amari and Polly, who carried baskets. But instead
of gently handing it down, he laughed and threw the peaches like
weapons, smashing the soft fruit against their heads. Hushpuppy
barked crazily at the bottom of the tree, chasing the peaches and
even eating some of them.

"Stop, Tidbit!" Polly cried with laughter. "Your mama's

gonna get you for wasting food."

"Polly, Polly Peach Pie!" Tidbit chanted from the tree.

Amari had grown to love having the boy around. It was almost like Kwasi's spirit had found her in this strange new world. "Climb down from the tall tree, my little one," she said in her own language.

Tidbit shimmied to the ground, a peach in each hand, and looked at her strangely. "That Africa talk?" he asked.

Amari nodded.

"My mama be tellin' me stories 'bout Africa all the time, but she do it when ain't nobody else listenin'. Where Africa be?" the boy wanted to know.

"Far away. Over ocean. Under sky," she replied in English.

"What does it look like?" Polly asked.

"It look like bright colors, like happy. Sunshine. Family. Chickens and goats. Not need much." Amari smiled softly, thinking back to the green seas of grass that she and Tirza ran through as girls, the red and green screaming jacana birds that awakened her, the annoying little monkey that would whisk into the village and steal papayas when her mother turned her back, the smell of the wood fire in front of their hut. She wanted to explain how *right* everything felt in a place where she was surrounded by mischievous children, overbearing cousins, and doddering elders who were all a part of her. The storytellers who had absorbed her history, the villagers who breathed the same air and dreamed the same memories—all of them were black. She did not have the words to express the depth of her loss. "Everybody black. Feel good," was all she said.

Amari remembered the utter safety she felt as a child in her village, knowing that if she fell down and skinned her knee, any woman close by would dry her tears, put a little mud on the wound, and send her on her way with a hug.

"Little boys like me be there?" Tidbit asked with genuine curiosity.

"I had a brother," she said slowly. "Little older than you be. Happy boy with laugh like gold." She had to close her eyes at the thought of Kwasi.

"Where he be now?" Tidbit asked innocently.

Amari's face crumpled. "Dead," she said. Tidbit looked at her and nodded with a look of almost adult understanding. The three of them were silent for a few minutes, the only sound being the trilling of warblers and swallows.

Tidbit then asked Polly, "Where you was 'fore you come here?"

Polly looked thoughtful. "I grew up not far from here—in the low country. I remember moving from place to place and never having enough money, but that never bothered my parents. They doted on each other, but I was their shining star." Amari was thankful Polly spoke slowly so she could follow along.

"What that mean?" Tidbit asked.

"You know how your mama looks at you just before you go to sleep? That worried look when you stay out with Hushpuppy too long?" The boy nodded. "That's how my mama and daddy loved me."

Amari understood as well, but it surprised her. She'd never really thought about Polly's loss or grief. She just figured that because Polly was a white girl, her life just had to have been easier.

Polly looked into the distance and kicked at the tree trunk. "My mother told me once that she wanted to be a lady—somebody who wore lace and rode in a fancy carriage. But it never happened," she mumbled. "So she wished it for me."

Amari wasn't sure of every single word, but she knew Polly missed her mother. She reached over and touched Polly's hand. She was surprised that Polly didn't jerk away.

"You ever goin' back to Africa?" Tidbit asked Amari.

"No," Amari replied quietly and sadly, and she knew that it was forever true. Tidbit nestled against her, as if he understood her sorrow.

The two girls, accompanied by an unusually quiet Tidbit, walked back to Teenie's kitchen in silence. They delivered the peaches to Teenie and returned to their chores without comment.

◆

IN SPITE OF TEENIE'S DIMINUTIVE SIZE, AMARI noticed that no one ever questioned her authority in the kitchen, not even the white people who lived in the main house. For a slave, that was power.

Isabelle Derby, the current mistress of the house, turned out to be surprisingly motherly and caring. Amari had heard whispers and rumors about her from some of the house slaves who stopped by Teenie's kitchen. Her husband controlled her every move and kept her away from everyone she had once known, they said. Amari noticed also that the household servants obeyed her without question—maybe because she was the only white person they knew who looked at them with a smile.

All the slaves also whispered about the fact that she was pregnant.

Each morning Mrs. Derby, dressed in white, as she usually was, came to Teenie's kitchen, greeted everyone with a cheerful hello, and planned the meals for the day. She would sometimes unlock the smokehouse so Teenie could choose a smoked meat if nothing fresh was available. Amari knew that Teenie would fix what she wanted to in spite of what Mrs. Derby suggested, but they had this conversation every morning anyway.

"It's a lovely day, Teenie," she'd always begin. She would always glance out of the narrow door and toward the horizon as she said that. It seemed to Amari that she wished she could be in another place.

"Yes'm. Gonna be hot again—hotter than buzzard's breath." A look of wistful sorrow crossed Mrs. Derby's face.

"Perhaps some iced tea for Master Derby at dinner would be refreshing." Mrs. Derby always frowned as she spoke of her husband.

"Yes'm. I be fixin' fresh chicken and snow peas and hush puppies. Anything else you be wantin' today?"

"Maybe some of your delicious peach pie?"

"Already done started it, ma'am. Be real good for you and that chile you carryin'. You need a little meat on them bones."

Mrs. Derby looked down at her swollen belly. "I pray for this child, Teenie," she said quietly. Amari watched as the woman gently rubbed her stomach.

"Yes'm. Maybe that chile make you happy for shure."

"Perhaps," Mrs. Derby replied, the wistful look returning.

Amari was fascinated with this white woman who seemed to be so pleasant and gentle. She tried to be in the kitchen area whenever Mrs. Derby came around, because the mistress of the house had a kind word for everyone and always smelled like flowers. Amari liked the fact that she didn't look at her as if she were ugly or an animal or a piece of flesh to be used. Mrs. Derby smiled at her with genuine compassion.

One early morning when the grass was still wet with dew,

Amari was returning to the kitchen with a bucket of water for Teenie. She didn't often get time alone, so she walked slowly, savoring each solitary moment, even though she knew Teenie would scold her for being late.

She looked up with surprise as she almost collided with Mrs. Derby, who was walking alone on the path that led to the woods. Dressed in a long billowing gown that accentuated her pregnancy and a white hooded shawl, she looked almost like a spirit to Amari.

"You are Myna, am I correct?" Mrs. Derby asked her, to Amari's surprise. Her voice sounded whispery.

Nervously, Amari replied, "Yes'm." She stared down at her own bare, dirty feet, which stood so close to the fancy white shoes of the mistress. Teenie had told her never to look the masters directly in their eyes, but Amari had stolen looks at Mrs. Derby as often as she had been able to.

"Are you adjusting to your life here?" the woman asked kindly.

Again Amari simply replied, "Yes'm." How could she tell this woman of the horrors of her forced nights with Clay or her gut-wrenching longing for her mother?

"It must be very difficult for you, dear," Mrs. Derby said, as if she had read Amari's mind. "I know what it is like to be unhappy."

Surprised, Amari looked up. This white woman was admitting a weakness to her—a slave? Mrs. Derby smiled and reached out to touch Amari's shoulder. Amari, startled by her kind touch, gazed into eyes so green, they looked unreal. She had never encountered anyone with eyes that color. Amari also noticed what might have been tears on Mrs. Derby's face, but perhaps it was just her imagination.

Mrs. Derby hesitated, then said, "I know about you and Clay."

Amari stepped back, her heart beating fast. What did she mean, "you and Clay"? Did this woman think she went to his room *voluntarily*? Amari didn't know what to say, didn't know *how* to say all the jumbled thoughts in her head.

"It is an unfortunate situation," Mrs. Derby said with feeling. "But I have no control over what he does. To tell you the truth, I have very little power over anything around here," she said morosely. "I just want to let you know I sympathize. I hope it ends soon."

Amari, whose face was hot with embarrassment, managed to mumble, "Thank you, ma'am."

"I must go now," Mrs. Derby said suddenly, looking nervously toward the manor house. She gave Amari one last look, then turned and hurried back to the house, her body a silhouette against the morning sun.

Later that afternoon Amari, peeling potatoes in the corner of the kitchen, listened as Lena, one of the house slaves, gossiped with Teenie. Grasping on to every word, Amari did her best to figure out the conversation. "Miz Isabelle be carryin' that baby real high, Teenie. I figger it's a boy."

"No, gal," Teenie commented. "It's a girl for shure. Miz Isabelle deserve a purty little girl to keep her company in that big ol' house. I feels sorry for her."

"How you feel sorry for a rich white woman?" Lena asked harshly.

"Money ain't everything, chile. And ain't none of his money belong to her—she got 'bout as much chance to use his money as you do."

"Yeah, but she ain't no slave," Lena insisted.

"Pretty close to it," Teenie said. "He decide where she go, who she talk to, what she wear—everything. She just sleep in a better bed than you do!"

Lena continued, "And Noah, that slave she brought with her, I heard tell she got legal papers all writ up for him, so when she die, he be free."

"Do say, now," Teenie replied, but she made no real comment. Lena had ambled out of the kitchen then, to tend to other chores.

Intrigued, Amari wanted to know more. "How old she be— Miz Derby?" Amari asked Teenie.

Teenie counted on her fingers. "Maybe round 'bout eighteen. She jest a young thing. She came to that marriage with her slave Noah, lots of land, and piles of money, which is what ol' Massa wanted." Teenie glanced at Amari, a look of warning on her face. "Now, don't you be mindin' white folks' business, you hear me, gal? Just get them 'taters peeled right quickly."

Amari nodded and tried to focus on the mountain of potatoes in front of her.

Several evenings later, just before darkness completely obscured the path, Amari, exhausted from the labors of the day, hurried to finish gathering kindling to stoke Teenie's fire during the night. Suddenly, she stiffened, for just off the path she heard soft voices— a deep male voice, speaking in hushed tones, then a female's whispered reply. The woman seemed to be upset or crying.

"Who there?" Amari asked, not sure what she was interrupting. She recognized most of the slaves on the place by now and knew they posed no threat to her. But she feared running into Clay.

She heard a rustling in the bushes, then footsteps retreating. Amari listened for a moment or two, but all was silent, so she hurried back to Teenie's kitchen. She had learned, in her short time on the plantation, never to ask too many questions. Some things were best left unsaid, so she did not mention the incident to Teenie or Polly.

At the end of each day Amari collapsed, exhausted, on the floor mat in their small cabin. At first she thought she was being selfish, taking the sleeping mat from Polly, but Polly actually seemed to prefer that lumpy, smelly mattress. Gradually, Amari had figured out that not everyone slept as she had back in her village.

Clay, for example, slept on a soft, clean feather mattress, with perfumed sheets and silken curtains around the four-poster bed. But the curtains hid his vile habits, the smell of the perfume made her gag, and the clean sheets stank of his sweat by the time he was done with her. Oh, how she hated the smells of that bed!

Amari didn't know how the other slaves managed, for after their day's labor, they returned to their huts to care for their children, tend their small gardens, and prepare their own meals for the next day. Sometimes she heard bits of their conversations and voices singing late into the midnight hours.

"Why do you think they sing?" Polly whispered one hot, humid night as they listened to the somber songs drift through the window.

"Songs float up to sky—fly free," Amari had replied simply. She sadly thought back to the music of her mother's voice. She fell asleep, and thankfully, on that night, she was not awakened by Tidbit.

PART FOUR

POLLY

POLLY WAS DETERMINED TO GET A POSITION IN the big house. The slave girl was adjusting, Teenie didn't really need her, and Polly was tired of working like a common slave. She waited for her opportunity, praying for a moment alone with Mrs. Derby to ask for a more suitable position in her household. But Teenie kept her busy from dawn to dusk doing what Polly considered to be slave labor—peeling potatoes, shelling peas, shucking corn, and carrying heavy stacks of kindling for the fire.

Lots of corn grew on the land, and Polly was consistently impressed by Teenie, who seemed to know thousands of things she could make from it, but Derbyshire Farms was actually a rice plantation. Rice was everywhere. Rice ruled.

"Do you think Mr. Derby gets his wealth from the rice?" she asked Teenie one humid afternoon.

"Lawd, chile, what you care about Massa Derby's money? All I knows is every year Massa Derby go to market and buy big strong male slaves directly from Africa, for to work in the rice fields," she explained. "I was surprised at first when he brung

Myna here—little biddy girl thing—she ain't no bigger than a rock-eatin' chicken. For shure she ain't strong enough to work the fields." She sighed. "But then I figgered out the reason why. I'm sorry, chile," she said to Amari.

Amari simply shrugged. "Why he buy Africa men?" she asked Teenie.

"They knows the rice 'cause they work it in their own country. They the brains of the whole project here. Massa won't admit it, but he need them men to keep this place goin'. They is what's makin' him rich."

Polly pondered this a moment, trying to find any opportunity to move from the kitchen to the house. "Perhaps Mr. Derby could use an assistant to help him keep his books. I can read and cipher, you know," she added with a bit of pride.

Teenie snorted. "Ain't much call for none of that round here. That's enough o' talkin' about the massa's money. I want y'all to head over to the rice fields and take this here water to the workers. Tote a little corn bread for 'em too. Lawd knows when they gonna git the time to eat or drink, though." She prepared a large wooden bucket for each girl to carry.

Polly groaned inwardly as once again she was given what she considered to be slave duties. *What is the advantage of being white if I have to work like I'm black every day?* she thought with consternation. *Mama would die if she saw me here!*

Teenie motioned to the boy. "Tidbit, you and that dog of yourn go with them and show them the way. But you stay outta that water, you hear? Gators get you!" Teenie wiped the sweat from her face.

"Yes, Teenie," Polly replied with resignation. She grabbed one of the buckets.

"Leave everything with Cato—if he ain't dead yet. He so old, he couldn't cut hot butter with a knife!" She laughed at her own joke. "And don't be all day down there—y'all got work to do back here."

Polly gritted her teeth, slowly repeated everything Teenie had said to Amari, even though she figured the girl had already understood most of it, and headed out of the kitchen and down to the river.

As they were walking down the path, Polly heard Teenie call out one final warning: "Y'all be careful of snakes, now!" Tidbit laughed, dropped to the ground, and pretended to slither like a snake. Hushpuppy, always ready for a new game, cavorted around Tidbit, barking wildly.

"Get up, silly boy," Polly said, her grim mood fading. "Your mama will get us if you get any dirtier." The boy got up, but he darted along the path like a little insect, picking up bugs and rocks along the road and tossing sticks for Hushpuppy to chase.

"I hate the heat of late summer," Polly remarked, her hair sticking to her face in the humidity. Amari didn't respond, but she seemed to be enjoying the warmth of the sunshine.

Polly had never been this far from the big house. She had heard of the rice fields, but she stood amazed at what she saw. Two dozen black men and women, knee-deep in thick mud, bent over the delicate-looking rice plants. There was no shade anywhere, and Polly could see thick rivulets of sweat running down their faces. They moved slowly, joylessly. *How can people live like this?* Polly thought.

"What y'all want?" a wrinkled, skinny slave sitting on the bank of the river asked. His hair, what was left of it, dotted his head like tiny clouds. "Hey, Tidbit! How be the little man and his dog?"

Tidbit bounded over to the old man and gave him a big hug. "Hey, Cato."

"Teenie sent corn pone and water for the rice workers," Polly told him.

"Hopes they get to eat 'em 'fore the bugs do!" He cackled, then almost choked in a spasm of coughing. "So how it be fer the new 'dentured gal?" he asked Polly when he got his breath. "That sunshine-colored hair of yourn gonna get you out of your indenture right quick," he predicted. "Alls you need is a lonely little white boy!" He laughed at his own comments, then coughed even harder.

Polly touched her hair but did not answer him directly.

Amari asked him, "You work hard today, Cato?" Polly had learned that Cato, the oldest slave on the plantation, always seemed to know everything that went on while managing to do very little work at all.

"They ain't got much choice but to let me do pretty much what I wants to nowadays, since they done 'bout worked me dry," he said, chuckling. "Right now I'm workin' at watchin' this here grass grow!" He laughed and coughed deeply.

Cato looked up at Polly then. "You two still workin' in the kitchen?" he asked.

Polly nodded.

"Not fer long, chile. You'se a white gal—soon they gonna have you sewing fer Miz Isabelle." Polly thrilled at the possibility. "But

Miz Africa here gonna be down here in the swamps with us—
soon as Massa Clay get tired of her." Amari let out a soft moan.

"How do you know this?" Polly asked.

"I ain't the oldest slave on the place fer nothin'. I hears things
and sees things."

"Maybe it is too soon for her," Polly said, frowning.

Amari looked at Polly, a look of surprise on her face.

"You don't have to convince ol' Cato. I'm just tellin' you what
I knows. Massa love to see the Africans workin' the rice."

"You ever hear tell of anybody goin' back to Africa?" Tidbit
asked.

Cato replied seriously, "No, little one. Don't nobody go back
to Africa. When they put you in the rice fields, you'll be dead in
five years, so don't matter no how."

"Five years? Why?" Polly asked, sounding genuinely shocked.

"Let me 'splain," Cato replied. "I spent eighteen years out
there—some kinda record they tells me. Every day the rice hands
be exposed to the burnin' sun. Sometime it seem like the very air
we be breathin' is hotter than human blood. Then there's the
malaria, and the new-monia and the snakes, plus the mosquitoes
and the flies and their maggots—all joinin' us to keep us company while we sweat. Pregnant women be havin' stillbirths, and
the babies that end up bein' born die young—like they sickly or
somethin'. That's why Massa keepa bringin' in new Africans—
they knows the rice, and they strong."

Amari inhaled deeply and looked at Cato, her eyes wide.

"Hey, boy!" Cato called to Tidbit as he heard the dog bark with
alarm. "Get away from that water! You want a gator to eat you?"

"Gator can't catch me!" Tidbit replied, but he ran back up on the grass.

"You know how rice be planted?" Cato asked the girls as he continued. They shook their heads. "One seed at a time."

"But rice be so small!" Amari remarked.

"Yep, that it is. You makes a hole in the mud with your toe. You drops the one tiny little rice seed in the hole. Then you closes the hole with the heel of your foot. Toe. Plant. Heel. All day long. Bendin' over. Knee-deep in swamp water." Cato coughed once more and looked down at the ground.

"And that's just the first part. Then you gotta tend to the plants and flood the fields and cut the stacks and thresh the seeds— seem like it go on forever. That's what be in your future, Miz Africa. And when he get old enough, this here boy's future too."

Polly looked at Cato in disbelief. "They'd put Tidbit out there?" she asked, horrified. The thought of little Tidbit sweating and working in the dangerous swampy water made Polly feel ill.

Amari put her hand to her mouth, barely holding back a sob. "What to do?" she finally asked.

Cato shrugged. "It might help if Miz Isabelle like you, but she ain't got no say-so over much round here. I s'pose you gotta keep on makin' yourself useful in Massa Clay's bedroom—that be all any slave woman can do," Cato explained sadly, "lessen she run away."

At that moment they heard a bloodcurdling scream coming from one of the slaves in the rice field. Cato moved astonishingly quickly for an old man, and he hurried down to see what happened. Polly, Amari, and Tidbit followed.

"Oh, my Lawd! Copperhead!" a slave named Jacob cried hoarsely. "My Hildy been snake-bit!"

Polly watched, horrified, as Jacob emerged from the swampy mud, carrying Hildy's limp body to the shore. He laid her gently on the grass. Polly could barely see the two small wounds on her leg; there was very little blood. Some of the slave women quickly daubed her leg with mud and wrapped it tightly with strips of cloth ripped from their own dresses. The woman's eyelids fluttered, she called for her husband, then she arched her back and was still.

"She be dead?" Amari asked, her voice barely a whisper. Tidbit, for once, was still and quiet.

"Not yet," Cato replied quietly. "Just passed out. But the poison likely to kill her by sunset. Copperhead don't play." Cato looked directly at Amari as he spoke again. "Two dead of snakebite this season. Two more died of the malaria. One gator bite. One drownt. Do whatever you can to stay outta this here place, gal. Ya hear?"

Amari looked terrified, Polly thought, and rightfully so.

As they left the rice fields, Polly could hear the workers being called back to work—no free time just because of a little snakebite.

WHEN POLLY AND AMARI RETURNED TO TEENIE'S kitchen, both of them clearly upset, Teenie didn't seem the least bit surprised. "How's Hildy?" she asked as she pulled Tidbit close to her.

"Cato told us she might die," Polly reported, tucking her shaking hands under her arms. Then she asked, "How'd you know?"

"I declare, chile. You oughta know by now that it don't take long for news to travel round here," Teenie said. "So, did Cato also scare you 'bout how gals like Myna here be endin' up in rice fields?"

Polly nodded, then frowned. This time last year, when she was back in Beaufort with her folks, she wouldn't have given a second thought to a slave going to work in the rice fields. That's what a slave was *supposed* to do. Who cared about the feelings of an ignorant slave, anyway? But this was someone she knew, maybe even felt sorry for. Somehow that made a difference.

"Cato speaks true," Teenie said solemnly. "But I got an idea. Let's see what we can do. The two of you go out back and wash yourself. Get back in here real quicklike."

The two girls returned with clean faces and hands, and Teenie handed them each an outfit worn by the house serving maids. "Flora, one of the serving gals, is Hildy's daughter. She done run down there to see to her mama," Teenie explained. "Massa don't allow such behavior, but he don't know yet. So you two gonna take her place at supper." Polly and Amari exchanged looks of surprise.

"Polly, you just do what Lena, the head serving gal, tells you to do. Say nothing except for 'yes, sir' and 'yes, ma'am.' Myna, you copy everything they do and act like you know what you doin'! You understandin' all this, gal?"

Polly was pleased that Amari replied as she had been taught, "Yes, Teenie." But she was thrilled about the chance to go work in the big house. Finally!

Teenie looked worried, however. "Don't you drop nothin', you hear! Now git!" she told them.

Polly changed quickly into the stiff black uniform, inwardly praying that perhaps this would be the start of her move up to the main house and out of the kitchen with the slaves. She then helped Amari tie the sash on her apron. Tidbit laughed out loud when he saw the two girls dressed as maids.

Polly shooed him away. "Have you seen Mr. Derby since the first day we arrived here?" she asked Amari as they prepared to take the food to the main house.

Amari shook her head. "Not see, which be good."

"Have you ever been inside the main house?" Polly asked. Then she gasped as she realized what Amari's answer would be.

"Only nighttime," Amari replied harshly.

"Oh, Myna, I forgot."

"I not forget," Amari stated, her voice sharp as broken glass.

"Do you think Mrs. Derby knows what Clay is doing?"

"She know," Amari said angrily.

"Maybe she can help you," Polly offered tentatively. "She seems to be very pleasant."

"She need help herself," Amari replied sharply.

Polly tried to understand, but she couldn't truly fathom the depths of Myna's apparent distress. Slave women were always called to the bedrooms of their masters—it was simply a fact of life. Myna should understand that by now and be getting used to it. But she let the subject drop as they prepared to carry the food.

Amari took a platter of venison, while Polly carried a huge, glistening corn pone on another large platter. They walked carefully up the path from the kitchen to the big house and entered through the back door.

Lena took one look at the two girls and rolled her eyes up to the ceiling. "Lawd have mercy, we gonna get in trouble for shure! Tell Teenie if I gets a beatin' over this, I ain't never forgivin' her. Now go on back and bring the rest of the food."

Polly and Amari dashed back several more times to get the rest of the food for supper for Mr. Derby and his wife. All of it was laid out on a sideboard, to be served as Lena directed.

Polly looked around the room in rapt curiosity. *Now, this is where I belong,* she thought with a smile, taking in the dark green curtains covering the windows to keep out the afternoon heat, the fine, pale green, embroidered carpet decorating each floor, and the pictures of ancient Derby relatives lining the walls. Fancy silver eating and drinking utensils lay in a huge cupboard on the other side of the room. Polly had never seen such finery. *Oh, how Mama would have loved this!* she thought.

Polly tiptoed to peek into the adjoining room, which was obviously Mr. Derby's study. She inhaled with pleasure. Shelves of leather-bound books filled one wall. She'd give anything to simply touch them; to have access to them would be heaven. Her mother had taught her to read using the Bible and occasional pieces of newsprint that came their way, but Polly longed for books of her own. *If I could get assigned to the main house,* she thought, *I would sneak into this room during every free moment.* She sighed and returned to the dining area.

Standing silently near the door of the dining room, almost like a statue, was the coachman who had driven the two girls here from the market just a few months ago. Once again he was dressed in an elegant coat and a shirt with lace cuffs. "This here is Noah," Lena explained. Noah nodded slightly but continued to stand stiffly and formally. "He's the coachman, the butler, Miz Isabelle's bodyguard, and prob'ly the fanciest house slave we got round here—best lookin', too!" Lena laughed. "Massa trusts him, and"—she lowered her voice to a whisper—"word is that Miz Isabelle done taught him how to read! He—"

Suddenly, Lena cleared her throat and snapped to attention. Polly and Amari did the same. Mr. Derby, dressed in a red velvet suit, escorted his now very pregnant wife into the room. Clay sauntered in behind them, gave a look of undisguised disgust to his stepmother, and sat as far away from her as he could. He seemed to be trying to get Amari's attention, Polly thought, but Amari had dropped her head and refused to look at him.

"Where's Flora?" Mr. Derby demanded as soon as he had helped his wife be seated.

"Her mama got snake-bit today, sir. Real bad. She done run to the quarters to see her," Lena explained quickly. "But we got something special for your supper today, yes we do. Polly, pour the wine like I showed you." Polly hurried to obey.

"Well, I hope she's not too badly injured," Mr. Derby said irritably. "I hate it when my workers are laid up."

Mrs. Derby spoke up, although barely audibly. "Shall I check on her tomorrow, Percival?"

"No, my dear. I really disapprove of you dealing with the servants. It's not wise in your condition, you know."

"She might need medical attention," Mrs. Derby suggested softly.

"I'm sure she'll be fine," her husband said. "It is *you* I worry about, Isabelle. Right now the most important things on my mind are your happiness and comfort," he said firmly, "and the safety of our child. I could never forgive myself if anything happened to that baby. I have not been this excited, or this happy, in many years." He took her hand in his. It seemed to Polly that he gazed at his wife with genuine concern.

Mrs. Derby smiled at him, touched her belly, and let the matter drop.

Turning to Clay, Mr. Derby said, "Son, run down to the quarters tomorrow and get one of the slaves from the fishing gang to take her place."

"It will be my pleasure, Father," the young man replied lazily, "but why not just send Noah? He's able-bodied. Perfectly good waste of a strong worker, seems to me." Polly saw Clay look at his stepmother with a wicked grin.

Isabelle Derby inhaled, then looked at her husband in alarm. "You promised, Percival. You promised when we married that I could keep my bodyguard."

Mr. Derby's face softened as he put his arm around his wife's shoulders and gave her what seemed to be a reassuring hug. "I think Clay is merely teasing you, my dear. I wouldn't think of upsetting you by doing such a thing. All I care about right now is your health and your happiness." To Clay he said, "Try to be kinder, son. You'll have a brother or sister soon."

Clay rolled his eyes, looked at Mrs. Derby with disdain, and drank another glass of wine. It was clear to Polly that he truly disliked his stepmother.

As they continued to serve the food, Amari looked nervous, so Polly tried to help whenever she thought Amari might not understand a command. She wasn't going to let Amari spoil her chance to impress the Derbys. Noah continued to stand like a sentry at the door, never moving, never displaying any emotion.

Mrs. Derby drank very little of the white wine that Amari had carefully poured for her. She had given Amari a pleasant smile, however, and had thanked her as Amari deftly slipped a white linen napkin onto Mrs. Derby's lap.

"You must eat more, my dear Isabelle," Mr. Derby said to his wife. "You want our child to be healthy, don't you?"

She looked up nervously. "Yes, of course you are right, Percival," she replied. She motioned to Polly to put a little more corn pone on her plate, but Polly noticed she only nibbled at it.

"Please tell Teenie the supper is delicious," Mrs. Derby said to Lena.

"Now, don't compliment the slaves on doing their jobs, my dear. Your kindness only makes them weak and careless." It sounded to Polly that Mr. Derby admonished his wife almost as if he were speaking to a child, but he also seemed to dote on her. He touched her constantly, fixing a ringlet of hair that had fallen into her face, brushing a speck from her shawl, and patting her left hand with his right.

As Lena skillfully served the stew, venison, corn, and beans to the Derby family, Amari and Polly were kept busy taking plates back to the kitchen, bringing up steaming baskets of bread, and, finally, a fresh-baked blackberry pie.

Mrs. Derby continued to pick at her food, and her husband sometimes stopped his conversation with Clay to cut a small piece of meat for his wife so she would eat it. "Now, don't you feel better?" he would say after she had swallowed it. She would smile wanly in agreement. It seemed to Polly that he treated his wife more like a delicate possession than a real person. Any genuine conversation he seemed to save for his son.

"I'm thinking we can bring in a few more slaves," he told Clay. "The rice crop will do well this year, and the market has gone up. Let's plan on making a bigger harvest next season."

Clay nodded, casting another glance at Amari. "That means expanding the fields by the river. We'll need fresh Africans for that—they know rice so well."

"How many, do you think?" his father asked.

"Three or four, at least," Clay replied. "They don't seem to last long out there."

"Well, I'll keep my eyes open the next time I go to market," Mr. Derby said. "We best be getting them soon, so they can be broken in by planting time."

They speak about buying slaves the same way they discuss the purchase of cattle or supplies, Polly noticed, surprised at how uncomfortable that made her feel. *When I am the mistress of such a place, will I discuss the purchase of people as they do?* She was not sure of the answer.

"Do you think we'll need to sell any slaves to get money for next year's supplies?" Clay asked his father.

"Not this season, son. I've monitored the books quite closely, and I think this year we will make quite a profit without selling any property." He seemed pleased.

Property. They call the slaves property. Polly thought about the slaves she had come to know since she had come to the plantation. The thought of one of them being sold distressed her in a way she had not thought possible. *Without Amari and Teenie and Tidbit, how awful it would be here,* Polly suddenly realized.

Clay stopped to scratch his head, then said to his father, "I hear talk in town of folks in the North starting to speak about ending slavery."

Mr. Derby, sipping his third glass of wine, snorted, "That will never happen. Those Northerners. They can't even *grow* the rice they love so much. They know nothing about how a business is run. Rice, tobacco, corn—where do they think it comes from?"

Clay, who had had even more wine than his father, leaned back on the two back legs of his chair carelessly. "Slavery just makes good sense to me. Anyway, our slaves are better off here than in some jungle eating bugs and slugs like savages."

"Of course they are. They need us, son."

Mr. Derby is right, isn't he? Living here has got to be better than a jungle, right? Polly wasn't sure anymore. She could see Lena grinding her teeth in anger. She glanced over at Amari to see her reaction, but Amari stared straight ahead.

Isabelle Derby sat pale and quiet, her eyes cast down through most of the meal. It was as if she were one of the many room decorations. Unhappiness seemed to ooze from her like perspiration on a humid day. Polly shook her head as she realized that being a fine lady didn't necessarily mean finding joy. Clay's antagonism toward Mrs. Derby was almost palpable—he glared at her every time she picked up a spoon or wiped her lips with a linen napkin.

Finally, the meal was over, and the last of the dishes were being removed. Polly, relieved that neither she nor Amari had done anything to call negative attention to themselves, congratulated herself on a successful evening. *I'm going to speak to Mrs. Derby right after dinner,* Polly vowed bravely. *This might be my only chance. I will offer my services as her personal assistant. Surely, with the new baby, she will need someone to help her.*

Mr. Derby finished a last glass of wine, then lit his pipe and stretched his long legs out from his chair just as Amari was walking by with the final platter of leftover blackberry pie. Amari, looking at Polly rather than the floor, tripped over his legs and fell. *No! No!* Polly breathed as the platter flipped and the pie careened to the floor. Purple-red berries splattered onto the pale carpet. There was a moment of absolute silence.

Amari cowered on the floor in obvious terror. Polly, too afraid to breathe, waited for the thunderous voice of the master.

"You stupid black wench!" he roared. "Lena, go get my whip!" Polly gasped at the same moment as Amari did. Polly knew Lena had no choice but to obey. She returned quickly and handed it to Mr. Derby, never looking at him directly. Coiled like a snake, the whip was made of leather. The tip of the lash was laced with wire.

Polly inhaled and held her breath.

Mr. Derby grasped the handle, drew his arm back, and fiercely brought the braided lash of it across Amari's back. She screamed, twisting with pain at his feet. Again he beat her. And again. Seven times he thrashed her. Ten. Twelve. The back of her new house-maid uniform was ripped to shreds, stained with her blood.

Polly clenched her hands into fists, furious at being so helpless and angry at her own selfishness as well. Because even though she flinched every time Amari was hit, she couldn't help but realize that this incident would forever ruin her chances of working in the main house.

Lena quietly murmured words of prayer. Horror distorted Mrs. Derby's face. Clay looked surprisingly uncomfortable and agitated. Only Noah never changed his stance or facial expression.

Finally, Isabelle Derby got up from the table and walked over to her husband. Noticeably trembling, she grabbed his hand as he lifted it to strike Amari again. "Enough," she said quietly. "The girl has learned her lesson. Make her clean up the mess and let her be. It is distressing to me to see such a scene. It might mar our child."

Mr. Derby, as if returning from another place, shook his head and coiled the whip. "You are right, my dear," he told his wife.

He took a deep breath. To Polly he said, "I put you in charge of this ignorant African. You have failed me. It is your fault she made such a fool of herself tonight. Clean the floor, then tend to her wounds. As soon as she's healed, she goes to the rice fields to replace Hildy."

Polly bowed her head and murmured apologies that she knew Mr. Derby would not hear. She dared to look at Amari, who lay deathly still, and at the carpet, stained with both blood and pie. Polly wasn't sure what to do first. She had never been so scared in her life.

Mr. Derby escorted his wife out of the room then. Clay, looking quite distressed, gazed at the bleeding and unconscious Amari for a long time before following after them.

Noah slowly left the room as well, as his job was protector of the master and his wife. "Vinegar," he whispered as he headed out of the door. "Vinegar will remove the stains from the carpet."

PART FIVE
AMARI

23. FIERY PAIN AND HEALING HANDS

HER BACK WAS ON FIRE. AMARI DIDN'T REMEMBER being brought back to the cabin, didn't hear Teenie's shouts or see Polly's tears. All she knew was that every breath made the pain intensify, every movement made her gasp and scream. She was dimly aware of voices above her, of hands carefully washing the bleeding, sliced skin on her back, of cooling salves being applied. Then, mercifully, she slept.

For three days she hovered between the darkness and the light. She dreamed of her parents, of her little brother, of the belly of the slave ship. And of the flames that devoured her flesh. On the third morning Amari felt gentle hands and cool water on her face. She opened her eyes and saw Polly.

"Welcome back," Polly said softly.

"Water," Amari whispered. Polly lifted Amari's head and gave her small sips of water from a cup.

"Hurt so bad," Amari said next. She groaned as she tried to move.

"Yes, I know. Let me put some more of Teenie's salve on your back. I don't know what's in it, but already the welts are starting to heal a little. At least the bleeding has stopped."

"So sorry," Amari said.

"Don't apologize. It's not your fault. Mr. Derby needs to have somebody give *him* a stiff lashing to let him know how it feels!" She stomped back and forth in their cabin. Amari, even in her dazed state, could feel that Polly's anger was too big for the small room.

"It be better soon," Amari said, trying to calm Polly a bit.

Polly picked up an empty wooden bucket and threw it across the floor. "Mr. Derby is horribly cruel. He probably tripped you on purpose! How could he beat you like that? It was just a spilled pie!"

"Must clean stain," Amari whispered, trying to move.

Polly placed her hand on Amari's arm. "Be still. Me and Lena cleaned it up so you would never know it was there. His precious carpet is unharmed."

"Thank you," Amari breathed out.

"All you have to worry about is getting better. I never thought I'd say this, but I miss having you around."

Amari blinked with surprise. She knew how much Polly yearned to escape from the kitchen—her desire to move on and her distaste for the work of slaves were very apparent. Amari grimaced as she moved her head. She looked at Polly with remorse. "Now you never get chance to go to big house. So sorry."

Polly placed another cool rag on Amari's head. "You continue to surprise me, Amari. I had no idea my desires were so obvious. You watch and you learn. That is very wise."

Amari tried to nod her head, but it hurt too much. After a

few moments she asked with a slight smile, "Teenie work you too much?"

Polly replied. "All I have to help me is Tidbit, and that's about as much help as a rabbit in the rice field!"

"You sound like Teenie," Amari remarked quietly.

At that Polly almost laughed out loud.

Amari was remembering what Mr. Derby had threatened, however. "Rice," she said bleakly. "He gonna send me to rice field." She couldn't stop the tears that began to trickle down her face.

Polly's face fell. "Yes, he threatened to send you to the rice fields. We just have to think of something to get him to change his mind. In the meantime, he won't do anything until you are well, so let's make sure your recovery is very, very slow!"

Amari knew, however, that it was just a matter of time before she would be toiling in the hot sun, up to her knees in water, planting the rice, one kernel after another. "Rice field come soon," she mumbled.

"I have to get up to the kitchen to help Teenie. I'll be back to check on you. You'll be all right for now?" Polly asked Amari, real concern in her voice.

Polly's voice faded as Amari drifted in and out of reality. Dreams of sunny days with Besa and the fiery sun over the rice fields floated above her. In her haze her mother was alive and laughing, dancing in front of her cooking fire. And, strangely, she dreamed of Mrs. Derby, whose face sometimes replaced her mother's in her dreams.

When she awoke, it was dark outside and Amari could smell a

hint of a pleasant, flowery scent. "Try to sip this tea, child," Mrs. Derby's voice whispered.

Startled, Amari almost knocked the cup over as she felt her head being lifted. *What is Mrs. Derby doing here?* Amari wondered. She felt instantly embarrassed because she hadn't bathed in days, she knew her wounds and salves probably stank, and she had proved herself incapable in the master's home. The tea, which tasted faintly like peppermint, she sipped slowly. "So sorry," Amari whispered.

"No, dear. I am the one who must apologize. I am so full of remorse for how badly my husband hurt you," Mrs. Derby replied. She continued to help Amari drink the tea until Amari felt herself drifting back to sleep.

Slowly, Amari returned to the world, sipping mugs of hot liquid, eating a little of the special foods that Teenie made for her, and staying awake for several hours at a time. Tidbit hovered, trying to make Amari feel better by making little jokes and silly faces.

One evening during the second week following the beating, after an exhausted Polly had returned to their cabin, Amari felt well enough to sit up. She did not let her back touch anything, but it felt good to breathe deeply and not lie prone for the moment. She tried to stand up next, but she found she wasn't quite strong enough yet. She groaned softly as she sat back down.

"Is the pain very bad?" Polly asked gently.

"Hurt much. Big much," Amari admitted. "But it be better."

"Is there anything you want me to do?" Polly asked.

Amari shook her head. There was nothing that anyone could do.

"You know Mrs. Derby came to see you every day, don't you?"

Amari nodded. "She smell like flowers."

"She always looks so sad," Polly commented.

"Baby come soon and she be happy," Amari said.

Polly smiled. "She deserves someone to love."

The wounds on Amari's back healed slowly, with the help of Teenie's ointment and Mrs. Derby's tea. Within another week, Amari was back to work with Polly in the kitchen. They had heard nothing more about Amari being transferred to the rice fields, so she worked as hard as she could and tried to make herself invisible to anyone in authority.

Clay had not called for her since the beating, and for that she was grateful. He had, however, ordered Tidbit to deliver a bag of sweets to Amari. They had obviously been purchased in town. *Why would he do this?* she asked herself with a shudder. She gave the treats to Tidbit, who ate them with delight.

"You feelin' all right today?" Teenie asked her one morning. "You still lookin' like a bird that done fell out the nest."

"Some better today." Amari lifted her arm up and touched one of the welts on her back. She winced. "Hurt to touch," she said.

"The pain gonna go after 'while, but them scars gonna be there forever," Teenie told her honestly.

Amari took a deep breath. "I know," she replied.

Teenie touched Amari gently on her head. "You got a strong spirit, Myna."

Amari just shrugged. She could see no reason for having such a strong spirit, nor could she see any hope in her future. She just survived each day. However, she couldn't help but think of Afi, who kept her alive during the horrors of the voyage to this place by telling her the same thing.

"Sometimes spirit die," Amari replied quietly while she stirred the pot on the fire.

CLAY SAUNTERED UNANNOUNCED INTO TEENIE'S kitchen one hot afternoon. Teenie, making crust for a pie, was shuttling back and forth, carefully watching over Polly, who was peeling apples, and Amari, who was stirring a mixture of apple juice and brown sugar over the fire. Tidbit sat on the floor, tracing the path of an ant in the dust of the floor with his finger. Hushpuppy growled softly and everyone looked up.

Amari cringed when she saw who had entered, the barely healed lashes on her back suddenly aching, but Clay did not even look at her.

"Y'all better keep that vermin dog out of the kitchen where my food is prepared," he said without warning.

"Yassuh," Teenie mumbled without question. "I told you to get that dog outta here," she said softly to Tidbit. "Take him out to the barn, you hear?"

"Yes'm," the boy replied obediently as he hurried to the door with the dog. Just as Tidbit got to the doorway, Clay grabbed the child, picked him up, and slung him over his shoulder.

Tidbit screamed with fear, while Hushpuppy barked fiercely. With one swift movement, Clay raised one heavy boot and kicked

Hushpuppy, propelling the dog out the door of the kitchen and into the yard. The dog yelped and limped away.

"What you gonna do with my boy, sir?" Teenie asked fearfully. To Tidbit she said, "Hush now, chile. Massa Clay ain't gonna hurt you. He just need your help." Her face showed she didn't believe a word she said, but Amari knew she had to calm the child so as not to provoke Clay's anger.

Clay grinned. "I have some friends visiting from Charles Town. We've decided to go alligator hunting this afternoon, and we need some gator bait!"

Teenie clasped her hand to her mouth. Amari saw desperation in her eyes. Finally, Teenie said, her voice full of pleading, "He be too young for such, suh!"

"He's just the right size," Clay replied, patting the boy on his backside.

"He can't swim, suh," she implored.

"Then he'll learn today," Clay replied. He glanced at Amari then. "Hey, Myna, you ever seen a gator hunt?"

Amari glanced at Teenie before saying, "No, sir."

"Then come and watch. I want my friends to see what I got for my birthday. Besides, I have missed your company," Clay said boldly.

Amari wasn't sure what was happening or what she should do, so she looked at Teenie again. The look on Teenie's face truly frightened Amari, because for the first time since she had arrived at the plantation, Teenie looked terrified.

"Go, chile," Teenie urged her. "I pray you bring my boy back alive."

"You never know," Clay said merrily. "Sometimes the gators are fast and sometimes they are slow."

Teenie wiped her hands on her apron over and over. "Please, suh, not my baby, suh."

Clay ignored her. "Myna will return in a couple of hours with either a boy who's ripe to be gator bait again next week or a few of his fingers and toes left over to bury." Then he turned on his heel, and with Tidbit still over his shoulder like a sack of flour, he headed across the yard. Amari followed, wondering what new cruelty Clay had in store.

Tidbit was only four, but he knew when to keep his mouth shut. He stopped struggling and crying out, although Amari knew he had to be petrified. His eyes searched for Hushpuppy, who lay in the yard licking his hindquarters where he had been kicked. When Tidbit saw the dog was all right, he kept his eyes on Amari as she hurried behind Clay.

Clay headed down to the river, whistling and stopping occasionally to spit. Amari had always hated that particular habit. Standing near the shore of the Ashley River ahead of them, Amari could see three young men about the same age as Clay. One, dressed all in leather, stood next to a handsome black horse that stamped its hooves on the soft grass. Another, who wore an elaborate lace collar and cuffs, looked overdressed even to Amari, who had no knowledge of the fashion of rich white youth. He gazed serenely at the water. The other young man, dressed more casually, had curly red hair like the sailor who had taught her words. He tossed rocks into the water as they waited for Clay. All four of them gave off an air of superiority and power that frightened Amari. Their presence made her even more wary of what might happen.

The young man with the ruffled collar held about a hundred-foot length of rope in his hands. Four muskets leaned against a tree, the branches of which hung over the water. Two other horses grazed nearby.

Clay called out to his friends as he got close, "Hullo! Feeling like a little gator stew tonight?"

"If we're lucky!" one of them replied. Evidently, the three young men thought that was so funny, they laughed uproariously. Amari understood enough English to know that Tidbit was in real trouble.

"I told you I knew where to find the best gator bait in the world!" he boasted as he lowered Tidbit to the ground. It seemed to Amari that Clay was trying a little too hard, talking a little too loudly, showing off for his friends.

"Just the right size," the owner of the black horse said as he poked Tidbit with his toe. Tidbit cringed. Amari wanted to reach out and comfort Tidbit, but she dared not.

The boy looked from Clay to each of the young men, and though his little body shook with fear, he didn't make a sound.

Taking the rope from his overdressed friend, Clay gave it to Amari and ordered, "Tie the rope around him, Myna."

"So who is this delicious slice of slave girl?" asked the young man dressed in leather. He reached over and patted Amari on her backside.

With sudden fierceness, Clay jumped between Amari and the young man who had touched her. "Keep your hands off her!" he snarled. "She is *mine*! That is why I named her Myna."

Amari was so surprised, she dropped the rope. The leather-clad friend backed away and held up his hand. "I have the pick of the women on my father's plantation," he said. "I was just asking who this one was."

Clay, seemingly calmer, replied, "She was my birthday gift this year. I wanted the three of you to see her." Again Amari couldn't understand why Clay acted as if he was proud of her, showing her off to his friends. She felt like an animal on display, almost as bad as the day she was sold at the market. She hung her head and wished she could disappear into the waters of that river.

To Amari, Clay repeated, "Tie the boy with the rope. Make sure it is secure."

Amari nodded and hugged the trembling child as she knotted the rope. She whispered into Tidbit's ear, "Be brave, little one, and hold your breath." She stood up and reluctantly handed the rope to Clay.

In control of the situation once more, Clay stooped down and said to Tidbit. "All you must do is swim, little nigger. You hear? If you can swim faster than those gators, you get to go home to your mama, understand?"

Tidbit quivered and nodded. He looked at Amari one last time before Clay picked him up and abruptly tossed him into the river. Clay held the rope while his friends laughed and cheered as the little boy swam for his life.

"Now, would you look at that," the tallest one called out, pointing to Tidbit struggling in the water. "The little nigger boy *can* swim!" Tidbit thrashed about hysterically, his tiny face wild with fear.

"I've never seen anyone move his arms and legs so fast!" Clay said, laughing.

"All that splashing ought to attract a gator soon," another one remarked.

As Amari watched Tidbit bobble in the water, for the first time since she had been captured, she felt angry enough to lash out and kill. She was sick of tears, of submission, of putting up with inhumane treatment. She knew if she couldn't do something to save Tidbit, she might explode. Finally, she could hold it in no longer. *"Stop!"* she cried hysterically. *"Please stop!* Bring Tidbit back. Please." She broke down, sobbing.

Clay's three friends stopped their cheering and stared in astonishment at this slave girl who had nerve enough to try to interrupt an afternoon's sport. Clay, with surprising calm, told Amari, "If you don't let us continue, your little friend is likely to get eaten. Now shut up!" He did not hit her as she expected him to.

Amari, defeated, looked from Clay to his friends in utter disbelief. This was beyond her grasp, to torture a child like this. *What kind of people are they?* And then she saw it—the dark figure of an alligator appeared in the water near Tidbit's splashing feet. She held her breath.

"Oh, look, here comes the first gator!" called out Clay's friend with the red curly hair. Instantly, their attention turned from Amari to the river again. In one smooth motion the lace-collared fellow snatched up his musket, cocked it, and fired.

Ka-boom! The musket shot sounded like an explosion as it was fired at the alligator. The water turned bright red as the animal rolled over in the water. The startled horses reared and pulled at the ropes that tied them to the trees.

"You got him, Conrad!" Clay shouted to his friend.

Amari could see only bloody water and foam in the distance. She couldn't tell if Tidbit had been shot or bit or had survived.

She didn't know what she would do if she had to return to Teenie without the boy.

"Good shot!" one of the others called out.

"Pull the boy in and let him catch his breath," Clay ordered. "The next gator will be mine," he said as he checked his gun.

Conrad hauled Tidbit in. The boy, dripping with blood and water, scrambled up the muddy shore next to them. He was shivering uncontrollably, but he seemed unhurt.

Amari ran to him, knelt down on the muddy riverbank, and hugged him tightly. As she felt his narrow shoulders shake, the fury she had felt earlier began to build once more. She wasn't sure how much more of this she could take. She whispered, in her native language, the same words of comfort that Afi had once told her: "In spite of all you must endure, my little Tidbit, the flame of your life spirit will not leave you." Then, because she knew he would not understand what she was saying, she told him, in English, "You will live. You are strong. Do you understand?" Tidbit nodded miserably.

"Enough of that!" Clay shouted. He pulled Tidbit away from Amari, made sure the rope was still secure, and pitched the boy back into the water. This time two alligators surfaced. Amari wanted to scream out once more, but she realized she couldn't distract the hunters. They *had* to shoot or Tidbit would be attacked. She wished she could run and snatch Tidbit out of the water and just disappear. Tidbit paddled furiously as the alligators circled him. Two shots exploded in the afternoon sunshine as both Clay and one of his friends fired at the huge reptiles.

Amari wondered for how much longer the child could be tortured so.

Twice more Tidbit was tossed into the bloody water, and twice more he barely escaped the jaws of the hungry alligators. It seemed to Amari that the young men always waited until the last possible moment to fire.

Tidbit almost seemed to be in shock by the time they finally decided their afternoon of enjoyment was over. He could barely walk. Amari ran and picked him up.

"It is getting late," Clay said to his friends as he untied the rope from around Tidbit's waist, "and this game is beginning to bore me. Let us retire to the house for supper, but I fear I no longer have a taste for gator stew!" The other three young men reacted with loud laughter as they readied their horses. The one who rode the black horse reached down and hoisted Clay up so he could ride with him.

Clay looked down at Amari and smiled as she tried to comfort Tidbit. "We'll have to do this again sometime. I had fun. Didn't you?"

"Yassuh," Amari mumbled. Her fists were tight as she held Tidbit.

"And, Myna?" he said, his tone changing from warm to cold in an instant. She looked at him in fearful expectation. "Don't you *ever* raise your voice to me again!"

"No, sir. Yassuh," Amari stuttered. She knew she had escaped another beating—or worse.

With that, Clay and his friends headed toward the north fields, where the corn was grown, whooping like children as they galloped off.

Amari and Tidbit headed slowly back to the house. Neither of them spoke. Halfway there Hushpuppy met them, limping a little, but wagging his tail energetically. Tidbit fell to the ground and buried his head in the dog's soft fur.

PART SIX

POLLY

25. BIRTH OF THE BABY

EARLY ONE MORNING, ABOUT TWO WEEKS LATER, the doorway of the kitchen was suddenly darkened by the unexpected shadow of Mr. Derby. He looked surprisingly agitated. Polly dropped the spoon she had in her hand. She watched as Amari moved swiftly to the back of the small room to try to make herself invisible. Tidbit ran behind his mother. Even the dog hid in a corner.

"Where's Lena?" Mr. Derby roared.

Teenie looked around in confusion. "She ain't here, Massa. I ain't seen Lena since last night," Teenie said truthfully.

"And what about Flora? I swear I'll kill her if she's not back at the house when I return!"

"I ain't seen her, neither, Massa," Teenie said as she stirred the kettle wildly. "I been cookin' all de mornin'."

"Why is it that when I need a slave, they all disappear?" He strode across the kitchen and swept plates and platters to the floor in a fury. He stopped directly in front of Amari, who cowered at his feet. "Why aren't you in the rice fields like I ordered?" he demanded.

Polly could see that Amari had no answer. She knew that Amari had learned that, when not given a direct order, a slave's best bet was to say nothing.

Mr. Derby looked at Polly. "Does the African understand English yet?"

"Yes, sir, a little, sir," Polly replied. *What is he going to do?* she wondered, her fear growing.

"Do you know anything about childbirth?" he asked Polly suddenly.

"Sir?" Polly asked, confused. Then she realized Mrs. Derby must be in labor.

Mr. Derby with concern edging his voice, said, "Isabelle is about to have the child. I have sent Noah to Charles Town for the doctor, but it will be several hours before they return." He wrung his hands. Polly had *never* seen him look helpless or afraid. "She's in a lot of pain. Can you help her?"

"Yes, sir. Of course, sir." Polly breathed with relief, for herself and for Amari as well. Amari would not to be taken to the rice swamps—at least not today.

"And you," he said, pointing to Amari, "get up and help her! Hurry! I'll ride to the next plantation for more help." He stormed out of the kitchen, leaving behind sudden sighs of relief.

"You ever helped birth a baby, chile?" Teenie asked Polly.

"Never," Polly replied frantically.

"What 'bout you?" Teenie asked Amari.

"Yes, many, many," Amari replied quickly.

"Both of you get up there and see to Miz Isabelle. Here's boiled water. Hurry!"

Amari and Polly rushed out of the kitchen and up to the big house—their first trip back since the night of the spilled pie. They climbed the stairs as quickly as they could without splashing the hot water and tiptoed down the highly polished wood floor of the upstairs hallway, searching for Mrs. Derby's room. Ordinarily, several slaves would be in the house, cleaning or washing, but today, oddly, there were none. Clay was nowhere to be seen either.

"Oh, Lord in heaven!" they heard Mrs. Derby cry out from the first room on the right. She lay in her bed, which was surrounded on all four sides with thin linen curtains. Huge pillows surrounded her pale face. She moaned in pain as Amari and Polly entered the room and pulled back the curtains. She looked at the two girls and tried to smile weakly. "You must help me," she said, desperation in her voice, "if the baby is, if the baby is . . ." She could not finish the sentence.

"Yes, ma'am," Polly replied. "We will make sure you and your baby will be just fine." Polly had never been so close to a woman who was about to have a baby, and she was more than a little frightened. The smell of sweat and body fluids was overpowering.

"You don't understand," Mrs. Derby said as another labor pain gripped her. "You must help my baby."

"Baby good thing," Amari said, trying to reassure her.

Mrs. Derby inhaled sharply, cried out once more, and tightly grabbed a handful of the sheet. When the contraction passed, she said urgently, "I will die, but you must save my baby."

"You not die, Missus," Amari said in her most soothing voice. "Babies be born every day."

"She's talking out of her head," Polly said to Amari. "Let's help her get more comfortable." They adjusted her blankets, set up clean cloths and towels close by, and made sure the hot water was ready in the basin. Polly hoped Amari knew what to do.

Amari touched Mrs. Derby's bulging belly and declared, "Baby come quick—very soon." The labor pains rolled faster and stronger with each contraction. Mrs. Derby was turning red with exertion and pain.

The girls massaged her hands, washed her face with cool water, and helped her through each contraction by talking to her gently and quietly. Soon it was apparent that the baby had no intention of waiting for a doctor or Mr. Derby or anyone else. Mrs. Derby arched her back, screamed, and passed out.

Polly lifted the blankets and saw the baby's head. She motioned to Amari, who gently eased the baby out. The infant cried—lusty, loud, and healthy.

Amari held the child with a look of wonder on her face. "Beautiful baby," Polly heard her whisper.

Polly brought Amari some wet towels to clean the baby off. It was a little girl, with bright green eyes like her mother and curly dark hair. Then she froze, her hand still extended.

"Oh, my Lord!" Polly exclaimed. "The child is black!"

"BLACK BABY. WHITE MAMA. BIG TROUBLE!" Amari said with fear tightening her voice as she carefully washed the child and wrapped her in the blanket.

Polly's jumbled thoughts careened from how this could have happened (rape, perhaps?) to how Mr. Derby would react (uncontrollable rage, to be sure) to how she felt about a proper white woman producing a black baby (mild disgust, at the very least). "What should we do?" Polly asked, almost panicked. "Tell Mr. Derby?"

"No!" Amari cried, alarm in her voice. "Get Teenie. Hurry, hurry."

Polly rushed out of the room, praying she would not encounter Clay or Mr. Derby as she ran to the kitchen. "Teenie!" she screamed when she got there. "Come quickly! We don't know what to do!"

"Is the chile borned yet?" Teenie asked as she ran with Polly back to the house.

"Yes, the baby is fine and healthy," Polly said, panting. "It's a little girl."

"Do it look like Mrs. Derby—all pink and perfect?"

"The child is not what anyone expected, Teenie."

"What you mean, chile? Is Miz Isabelle ailin'?"

"No, she's sleeping. She doesn't know yet."

"Know what? You ain't makin' no sense, Polly!"

By that time they had reached Miss Isabelle's room. Amari was sitting in a chair with the baby in her arms, cuddling it close to her. Teenie stared at the baby in shock.

"Oh, Lawd, Lawd, Lawd!" Teenie exclaimed as she sucked in her breath. "It be Noah," she announced with finality. "No wonder everybody be scarce as hen's teeth today."

Noah? Polly thought. *Noah! Of course! It all makes sense now. But how could she? Why would she?* Polly's stomach churned as she tried to figure out the magnitude of this problem.

At that moment Mrs. Derby opened her eyes. She looked around in fear. "My baby?" she asked desperately.

"You got a purty little girl child, Miz Isabelle. But you got a big problem, ma'am," Teenie told her with concern in her voice.

"May I see her?"

Amari placed the sleeping baby in her mother's arms. Mrs. Derby gazed down at the child, her eyes brimming with tears. "My beautiful baby," she murmured over and over. Finally calmer, she looked up at Teenie and the girls. "I must explain," she whispered, "before I die."

"You ain't gonna die, Miz Isabelle," Teenie assured her. "You is fit and fine. Everybody feels a little poorly after havin' a baby."

Tenderly, Mrs. Derby touched the infant's velvety brown face. "You don't understand. My husband will kill me," she said with certainty.

"He adore you, ma'am," Teenie said reasonably. "Anybody who look at him can see that. He ain't gonna hurt you."

Mrs. Derby blinked back tears. "Even though he married me for my money, I know he really has come to feel real affection for me. But I love Noah—I have for many years. And he loves me. But now Noah will die, and so will I. My husband is going to kill us both—and our baby."

"He would never do such a thing!" But Teenie knew that Mr. Derby was probably quite capable of murder and would be within the limits of social acceptability to do so for this impropriety. Her mind was reeling.

"What to do?" Amari asked in a whisper.

"What should we tell him, ma'am?" Polly asked.

Mrs. Derby pushed herself up into a sitting position. She suddenly looked excited. "Tell him the baby died! Tell him it was a stillbirth! You must take my baby away to safety. Here, take her," she urged them. She lifted the baby up, but when Amari reached for the child, Mrs. Derby drew the child to her chest once more.

"He gonna want to see the baby's body, ma'am," Teenie tried to reason.

"Tell him it was deformed—a monster! Tell him anything! Just keep my baby safe!" She kissed her daughter gently and snuggled her closer.

"We best get you cleaned up 'fore the massa get back. He only went to the next plantation," Teenie declared. "I got a bad feelin' 'bout this. We all gonna hang 'fore nightfall!" she muttered. "Lawd, Lawd, Lawd. What we gonna do? We done fell out the trouble tree and hit every branch on the way down!"

Polly, Amari, and Teenie moved quickly to help Mrs. Derby get cleaned up and ready to face her husband. The baby nursed peacefully at her mother's breast, her cocoa brown skin a sharp contrast to Mrs. Derby's pinkness.

Mrs. Derby patted the baby, held her close as she slept, and brushed away tears. Finally, she handed the infant to Amari. "Protect her," she said simply.

Amari blinked to keep away her own tears and took the baby with great seriousness. Polly watched as Amari held the perfect little infant close to her breast.

"We must go now, Missus," Teenie said with quiet alarm. Mrs. Derby nodded with sad resignation as Polly, Amari, and Teenie left with the baby.

As they crept down the steps, Teenie whispered to Amari, "Sara Jane just borned a baby 'bout three months ago. She got lotsa milk. That's where we'll hide her for now." They tiptoed down the hall.

Only Polly noticed Clay through a window as he approached the other side of the house. She signaled for Amari and Teenie to be still. He seemed to be looking in the other direction. She prayed he had just arrived back home and had not seen anything. When they heard him enter the back of the house, they exited quickly through the front.

"Tidbit!" Teenie called as they reached the kitchen. The sleepy boy and his dog jumped up from the pallet they shared near the fireplace. "Take Myna and Polly down to the quarters to Jubal and Sara Jane's place. And don't ask no questions!" The child looked at his mother's frightened face and seemed to realize this was no time for foolishness.

Teenie told Polly, "Don't tell her nothin' except this baby's mama is dead and she gotta nurse it. Of course, don't take no genius to figger out whose baby this be. Lawd, what a mess! Hurry!"

Amari and Polly dashed out after Tidbit, Amari clutching the child close to her.

"Baby be safe with Sara Jane?" she asked Polly.

"We have no choice. The baby's life is at stake," Polly replied, trying to sound hopeful.

Sara Jane's large, loving arms took the baby girl with no questions. "She be fine, chile," Sara Jane said to Amari. "Sara Jane will keep this little one safe. Now y'all get on back to the kitchen. Tonight be full of danger."

Polly shivered as they hurried to Teenie's kitchen. *Will this work?*

As soon as they got back, Teenie told her, "Get on up to the house and see to Miz Isabelle, Polly. Amari, you stay here with me. I still got supper to fix." She began pulling down pots noisily, mumbling, maybe praying, to herself, Polly figured. She hurried off to the main house.

Polly had just made sure that Mrs. Derby's hair was brushed and that she had on a fresh dressing gown when Mr. Derby returned. Polly heard him rush up the stairs. She braced herself. He burst into the room, where he found his wife fast asleep. Polly, sitting in a chair next to her, pretended to be weeping. Her heart thudded in her chest. She prayed she could convince him.

"Where is the baby?" Mr. Derby demanded. He looked around in confusion.

Polly, eyes full of honest fear, told him sadly, "The baby was stillborn, sir. I'm so sorry. But your wife is fine," she added.

"What?" He took a few steps back. "It died?" He raked his fingers through his hair. His face seemed to crumple. "Was it a boy or girl?" he asked, barely able to choke out the words.

"A girl, sir."

"I want to see her. I want to see my baby." His voice broke.

"You don't want to do that, sir," Polly said, stammering a little. "The child was, uh, not normal. It is better to bury it quickly."

Anguish ripped Mr. Derby's face. "Don't you try to tell me what I want to do! Bring me the body of my daughter." He blinked furiously, but Polly could see the tears in his eyes.

She didn't know what to do. At that moment his wife's eyes fluttered open. She looked around, confused for a moment. When she saw her husband, she said with a sob, "The baby never took a breath, Percival. I'm so sorry."

"Are you all right, my darling?" Mr. Derby asked her gently as he leaned over her.

She reached up and touched his face. "I am fine."

"Did you see her—our daughter?" he asked.

Mrs. Derby hesitated. "Yes, I did. She was . . . she was . . . deformed." She took a deep breath and closed her eyes. Polly was impressed with how effective she was.

Mr. Derby narrowed his eyes. "Something doesn't make sense here," he said suspiciously. He paced the room and looked at Polly sharply.

"I prayed every day for this baby," Mrs. Derby whispered.

That much Polly knew was very true.

"I could not have fathered an imperfect child," Mr. Derby

declared. He seemed agitated. "I must see her—if nothing else, to say good-bye."

Mrs. Derby spoke up frantically. "I instructed the servants to wrap her and bury her far away from our home."

"Nonsense! Our daughter, regardless of any infirmity, must be buried with honor in our family plot," he told her. "How dare you discard my child like that?" he scolded, anger and sorrow lacing his voice. Polly found herself feeling sorry for the man.

"I'm so sorry, Percival," Mrs. Derby whispered again. "Please do not bring her into my presence again. Just thinking of her is more than I can bear." Polly thought she looked more terrified than sorrowful.

He leaned over and kissed his wife on her forehead. "I share your grief, my dear," he said to her. "You just rest for now, and I will take care of these unpleasant details." As he was leaving the room, he said to Polly, "Bring me the body of my daughter. When the doctor gets here with Noah, he will want to examine her." Polly curtsied, and he slammed the door behind him.

Mrs. Derby whispered to Polly, "Is my baby safe?"

"Yes, ma'am," Polly replied. "For now. But when the doctor gets here, we have to show him something."

"Perhaps the doctor can be delayed," Mrs. Derby suggested. "Can you get word to Noah before they return?"

"I'm not sure, ma'am. Will you be all right for a while? I must check with Teenie and see what can be done."

"Yes, of course. Please go and do what you must. You move beyond kindness to help us. I shall forever be grateful." Polly hurried down the stairs and out to the kitchen, desperate to avert a tragedy. *How has it come to this?* she thought. She realized then how deeply her life was entangled with those of the slaves she had once so despised.

27. DEATH IN THE DUST

AMARI WAS WAITING FOR POLLY IN THE KITCHEN. "Is the baby safe?" Polly asked her.

Amari nodded, then asked, "What Massa say?"

Polly looked at her and said, "It's very bad. Mr. Derby wants the doctor to see the body of the child."

"What we do?" Amari asked, turning to ask Teenie for advice.

"We must stop the wagon with Noah and the doctor before it gets here," Polly declared.

"Ain't no 'we' about it," Teenie replied as she shucked a basket of corn. "You a white gal. You the only one that be allowed on the road after dark."

Polly took a deep breath. "All right, I'll go. Tell me what to do."

"Whatever it take to turn that wagon round!" Teenie said without conviction. "Ain't gonna be easy."

Dusk had fallen. Polly left the kitchen and headed down to the main road, the road that had brought her to this place with Amari. *So much has changed since then,* she thought. She half walked, half jogged about a mile, the darkness so thick that it seemed to smother her, when she heard the wagon approaching.

As it got close to her, she ran toward it, startling the horses.

"Please, sir," Polly began. "Are you Dr. Hoskins?" She did not look at Noah, although she had a feeling he knew what was going on.

"Yes, I am. Is Mrs. Derby all right?"

"Oh, yes, sir. She's just fine—and the baby, too—crying and nursing and being sweet like newborns always are, sir." Polly knew she was babbling, but she couldn't find the words to make him turn around. "That's why I came out to meet you, sir—to tell you that the baby has been born with no complications, Mrs. Derby is fit and fine, and your services are no longer needed. Mr. Derby wanted to save you an unnecessary house call." She spoke very quickly, glad that it was dark and that they couldn't see how scared she was.

Noah seemed to understand immediately that it was not a good idea for the doctor to make it to the plantation, for he spoke up to say, "I'll be glad to drives you back to Charles Town, suh. No trouble at all, suh."

"Nonsense!" the doctor replied gruffly. "No, you will not drive me back—it took us four hours to get here! I shall see to my patient and her infant, I shall eat a fine meal prepared by Derby's servants, and I shall spend the night here and return refreshed to Charles Town in the morning. We shall proceed to Derbyshire Farms!"

"But, sir—," Polly tried weakly.

"Who are you, my dear, and why are you out here on the road after dark?" He offered Polly his hand and helped her up onto the wagon. "It is not safe, you know—highwaymen will slice your throat in a heartbeat."

Defeated, Polly replied, "My name is Polly Pritchard. I work for Mr. Derby."

"Did he send you out here to send me back?" Dr. Hoskins asked.

Polly wasn't sure whether to lie or tell the truth. So she said nothing in reply. The wagon moved slowly toward the house. Polly prayed, silently fingering the tie strings on her bonnet.

Mr. Derby waited near the big circular pillars at the front of the house. He looked grief-stricken. "Thank you for making this long drive, Hoskins," he said to the doctor as he stiffly stepped down from the wagon, "but I'm afraid your trip was in vain. Isabelle is fine, but the baby was stillborn." He choked on the words.

Dr. Hoskins looked confused. "Stillborn? This young woman here told me the baby was fine and healthy. What's going on?"

Polly tried to jump down from the wagon, but Mr. Derby grabbed her arm, the anguish on his face turning to anger. "What is going on here? I told you I would never allow any insubordination in my household. You explain what is going on this instant!"

Polly's heart pounded. She opened her mouth to speak just as she heard Lena's voice behind her, yelling from an upstairs window. "Oh, Massa, come quick! Miz Isabelle done fainted!"

Mr. Derby released Polly and ran with the doctor into the house. Polly collapsed on the ground with relief. *This night is not going to end well,* she thought fearfully.

Amari ran out of the kitchen as soon as the two men had disappeared. She looked directly at Noah, who was staring toward

Mrs. Derby's window with concern. "Baby is black," Amari told him bluntly. "Pretty girl child."

Noah groaned and covered his head with his hands. "Is Isabelle all right? The baby is alive?" Polly was surprised by the seeming depth of his anguish.

Teenie had come out of the kitchen to join them. She wiped her hands on her apron. "Yeah, they both alive for now. But it won't take long for Massa to figger out what really happened. We's all in big trouble, tryin' to cover up yo' mess." Tidbit ran from the kitchen and toward his mother. She yelled at the child fiercely, "You go git in the kindlin' box and hide there, you hear? Don't you come out till I come git you!" The boy took a long look at her face and hightailed it back to the kitchen.

Noah sat on the ground in the dirt. It seemed to Polly he was overwhelmed by the evening's events. "We growed up as children together," he explained. "She was the mistress, of course, and I be the slave, but that didn't make us no matter at all. We'd go fishin' and runnin' through the woods—just likin' each other, you know?"

Teenie grunted and kept glancing at the window to the upstairs room where Lena and Miss Isabelle were trying to stall the doctor and Mr. Derby.

"What was you thinkin'?" Teenie asked finally, annoyance and amazement in her voice. "Just 'cause a chicken got wings don't mean it oughta fly. Y'all shoulda known better!"

"As she got older," Noah continued, ignoring Teenie, "she turned down every good-lookin' boy who come to court her. Her daddy finally put a stop to that young-girl foolishness and married her off to Massa Derby. She cried for days before the weddin'." Noah stopped. His shoulders drooped.

"When Massa Derby move her here, she insist I come with her. Her daddy didn't see no harm, so she and me was real happy. When she found out she was with child, we figgered the baby belonged to Massa Derby. At least that what we was hopin'."

Mistress and slave—falling in love! Polly realized with a start. *I didn't think such a thing was even possible.* "Has something like this ever happened before?" Polly asked.

Noah shook his head. "I don't know, missy. No one's done lived to tell 'bout it."

"You got to run away, Noah," Teenie told him clearly. "Massa gonna kill you for shure."

"I ain't runnin. I love her," he replied simply.

Teenie snorted. "Love don't mean pig spit round here." She had no more time to argue with him, for at that moment Mr. Derby emerged from the front door of the house, angrily holding up a weak and sobbing Mrs. Derby. In his right hand he held a gun. The doctor, noticeably, had remained inside.

Polly, Teenie, and Amari drew back at the fury on Mr. Derby's face. Noah stood slowly and with dignity. He looked at Isabelle Derby with a look of absolute love on his face. She seemed to relax as she gazed at Noah. She smiled at him, then reached out to him with her free hand. Her husband slapped her arm down. "Isabelle!" he barked, his voice tight with fury.

Coming from the opposite direction, from the slave quarters, the sharp wailing cry of a newborn could be heard. As they all turned in that direction, they could see Clay Derby strolling toward them, carrying the baby girl. The infant had been stripped of her blanket, and she protested loudly in the chill night air.

Polly was having difficulty finding each new breath. She had to force herself not to reach out and grab the baby from Clay.

"Looking for something, Father?" he asked with a grin. "I found this baby down at Sara Jane's place. She swears it's her baby, but it looks to be newborn, and her little picaninny must be about three months old. Seems a bit impossible, don't you think?" Polly could tell that Clay was actually enjoying this!

She and Amari watched, horrified, as Clay lay the naked, screaming baby on the dirt in front of his father. Polly grabbed Amari's hand and squeezed it. She wanted to run to the child and pick her up, but she dared not move.

A look of revulsion crossed Mr. Derby's face as he stared at the perfect brown features of the infant. Isabelle Derby cried out, "My baby!" and reached for the child on the ground in front of her, but her husband held her firmly. Noah, impassive once more, showed no outward emotion, but tears slipped down his face.

Mr. Derby, his voice full of self-control, spoke calmly and clearly to his wife. "I loved you," he said, almost plaintively. "You were so young and beautiful—like springtime all year long. I just knew you would erase all the sorrows from my past."

Mrs. Derby shuddered, her head hung low.

"But you chose to betray me," her husband said, venom returning to his voice. "You are not even worthy of my vomit." He inhaled. "But I shall not kill you," he continued in a low, eerily controlled voice. She looked at him in surprise. "Instead, I shall refuse to let you die."

Polly was confused. She did not understand what he meant, but soon it became terribly apparent.

Mr. Derby pulled his wife over to where Noah stood. Then, with one hand, he cocked the musket and aimed it at Noah's broad chest. He spat at Noah, then glanced at his wife. He made sure she was watching. Then he fired.

Noah's blood splattered them all as he fell to the ground not far from his child. Polly screamed, Amari cried out, and Teenie fell to her knees mumbling, "Oh, sweet Jesus!"

The noise of the gunshot startled the baby, who cried even louder from where she lay on the ground. Mrs. Derby, shrieking and twisting like a madwoman, fought to get free of her husband's grip. Mr. Derby suddenly released her in a heap on the ground as he calmly but swiftly reloaded the gun.

Sobbing hysterically, Isabelle Derby scrambled in the dirt toward her baby. She had almost reached the infant when another gunshot exploded in the darkness. The baby was suddenly silent.

28. PUNISHMENT

NOT SINCE THE DAY HER MOTHER DIED HAD POLLY felt such agony. She gasped in disbelief, unable to catch her breath. Head spinning, she clung to Amari, who was choking on her sobs. Mrs. Derby threw herself onto her child, then fainted, this time for real.

Mr. Derby dropped the gun, then looked at his hands. He seemed stunned. He turned to Clay and said quietly, "Go tell old Jubal to get up here and take care of . . . of all this." He would not look at the bodies. "And make sure Sara Jane gets punished," he added without emotion. Polly watched Clay disappear into the darkness with a look of satisfaction on his face.

Dr. Hoskins peered out of the door then, unsure of what he might encounter. "Come get my wife, Doctor," Mr. Derby called. "I believe she's fainted again. Unfortunately, she had to witness the disciplining of some unruly slaves, and it proved a bit much for her. See to her, will you, old fellow?" Mr. Derby took a deep breath and smoothed his doublet.

The doctor crept slowly to the bloody scene, observed it all, but made no comment. He picked up Mrs. Derby in his arms and carried her back to the house. Lena waited at the door to assist him, her eyes bright with fear.

Then Mr. Derby turned his attention to Teenie, Polly, and Amari, who huddled together. "Follow me," he told them curtly.

He led them down the familiar path to Teenie's kitchen, where he stopped. "Where is the boy Tidbit?" he asked Teenie.

She hesitated. "I don't rightly know, suh. He done heard all the noise, and I guess it scared him. Maybe he run off to the woods."

"Call to him. You better hope he answers."

Polly could see that Teenie was not sure what to do. "Tidbit," Teenie whispered softly.

"Call him so he hears you!" Mr. Derby demanded.

"Tidbit, honey, you in there?" Teenie called, her voice quavering.

A faint rustling could be heard coming from the kindling box. Mr. Derby marched over, tossed aside the small pieces of firewood, and pulled the boy out of the box by one arm. The dog growled softly. "Mama?" Tidbit called out.

When Mr. Derby dropped the boy to the ground, Tidbit ran quickly to the skirts of his mother. She picked him up and held him close to her body.

Mr. Derby spoke then. Polly sensed he was just barely in control of himself. "Follow me," he demanded once more, and he led them a few paces from the kitchen to the smokehouse. He pulled out a key, unlocked the door, and turned to look at the frightened group in front of him.

"You," he said, pointing at Polly, "are a liar! I will not have such a person in my household!"

Polly cowered before him, her hands held up in front of her face. "Have mercy, sir," she whispered. He ignored her.

"And you," he said to Amari with consternation, "have been trouble since I was kind enough to bring you here." Amari looked frightened, Polly thought, but furious at him as well. That gave Polly courage to stand a little straighter in spite of Mr. Derby's fury.

"And finally you," he said fiercely to Teenie, "I trusted to obey me. Your responsibility was to me and you failed."

"I so sorry, suh," Teenie mumbled.

"Too late," he said harshly. He thought for a moment. "When Dr. Hoskins leaves in the morning, he will have three passengers. I'll send Clay with him to make sure there are no more problems. If it were not for my son, I might never have discovered the whole truth."

Polly searched for the words that might calm him down or change his mind. "Sir," she began.

But Mr. Derby ignored her as he firmly pushed each of them into the dark, windowless smokehouse.

Polly, Amari, and Teenie looked at one another but did not fight him or object—they did not want to do anything to further incur his anger. Mr. Derby slowly closed the door, then opened it again.

"Tomorrow is a market day in Charles Town," he said. "Polly, I plan to sell your indenture to a whorehouse in New Orleans. You'll bring a pretty penny. They like them young down there." He uttered a short, harsh laugh.

Tears welled up in Polly's eyes, but she shook her head and refused to cry. Anger began to replace her misery as she looked at Mr. Derby with steely-eyed fury.

"And, Myna, I can find another toy for my son to play with. I'm sure I can get more than I paid for you—a broken-in African is highly sought after."

Amari looked devastated, but she, too, seemed to have run out of tears. She faced Mr. Derby with quiet resolve. The two girls stood there, stony and silent.

"You'll leave at first light." They heard the lock fasten firmly in the latch and his footsteps as he headed back to the house.

"What 'bout me, suh?" Teenie called out through one of the wooden slats of the smokehouse. "Who gonna cook yo' food if you sells me?"

The sound of his boots stopped. "Oh, Teenie, " he called back, "I'd never sell you. You're much too valuable."

Teenie breathed a small sigh of relief. She clung to Tidbit fiercely in the darkness. "Oh, thank you, suh," she whispered.

"I'm selling Tidbit instead," Mr. Derby's voice said clearly. The sound of his boots on the hard dirt disappeared as he headed back to the big house.

Teenie's wails echoed in the darkness.

"OH, LAWD, WHAT WE GONNA DO?" TEENIE MOANED miserably. She sat on the dirt floor, holding Tidbit close to her. "He be my onliest chile. My baby boy," she whispered into his hair. "My baby boy."

Polly could hear Tidbit whimpering, "Whassa matter, Mama?" She knew he couldn't possibly comprehend the enormity of what was about to happen to him.

"Is there any way out of here?" Polly looked around, but the smokehouse was so dark that she could distinguish only the shadowy figures of a couple of hams hanging from hooks.

"No, chile. The smokehouse was built secure so can't nobody come in here and get free meat. And ain't but two keys—Massa got one and Miz Isabelle got the other." Teenie continued to rock Tidbit on her lap.

Amari, who sat on the floor near the door, suddenly asked, "Slaves ever run off?"

"Shure, they runs off—any chance they get," Teenie replied. "But mostly they gets brought back. They got dogs that can smell a person in the woods and folks whose job it is just to catch runaways and bring 'em back."

"Has anybody ever succeeded?" Polly asked.

"Yes, chile. Far as I knows. They mighta got killed on their journey, but they never came back here, so in my mind, they got to the North safely."

"What is North?" Amari wanted to know.

"North is where freedom lives, chile. They got slaves there, too, but I've heard tell of black folk livin' up North with jobs they gets paid for and houses that belong to them, and don't nobody own them at all!"

"So why don't more slaves run away?" Polly asked.

"It's hard to hide when yo' skin is black and everybody else got white skin," Teenie explained. "Now you, chile, could run off and fit right in. You could leave Myna and my Tidbit here and have you a chance to be free."

"I'd never leave them!" Polly blurted before she could even think about it. Yet, once she said it, she knew it was true.

"Easy to say while we's all locked up," Teenie commented quietly.

"Do they chase runaway indentured servants as well?" Polly asked her.

"Couple of years back, Massa had a 'dentured boy who run off. Massa brung him back after a few days, and he put a iron collar round the boy's neck so folks would know he was a runaway and not free to be on the roads."

"Where this boy now?" Amari asked quietly, touching her neck, which still held the scars from her own iron chains.

"He drowned that summer—I believe he let that iron collar just take him on down," Teenie told her.

"North," Polly mused. "We could all be free." She wondered

what freedom would mean to Amari, who could never get back to what she had lost.

"Shhh, what that noise?" Amari suddenly whispered. They all heard it—a faint scratching on the back wall of the smokehouse. They all moved quietly to the back of the small room.

They heard the scratching again, then Cato's whispered voice. "Y'all all right?" Polly smiled as she heard him clear his throat and cough.

"If they catch you here, they kill you for shure," Teenie whispered to Cato.

"If they kill me, at least I be free at last. I ain't worried 'bout it." Cato laughed quietly. His voice got serious then. "Teenie, you got to let the boy go with them purty lil gals. Yo' boy got a chance to be free."

"How you figger?" Teenie asked, skepticism in her voice.

"Doc Hoskins don't believe in no slavery."

"How you knows this?" Teenie asked suspiciously.

"How many times I gotta tell you that I just knows stuff? Lissen, Doc Hoskins ain't got it in him to sell nobody."

"But Clay is going with us!" Polly exclaimed. "I think it would give him pleasure to see us sold."

Teenie shifted her weight and handed Tidbit to Amari. "Hold him for a hot minute, chile. I got an idea." To Cato she whispered, "Go to my kitchen. Look out back under that big rock by the persimmon tree. You'll find a rag with a passel of seeds in it. Put just two seeds in Massa Clay's midnight wine." She was silent a moment. "Maybe three."

Polly heard Cato grunt. "I hear you. You jest leave Clay up to ol'

Cato. Last I heard, he was down in the quarters beatin' the sweet Jesus outta Sara Jane. I best hurry if I'm to fix him his usual bedtime glass o' wine. Get the boy ready, Teenie," he told her.

"I ain't partin' with my baby!" Teenie said emphatically.

"You wants that boy to be a slave like you? You wants to see him be gator bait again?"

Teenie groaned. Polly could almost touch the anguish in her voice. "I wants a better life for him, that's for shure."

"You gotta trust these gals and trust the good Lord and trust the spirits of hope," Cato said philosophically, still whispering through the wall. "You gotta let him go. You gotta give the boy the chance to be free."

"Cato," Teenie called out in a strained voice.

"I be here," Cato replied.

"Be real careful with them seeds. I'm gonna need a big pile of 'em soon. Yassuh, Massa Derby gonna have himself a right good meal pretty soon. I got a mind to fix him a stew he ain't never gonna forget—ain't ever gonna remember."

Polly wasn't exactly sure what she meant, but Cato whispered in reply. "I hears you."

Teenie took the sleeping child from Amari and held him closely.

Polly still could not see how leaving with the doctor in the morning, heading to the slave market, would lead to a chance for freedom.

Amari asked through the wall, "Where be North, Cato? Where is free?"

Cato answered clearly. "Do not go north. That's where they be lookin' for you."

"That makes no sense," Polly interjected. "What do you mean, don't go north? If we go south, we get deeper and deeper into slave territory. Our only chance for freedom *must* be in the North!" Surely he could see that.

Cato repeated, "Do not go north. Tracker dogs search the roads headin' north. Runaway papers be posted in the North." He coughed again.

"Where we go?" Amari asked.

"Head south. Find a place called Fort Mose. It be in Spanish Florida. I hear tell it be a place of golden streets and fine wine. Spaniard folk run it, and any slave who get there be set free!"

"'Dentured gals, too?" Amari asked.

"The ways I hears it, the folks at Fort Mose got open arms to slaves, 'dentured folk, even Injuns!" Cato told them.

"It sounds too good to be true," Polly commented.

"Ain't nothing gooder than freedom," Cato replied, almost too softly to be heard.

"Much danger?" Amari asked.

"Yes, chile, much danger. Swamps and alligators and bears and bugs to start, plus not knowin' how to get there, plus the fear. It be a long, hard trip."

"How we not get lost?" Amari asked, her voice trembling.

"Follow the river south, then leave it. All rivers run to sea, and you must travel by land. Stay way inland from the ocean. Else you have too many rivers to cross. That's all I knows to tell you. When you find them streets of gold, think of ol' Cato." His footsteps and his cough disappeared into the night.

Polly leaned against the wall, trying to think. *None of this makes any sense. Trying to escape by running south? Rivers? Bears? Swamps? Impossible!* She wished desperately that she could ask her mother for advice or just curl up in her arms and not have to worry about difficult decisions.

But she sat on the dirt floor of a smokehouse, surrounded by the dried carcasses of two pigs, a cow, and a deer, feeling scared and powerless. She glanced at Amari, a girl who just a few months ago had seemed dirty and disgusting. Now they were caught up together in a situation that was so awful, she had to grab her head to erase the bloody images from her mind. *Mr. Derby murdered a baby! What kind of man could do such a thing?*

Polly watched as Amari, wrapped in her own private thoughts, finally slept. Teenie cradled her son, whispering to him, singing to him, telling him stories. She heard Teenie murmur over and over, "Long as you remember, chile, nothin' ain't really ever gone."

Polly thought with compassion of Teenie's sorrow and the anguish Mrs. Derby must be enduring right now—it was enough to drive someone mad. She wondered what the morning would bring.

POLLY SHOOK HERSELF AWAKE AS SHE HEARD voices outside the smokehouse. Sunlight filtered through the slats of the wooden structure.

"Isabelle will recover quickly from the trauma of having a still-born baby," she heard Mr. Derby say. "Already she speaks of us having another child."

The doctor's voice sounded unconvinced. "Yes, of course. Make sure she gets plenty of rest."

"I intend to keep a close eye on her," Mr. Derby replied, his voice laced with barbs.

Polly poked Amari, who was still asleep on Teenie's shoulder. Startled, Amari looked around in fear. Teenie, who perhaps had not slept at all, was whispering to Tidbit.

"You remember all them stories I tolt you 'bout my mother and the Ashanti and the monkey and spider stories?" she asked the boy, desperation in her voice.

"Yes'm," the boy replied, sounding as if he wasn't sure why his mother was telling him all this now.

"You remember the drums that talked like thunder? And the

sun that shone like copper over the valley? You remember what I tolt you 'bout my mama and how she grabbed a piece of her own mother to take with her?" Polly heard Teenie saying.

"Yes, Mama, I remembers," Tidbit said, a whispering dread in his voice.

"You takes this piece of cloth, you hear, boy? Keep it safe, 'cause all my memories be tucked in it. You promise me you will never forget?" she asked him plaintively as she hugged him close to her. Polly watched her tie a leather string around the boy's neck. A tiny leather pouch hung from it. Teenie tucked a colored piece of fabric into the packet and closed it tightly with a drawstring.

"I remembers it all, Mama," Tidbit said, his voice sounding truly frightened now.

"You gonna grow to be a man—a free man."

"I don't wanna be no man," Tidbit protested. "I just wants to be yo' lil boy."

"You gonna always be my baby boy," Teenie said, though her voice was thick with grief. "Always."

Polly thought back painfully to the night her mother died, how she had whispered to Polly with her last bit of strength, "You make yourself a lady, you hear, my darling? I will always be with you." Polly knew that Teenie's heart felt as if it were being slashed into pieces.

"You goin' with us, Mama?" the child asked.

"I'll be along directly," Teenie lied. "You stay close to Myna and Polly till I gits there, you hear?" The boy agreed quietly, but he seemed to sense that something was wrong because he started crying. "You mind them and do what they says, you hear?"

"Yes'm," Tidbit replied in a small voice.

They all heard the lock removed, and the bright sun shone in like a harsh surprise after the darkness of the smokehouse all night. Mr. Derby stood outside the door and called to them, "Come on out of there now. You have a long journey ahead of you, and, Teenie, I expect to have breakfast on the table in half an hour!"

"Yes, suh," she replied sullenly as she emerged from the small room. Teenie squeezed Tidbit's small hand tightly into hers. Amari and Polly came out next, blinking in the bright sunlight. When Amari reached for Polly's hand, Polly took it.

The wagon stood hitched and ready. Dr. Hoskins sat on the seat, looking straight ahead, not at the hapless group standing near the wagon. Clay was nowhere to be seen.

"My son is ill," Mr. Derby said to the doctor, "so I'll entrust to you the transactions for the sale of these three." The doctor nodded silently.

Polly and Amari exchanged looks. Evidently, Teenie's seeds had been effective.

"Would you like me to check young Clay before I leave?" Dr. Hoskins asked halfheartedly.

"No, I believe he simply drank too much wine. He will sleep it off."

Dr. Hoskins looked relieved. "I will make sure your money from the sale of these three is safely delivered to you by a courier from Charles Town. He will return with your wagon."

"It's good riddance to the lot of them," Mr. Derby replied, a look of disgust on his face. To the frightened group in front of him he yelled, "Get in the wagon—and be quick about it!"

Polly climbed in first. "Yes, sir," she whispered. It was the same wagon that she and Amari had arrived in. Amari climbed in behind her.

"Myna, take this child," Mr. Derby commanded. He grabbed Tidbit from Teenie and slung the boy onto the wagon behind Amari.

Teenie exploded in grief. "Don't take my baby! He my onliest child! Oh, Lawd, please don't take my baby from me!" Tidbit, seeing his mother so upset, began to wail, reaching for her and trying to squirm out of Amari's arms. Hushpuppy barked frantically, adding to the uproar.

Mr. Derby, his face red, slashed at the dog with his whip. It ran yelping toward the rice fields. Mr. Derby then stung Teenie with the whip as well. "Get to your kitchen and to your duties. You have no more business here!" He pushed her in the direction of the kitchen, but she continued to scream in protest, inconsolable.

Polly huddled in the wagon, wishing she knew a way to vent the anger that she needed to expel. But she was as helpless as the others.

"I believe it best if I leave quickly," Dr. Hoskins said over the noise.

"I agree," Mr. Derby replied. He smacked the horse on the rump. It whinnied, then began to amble on its way. The doctor directed the wagon toward the road. Tidbit shrieked as he realized that he was really being taken away from his mother. Teenie fell to the ground, yelling her grief to the sky. Mr. Derby whipped her again and pulled her to her feet. He half dragged, half walked her back to the kitchen. Hushpuppy continued to bark frantically in the distance.

"Mama!" Tidbit screamed hysterically. "Mama!"

They turned past a bend in the road, and although she could still hear Teenie's anguished cries, Polly could see her no more. Amari held Tidbit, trying to soothe him, but Polly knew that nothing she could say or do would make the child feel better.

PART SEVEN

AMARI

31. THE DOCTOR'S CHOICE

THE WAGON LUMBERED SLOWLY DOWN THE ROAD. Most of the leaves of the trees, Amari noticed, were turning golden and copper with rusty hues. The sun shone brightly over, the wind blew gently from the east, but a storm of turmoil hovered over the small wagon in which they rode. Polly sat with her arms wrapped tightly around her body. Tidbit still cried for his mother, burying himself in Amari's arms. Amari, feeling bereft and empty inside, held the child and stared at the thick woods on either side of the road.

I'm to be sold once more? Is this the way it will be forever? To be passed from one owner to another like a cow? Afi had constantly talked about her bright spirit and her future. But Amari could see nothing but the darkness; she found she did not have Afi's strength.

After an hour or so Dr. Hoskins, who so far had said nothing at all to the passengers in the back of the wagon, slowly pulled over to the side of the road. The horse snorted and grabbed mouthfuls of soft grass.

The doctor was silent for a moment, then he turned around to look at his three passengers. He took a deep breath, then said quietly, "I am ashamed to be a human being this morning. I witnessed not just murder last night, but violence and cruelty and vicious hatred. By saying nothing, I feel I am as responsible as my so-called friend who pulled the trigger."

Amari and Polly exchanged stunned looks.

Dr. Hoskins continued. "I am just one man. I don't know how to fight everything that is happening around me. I don't understand how one man can own another. And I don't know how to stop it." He looked around at the deep woods and the darkness within them. "But I can help the three of you."

"How, sir?" Polly asked immediately.

"I plan to give you at least a fighting chance." He kept looking around him, as if someone would come down the road and discover what he was doing. "I have a little money and some food that Lena made up for our journey this morning." He pointed to a small bundle beneath the seat of the wagon.

"You not take us to town to be sold?" Amari asked, her voice hopeful.

"No, child. I'm not."

"What do we do, sir?" Polly asked.

"The Ashley River runs parallel to this road," he said, pointing to the west. "Find the river and follow it north. You will have to stay hidden during the day and travel only at night. Can you do that?"

"Oh, yes, sir!" Polly replied with enthusiasm.

"You'll have at least a day before they discover you're missing. I'll wait until tomorrow evening before I will be forced to report your 'escape' to Mr. Derby. If I could come up with the money to pay the purchase price for the three of you, I'd do it gladly," he said, "but unfortunately, I have no such means. All I can give you is time."

Amari frowned as she tried to make sense of the doctor's words. He spoke very fast, and she had to take her time to make sure she understood.

"How we gonna 'scape?" she asked, still unsure of the doctor's plan.

"I am setting you free," the doctor replied.

"We be free?" Amari asked, hardly daring to believe it. The word itself stunned her.

The doctor replied, "Well, I'm going to try to give you one small chance to be free. It's up to you and to the spirits of hope and possibility."

That much of the conversation Amari understood clearly. She thought of Afi and her unfailing faith in the future.

"We are so grateful for this opportunity, sir," Polly said, her voice breaking. "You are saving our lives!"

"This could just as easily destroy your lives," he warned. "There will be patrols out and documents posted for your arrest and dogs following your trail."

"How do we hide from dogs?" Amari asked.

"You can't. Dogs are trained to trace your smell and attack you when they find you. I'm not going to try to sugarcoat the danger."

"What happen to you when Massa Derby know you help us?" Amari asked.

"Me? I'll tell him we were attacked by highwaymen. I'll fake an injury to make it seem real. Don't worry about me—I'll be fine." Amari stared intently at the kindly, silver-haired doctor; she never would have imagined a white man willing to help her.

"You gonna tell Teenie her chile not get sold?" Amari asked as she held Tidbit's hand.

"Of course. But it won't be soon," he warned. Amari breathed a sigh of relief. She couldn't bear to think of Teenie's misery.

The doctor looked sadly at the three young people in the wagon. "You're just children," he mused, shaking his head. He reached under the seat and pulled out an old feed sack. From it he took a small bundle of food, a couple of coins, and a flintlock musket. Amari gasped at the sight of the gun.

"Use this only to save your life—not for hunting. You do not want to draw attention to yourself."

"How it work?" Amari asked.

Polly spoke up quietly. "I know how to use it—my father taught me. You half cock the hammer, pour in the gunpowder, wrap the lead ball, then stuff it into the barrel and fire." Amari was impressed.

The doctor nodded with approval. "Are you a good shot?" he asked.

Polly looked away. "No, sir, not very. My father tried to teach me, but I could not shoot straight."

The doctor shook his head. He gave Polly a small pouch that held the ammunition, as well as the sack. "You have enough gunpowder for only one shot. Make it count."

"Yes, sir, I will. Thank you, sir." She carefully replaced the gun into the bag and hoisted the sack over her shoulder.

"Hurry," the doctor said, glancing around worriedly. "Get

out of the wagon and as deeply as you can into the woods."

Amari looked up at him and smiled as she and Polly climbed out of the wagon. They both helped Tidbit jump down. "Thank you, sir," Amari said. She never thought she'd be thanking a white man!

"May God have mercy on all of you," the doctor replied. The wagon disappeared into the distance. The three children stood wordlessly for a moment, watching it, then, realizing their danger, darted into the darkness of the woods.

32. THE JOURNEY BEGINS

AMARI, POLLY, AND TIDBIT MOVED SLOWLY BUT
steadily through the woods, as if they knew where they were
going. Although the road had been brightly lit with the sunshine
of the morning, the woods were shadowy and dim under the
thick canopy of trees. Amari, somehow feeling very much at
home among this greenery, led them deeper and deeper until
they reached a point where no path was apparent, and the trees
and bushes grew so closely together that not even Tidbit could
squeeze between the thick green growth.

"Myna, let's stop for a bit and get our bearings," Polly suggested.

Amari nodded in agreement, and they all sat down on the
ground and caught their breath. Finches and swallows chirped
high above them, but otherwise the forest was surprisingly silent.
Polly closed her eyes and leaned against an oak tree.

Tidbit whispered, "Myna, I got to pee!"

Amari looked at the boy fondly. "Go quick—behind that tree."
The boy ran and returned shortly to the security of Amari's arms.
Amari gave him a reassuring hug, then she looked at Polly, who

sat next to her, scratching the mosquito bites on her arm. "My name be Amari," she informed the two of them.

Polly opened her eyes and looked at Amari with a slight frown. "What's wrong with the name they gave you?" she asked. "We're used to it now."

Amari took a deep breath of the woodsy air. "Not Myna no more. Amari." She spoke with clarity and certainty.

"If you say so," Polly said with a shrug. "I suppose it is a good name for a free woman."

"Free!" Amari exclaimed in quiet exultation. She had no intention of ever using that slave name again.

"I want my mama," Tidbit whimpered. He fingered the pouch that hung around his neck.

"You be free too, small one," Amari whispered to him. "You make your mama proud, you hear?" The boy just buried his head in Amari's arms.

"Which way do we go now, Amari?" Polly asked. "It's so easy to get turned around. I think the river is that way," she said, pointing to her left.

"No, river that way," Amari replied, pointing to her right. "I be smellin' muddy water."

Polly sighed. "How will we ever get to the North if we can't even find the river?"

"We not go north—we go south," Amari said defiantly.

"But Dr. Hoskins said to follow the river to the North. That's where we have a better chance at freedom," Polly insisted. "He's a doctor—he's got to know what's best for us."

"Cato say go south," Amari insisted.

"And he also said the streets were paved with gold. I think Cato's story is just an old slave's tale about a place that doesn't even exist!"

"I believe Cato!" Amari said emphatically. Her heart pounded—she had no intention of giving in to this white girl. "He be right about Massa Clay. He be right about doctor." She crossed her arms across her chest.

"But he *knew* them," Polly insisted. "This place he called Fort Mose is just a pretend place he's heard of—like the Promised Land—a place you go when you die. And I don't want to die—not yet!" Her face reddened in anger.

"We die if we go north," Amari said quietly.

"You will forever be a slave if we go south," Polly insisted.

"You want go north? Go alone," Amari said with a fierceness she hoped she had the courage to back up.

Polly inhaled sharply. After a long pause she replied, "We would all die if we split up."

"Choice up to you. Me and Tidbit goin' south. You come if you want." Amari bent down and picked up the small bundle of food. She hoped that Polly wouldn't go off on her own, but she just knew she had to go south.

"Slavery's not so bad up north," Polly said slowly. "I hear tell that lots of black folk are free up there."

"I free here. I free now," Amari replied, digging her toe into the dirt. Then, without looking at Polly, she added, "You white gal. You not need us." She knew that Polly could make it alone and would certainly find refuge quicker without the presence of two runaway slaves.

"I think we need each other," Polly said with quiet resolution.

Amari started to reply, but a noise from behind them made her pause. A twig broke. Then another. Amari held Tidbit tightly and held her breath. None of them moved. Someone was approaching. She motioned for them to be absolutely silent.

Suddenly, emerging triumphantly from the trees, lunged a dirty and burr-covered Hushpuppy. The dog rushed to Tidbit, licking his face and yelping with obvious joy. "Hushpuppy!" the boy exclaimed with happiness as he hugged his dog. "You found me!" The dog flopped down at the boy's feet and began to lick them, too.

Perhaps this was a sign of good fortune for their journey, Amari thought. And Polly must have thought the same thing, because she looked at Amari and smiled.

"Do you truly believe there is a place called Fort Mose?" Polly asked her.

Amari nodded. "I feel it—here," she said, pointing to her heart. "It be place where, if you get there, you be free inside and outside."

"I hope Cato is right," Polly said slowly. "But going south makes no sense to me."

"Patrols be lookin' north," Amari reminded her.

"How will we ever find our way to a place we are not even sure exists?" Polly asked.

"Spirits will lead us."

"I don't believe in all that spirit talk," Polly said quietly. "And it is such a long way."

"Long walk anyhow," Amari replied. Then she asked, "You not trust Amari?"

Polly looked at her for several moments, as if she were weighing her decision. "Well," she said finally, "we should get started."

Amari nodded in approval. "No talk," she reminded Tidbit. "We must move quiet like snakes."

"Silent snakes," the boy whispered back.

The three of them picked their way through the forest for the rest of the afternoon, stopping only to drink from the streams they crossed. Amari led them slowly and carefully through a maze of oak and elm and maple trees. Rabbits darted across their path, and deer looked at them with large, surprised eyes. But no voices followed them and no people approached. The dog, as if he knew silence was important, did not bark once.

For the first time since her capture in Africa, Amari relaxed. Even though her feet were bare and the ground was covered with sticks and pine needles, she felt no pain, for this walk was leading her, perhaps, to that destiny that Afi kept speaking of.

As dusk approached, Amari signaled for them to stop. "River be very close," she whispered. "We follow water in dark time."

"Tidbit tired," the boy whined quietly. "I wanna go back to my mama!" He rubbed his eyes and sat down with a thud. "I don't wanna walk no more!"

Amari knew she had to let him rest. "We stop here," she said. "Sleep some, for we walk much soon." She gave him a small piece of meat from Lena's bundle, and he promptly fell off to sleep, his head resting on Hushpuppy.

The girls could see the river in the distance and smell its earthy, wet shoreline as they hid in the darkness of the trees. Amari could hear laughter of men on boats and slow, sad chants of slaves working in the rice fields nearby, finishing up their labors for the day.

"We got to leave river," Amari whispered to Polly.

"Why?" Polly asked. "I thought the plan was to follow the river."

"All rivers run to sea," Amari explained, remembering what Cato had said. "We gotta go by land."

"How will we know which way is which?" Polly asked, looking perplexed.

"Moss grow on north side of trees," Amari explained, trying to remember exactly what Teenie had once told her. "So we follow other side of tree!"

"We can't see moss at night," Polly said reasonably.

"Stars lead us," Amari replied with confidence.

Polly shook her head, but she stopped arguing. The two girls rested their heads gratefully on twin tree trunks, but only for a short time. Amari knew they needed to travel in the safety of darkness. Tidbit fussed when she awakened him, but he soon rubbed his little eyes bravely and marched with them into the darkness without much complaint.

Fireflies blinked in the thick saw grass near the edge of the river. Bullfrogs erupted with tuneless burps. Mosquitoes swarmed in full force, and the three travelers swatted them constantly, their arms and bodies becoming covered with itching bites. A nightingale called far in the distance.

Amari lifted her head to the night sky. Bright stars decorated the darkness above, and she wondered if they were the same stars that had winked at her so far away in her homeland.

33. DEEP IN THE FOREST

MORNING DAWNED SLOWLY, BRIGHTENING THE forest. Amari, unusually weary but not willing to admit it, was glad when Polly suggested they find a thicket of trees to rest in. The girls had taken turns carrying Tidbit during the last hours of the night, and he was much heavier than he looked. Even Hushpuppy seemed tired.

Amari led them to the darkest part of the forest—a place where three huge trees had fallen together, and the hollow beneath them was just big enough for the three tired travelers.

"I hope the foxes or deer that usually rest in this spot won't be offended," Polly said gratefully, and she snuggled into the narrow indentation.

"Might come back," Amari suggested nervously as she nestled in next to Polly.

"Tidbit too tired to care," he said as he and Hushpuppy squeezed in next to the girls.

As the day grew brighter and warmer, the hidden children tried to sleep, but ants and mosquitoes feasted on their bodies while the growing heat of the day made them damp with sweat.

Near nightfall, they shared the last of the corn bread and ventured to the river to gather some water.

"One day free," Amari announced as she scratched the numerous bites on her body.

"How far freedom be, Amari?" Tidbit asked fretfully.

"Many, many days, little one," she told him gently.

He squirmed. "What this freedom we runnin' to, Polly?" he then asked. It was clear to Amari that he didn't understand such a grown-up concept.

Polly pulled a leaf from an oak tree. "Freedom is a delicate idea, like a pretty leaf in the air: It's hard to catch and may not be what you thought when you get it," she observed quietly.

Amari replied with a nod, not exactly understanding what Polly had said but comprehending the idea. It seemed to go over the boy's head.

Tidbit put his small fists to his eyes. "I just be wantin' to see my mama," he said, pulling his dog closer. "I know she be missin' me right 'bout now."

"Your mother is very proud of you, Tidbit," Polly told him. "You don't want to disappoint her, do you?"

"I don't care. I wanna go back to my mama's kitchen!" Tidbit cried loudly. "I be hungry and hot, and I don't like it here!" He plopped down on the ground.

"Shhh," Amari said, trying to soothe him. "Gotta stay quiet, little one. You want bad mens to catch us?"

Tidbit, looking miserable, shook his head.

"You gotta protect Hushpuppy," Polly told him. "Can you do that?"

The boy looked glum, but he stood up, stroked the dog, and scratched his legs.

Polly and Amari looked at Tidbit with concern, but they had no choice but to move on. They covered their tracks with leaves and headed into the darkness once more.

By the fifth day of their journey they were all tired and hungry, and their feet, scratched and swollen, cried out for relief. Occasionally, Amari suffered mild bouts of dizziness, and she had to ask the others to stop so she could clear her head and catch her breath.

"Hunger make me little bit weak," she said with embarrassment one morning.

"You're not completely recovered from that beating," Polly reminded her. "Take your time."

"No time to go slow," Amari replied. "Must get far, far away."

"You be all right, Amari?" Tidbit asked.

"I can still beat *you* running!" Amari told him with a laugh as she got up to chase him. He giggled and darted off.

Now and then they found nuts and berries in the forest, but hunger lived with them every day. Amari's mother had taught her a few things about gathering food, and Amari wished she had listened better. But she *had* listened to Teenie, and one evening she left Polly and Tidbit for an hour and brought back a pouch full of nuts and berries that she had gathered—walnuts, pecans, and boysenberries—as well as roots and herbs she had dug. "Good to eat. Give us strength," she told the others.

"How do you know which roots to pick, which herbs are safe?" Polly asked as she nibbled on the fruit of a mayapple, which looked a little like a lime. "I remember seeing these bloom in the spring back in Beaufort. But I don't recall ever eating one."

"My mother teach me," Amari replied simply, "and Teenie, too. But I not sure about plants grow here. Some I never see before." Amari picked those plants she recognized and others that just looked tasty, but she was very aware that some berries, like the ones Teenie kept hidden in her garden, could be lovely to look at but very dangerous to eat.

"This one taste funny," Tidbit commented, but he ate the mayapple hungrily. When he was done, he asked, "Why you not bring more?"

"Never take all," Amari explained. "You dig one plant, leave two plant; dig one, leave two. So plant come back next season. And ask plant permission."

"Ask permission?" Polly asked. "Why?"

Amari wondered how she could explain the need to work in harmony with the natural world. She tried to find the words. "Plant die. People live. Hunter ask animal before kill it. Then give thanks. Animal die so village live."

"So it is like showing respect for nature?" Polly asked, a look of approval and understanding on her face.

Amari nodded.

"I still hungry!" Tidbit exclaimed softly, pulling on Polly's arm.

"We'll find some good food soon," Polly told him. "Maybe beyond those next trees on that hill," she said, vaguely pointing to some trees in the distance.

He looked in that direction, but he clearly did not believe her. He whimpered and dragged the rest of the night, often having to be carried. Amari's arms ached from carrying him.

A couple of hours later Tidbit said, "I don't feel so good." He bent over and held his stomach, then ran off behind a tree.

Amari, who also had been feeling quite nauseous, looked at Polly. "You feel sick too?"

At that moment Polly doubled over and ran to find another tree.

Amari threw up. Even though she felt hot, when she touched her face it felt clammy and damp. She made her way to a pile of soft branches and lay there, her stomach cramping terribly. Tidbit came back and lay down near her. "I sick, Amari." She rubbed his little stomach; it felt tight and hard against her hand.

Polly took in deep breaths and asked heatedly, "What did we eat that made us sick? I thought you Africans knew all about plants and herbs!"

Amari tried to think, but her head was spinning. She felt terrible that she had made them all sick, but Polly's accusations made her angry. *She* certainly had not made any efforts to find food. Amari opened her mouth to retort but grabbed her stomach in pain instead. "I so sorry. I not sure—I bring back many kinds." She was going to apologize again, but she had to run to another tree to throw up once more.

The three of them spent a day and a night in that area, trying to regain their strength after numerous bouts of diarrhea and vomiting. Tidbit didn't seem to blame Amari, but Polly remained furious. "It's bad enough I'm lost in the forest with a couple of runaway slaves!" she told Amari. "But now you go and nearly kill us!"

In spite of her weakness, Amari tensed with anger. "I knows you ain't no slave. You free, Polly," Amari told her coolly. "Free to leave us when you wants to. Free to go back to Massa Derby. He say he sell you to be whore," she added sharply. She turned away from Polly.

Polly hung her head. "We're in this together, Amari," she answered softly.

Amari knew it was hunger, illness, and fatigue that made Polly so upset, but she also knew that Polly spoke what was truly on her mind. All of them needed proper food, and soon.

"We gotta eat," Amari announced later that night. She looked around the forest floor until she found what she needed—a sturdy stick that was pointed at the end and a sharp stone. She slowly sharpened the stick until the point gleamed in the moonlight. "I go to river to find food maybe. You be here when I get back?"

"I'll be here," Polly replied quietly.

"I be back soon," Amari said without acknowledging Polly's reply.

Amari disappeared into the darkness.

When Amari returned a couple of hours later, her feet were covered with mud. In her hands, however, she triumphantly held up three large, shimmering catfish.

"I don't believe it!" Polly exclaimed. "How did you do it?"

"Fish fast. I be faster!" Amari replied with a chuckle.

"But how will we cook them?" Polly asked. "If we make a fire, someone may see us."

"We eat raw," Amari said with authority.

"Raw?" Polly asked. "But won't that make us sick again?"

"Raw." Amari took the sharp stone and cut each fish open from tip to tail. She deftly removed the bones, then cut the fish into bite-sized pieces. The heads and tails she tossed to Hushpuppy, who gobbled them greedily.

Polly made such a face that Amari had to laugh. But she picked up her portion and bit into it. "Not as bad as I thought," she said as she swallowed carefully.

Amari bit into her own portion. She chewed slowly and deliberately. Amari woke Tidbit, who tried to turn up his nose at the idea of eating the raw and bloody fish, but his hunger took over and he gobbled his piece, even licking his fingers when he finished. Then he made a face. "You ask permission of this fish?" he asked.

"Fish happy to die for you this night," Amari answered with a smile. "He tired of swimming."

"Let's see if we can get moving again," Polly suggested.

"I got power of fish in me—feel more better," Amari said as she tried to stand up. She was genuinely surprised when Polly reached out and grabbed her hand to help. The two girls looked at each other with renewed understanding.

Amari and Tidbit helped to bury the fish bones, and the three of them prepared, with fresh determination, to continue in the darkness.

34. LOST HUSHPUPPY

AS DAYS WENT BY, AMARI HAD NO FURTHER luck at catching more fish. She was starting to feel overwhelmed with exhaustion. Her head hurt all the time, and even though the others seemed to have recuperated from the mayapple incident, she didn't want to tell them that she still felt dizzy and nauseous.

The forest had thinned, and hiding places were getting harder to find. Occasionally, Amari heard wagons on the road to the east of them and the sounds of farmers or their slaves working nearby, so the trio moved only in the darkest of night and thus made very poor time as they traveled.

Amari didn't try to find any more berries or fruit, worried that she would make them all sick again. Instead of eating, hunger ate at them. One evening, just before sunset, Amari stumbled over a fallen log and toppled to the ground in a heap. "Ow!" she cried as she rubbed her foot.

"Are you hurt?" Polly asked, concern in her voice.

"No, feet just be tired of walkin'," Amari replied with a short laugh. She leaned against the log, planning to get back to her feet, when something made her decide to look underneath it.

Dozens of insects, worms, and grubs squirmed in the unaccustomed light. Amari took a deep breath and grabbed a handful of white, soft grubs. "Safe to eat," she said, "I think." She closed her eyes, put some in her mouth, and chewed slowly. "Taste like chicken," she said, trying to make Tidbit smile.

She offered Tidbit and Polly some grubs as well, and surprisingly, they ate them without complaint, as well as some of the earthworms. It was a matter of survival.

Night after night they walked, afraid of every hoot of the owl and howl of the coyote. Some nights they crossed small streams, which gave them a chance to refresh themselves, quench their thirst, and soothe their aching feet. Sometimes they found small water creatures like crabs or clams to eat. By day they tried to sleep—under logs, in caves, in thickets. Their faces, arms, and legs became hardened with insect bites and scratches. Amazingly, however, they had heard no voices, met no other humans in the woods, nor were chased by patrollers who were looking for runaways. Perhaps Cato had been right, Amari thought.

One morning, just as dawn broke and they hurried to find a hiding place for the day, Tidbit cried out in alarm. "Where is Hushpuppy?"

Most of the time Amari scarcely noticed the dog—he rarely strayed far from Tidbit.

"Hushpuppy must be looking for a mouse for his dinner," Polly said to Tidbit.

"Can I call him?" Tidbit asked tearfully. "Maybe he be lost."

"No, child. You can make no noise. Too dangerous," Amari told him. "Hushpuppy come back."

Polly tried to console him as well. "A dog can always find the boy he loves. He'll be back."

But the dog did not return that morning, or by that afternoon or that evening. At that point Tidbit began to cry. He refused to get up and prepare for the night's travel.

"Hushpuppy will find us," Polly tried to tell him. "He found us all the way from Mr. Derby's house, didn't he?"

"I ain't goin' without Hushpuppy." Tidbit spoke to the dirt he dug his fingers into.

"Tidbit, we gotta go now," Amari said a little impatiently as she lifted the child to his feet. "Hushpuppy gonna come back." They headed out once more, but Tidbit dragged his feet and kept turning around to look for the dog.

The nights had grown more difficult lately, for the warmth of the sun during the day barely lasted past dark, leaving the nights cold and clammy. "Rain soon," Amari commented as she clutched Tidbit's hand, almost dragging him along. In her other hand she carried the sharpened stick, which she used as a walking staff.

"Rain will feel good," Polly said tiredly. "I don't think I've ever been so dirty!"

"Hushpuppy never find me now," Tidbit wailed miserably.

Amari leaned down and picked Tidbit up, wrapping his legs around her waist, and they headed south into the wet, damp night. Amari began to wonder if she was doing the right thing. It had been her decision to come south, and she was feeling increasingly responsible for them all. What if they were simply going in circles? What if Fort Mose didn't even exist? And she was tired, so very tired.

She also didn't know how to console Tidbit, who was crying

softly and begging for his mother and his dog. Finally, when she feared she could not take one more step, they came to a small cave. Amari looked at it as if it were a castle.

"Do you think it's safe to build a fire?" Polly asked. Polly, too, was trembling with cold.

"Think so," Amari replied.

"Do you know how to start a fire?" Polly asked then.

Amari looked around the floor of the cave. "Not sure. Not like home."

Polly grew thoughtful. "My father used to boast he could start a fire with just a stick, a leaf, and a shiny bug!"

"Sound like tall tale," Amari said with a smile.

"Well, we have to try something," Polly said as she began to gather dry twigs from the back of the cave, looking hopeful. Amari found a big branch and dragged it to the center.

With lightning quickness, Amari began rubbing her sharp stick between her hands, twirling it in the center of a larger branch, the way she remembered her mother doing it. But nothing happened. Her fingertips, numb from the damp, chilly air, weren't able to twist the stick fast enough. In her homeland she had started many fires, but usually with a burning stick from someone's cooking fire. Even Teenie's kitchen had a fire that never went out—those hot coals had been carefully tended at night.

Still, she rubbed and rubbed. Polly and Tidbit hovered close. After what seemed to be a very long time, a faint whisper of smoke snaked up from the twigs and leaves. Amari blew on it gently, and soon a small flame flickered in the darkness.

"Fire," Amari said quietly.

"Glory be," Polly whispered. She slowly fed the flames leaves and small sticks until it became large enough to ease their shakes and shivers.

Amari gloried in its warmth, for her head felt thick, like it had been packed with straw. She felt weak and dizzy. She knew she had to find them some real food soon.

"Maybe we use gun to get food?" she asked Polly tentatively.

"We only have one shot," Polly reminded her. "Suppose we miss or someone hears it and finds us?"

Amari nodded reluctantly.

"Do any animals live here, do you think?" Polly asked as they stared into the flames.

"Maybe animal share with us this night," Amari said with a half smile.

Tidbit fell into a fitful sleep in Amari's arms, his face drawn.

Amari sat close to Polly for warmth and companionship, looking at the fire, thinking not of the horrendous fire that had destroyed her village, but of the smoky cooking fires that decorated the front of each household as the women prepared the evening meal. If she closed her eyes, she could almost smell the pungent fish stew.

Suddenly, Amari could hear the footsteps of an animal pacing outside of the cave. She grabbed Polly's arm, and they peered into the darkness. They could get only glimpses of the creature, but it seemed to have a huge, furry head. And it seemed to be looking for a way to get past the fire. It smelled of wet fur and fresh blood.

"Fox?" Amari whispered.

"Foxes have small heads; this one is huge, whatever it is," Polly whispered back anxiously.

"Could be bobcat," Amari guessed.

"Maybe we are in its home," Polly offered. "I don't think it wants us here."

Amari looked around nervously. "We got 'nuff wood to keep fire going?"

"Not much," Polly replied softly. "Where is your stick?"

Amari looked stricken. "In fire. What if it be bear?"

The animal continued to pace. As the fire dwindled, the two girls huddled even closer together. The animal edged forward. Amari barely breathed. The scraping and sniffing and growling sounds were right at the entrance now.

Suddenly, the creature bounded over the fire. The girls screamed.

Tidbit startled awake and shouted with joy, "Hushpuppy!" The dog dropped what it had been carrying and leaped joyfully on the boy.

Amari, so relieved that it wasn't a bear, started laughing. "I never be so glad to see a dog!"

"Where you been?" Tidbit asked the excited dog. He ran over to the thing Hushpuppy had been carrying and dragged it over to the girls. It was the biggest, fattest rabbit any of them had ever seen.

"So that's why we didn't recognize him!" Polly commented. "He looked so much bigger carrying that."

"And he smell like blood," Amari said as she examined the rabbit.

"We gonna eat it raw like the fish?" Tidbit asked with a grimace.

The thought of another meal of raw meat made Amari feel utterly queasy. "No, little one. We cook. We be safe in cave for now."

Polly and Tidbit ran out of the cave and searched under logs for dry twigs to feed the fire. Amari found a sharp rock and was able to skin the rabbit, careful to save any part of it that might be helpful on their journey. The skin would make a good pouch, and she remembered her mother once saying that the entrails could be dried and used as string. Hushpuppy was given a huge pile of the leftover parts, which he ate with gusto.

Amari carefully pierced the meat with a stick Tidbit had triumphantly brought her, and after the fire had been built up again, each girl took turns slowly turning it until it was cooked to perfection. Even the drippings were saved. They ate well for the first time since they had begun their journey.

Licking his fingers, Tidbit said softly, "I miss my mama."

Amari pulled him close. A sudden image of her own mother and all that she had lost overpowered Amari for a moment. Tonight, however, she reminded herself, she must concentrate not on what was lost, but on what must be found.

THE NEXT EVENING, FEELING FULL OF ENERGY, the three young travelers headed out with renewed enthusiasm. The forest had turned to deep pine, the tall evergreens casting thin shadows from the moonlight. In the distance lights from farmhouses flickered.

"Hushpuppy seems to know he is the hero of the moment," Polly said with a smile as the dog bounded after every unfortunate rabbit or squirrel that crossed their path. "But he's too full to catch much now."

Amari laughed softly. Tidbit chased the dog merrily, his high spirits returned, and they all seemed to relax as they made their way slowly through the cool, dark night. They crossed another shallow waterway, where the soft river mud soothed their tired feet.

For four more nights they traveled smoothly, heading ever farther away from the plantation of Percival Derby. They had no more huge feasts, but the leftover pieces of the cooked rabbit lasted a few days, and roots and tubers were plentiful every time they reached a river. Amari was glad that it was not the rainy season—the small streams they crossed would have been roaring rivers. In addition, Amari figured out a way to catch crayfish in the shallows, the tangy flesh a delicious treat as they began their seemingly unending nighttime treks.

But she was tired—tired of walking, of being uncertain, and of feeling sick all the time. Every muscle in her body cried out for rest. The night was unusually warm, and Amari had broken out in a sweat. She didn't think she could keep this up much longer. She had no way of knowing how far they had gone or how much farther they still had to travel. She had nothing to grab on to for support. It reminded her of being on the ship, where it was impossible to determine time or place—just the endless sea.

She was fearful also, but she did not want to share her worries with the others. What would happen if they were found? She wiped her brow and tried to think positively, showing brave smiles to Polly and Tidbit. Just as she let herself relax, however, her worst fears became reality.

As they walked on, Amari could see nothing but shadows—some lighter than others. The trees—long, slim silhouettes—seemed to guide them most of the time, but sometimes the branches looked like arms with hands of many fingers, ready to attack.

And then, suddenly, the branches of a short, sturdy tree moved. Just as Amari jumped, one branch grabbed her wrist. She cried out and tried to pull her arm free. Polly instantly grasped Tidbit's hand and pulled him into the darkness.

Amari screamed again and tried to turn, but she couldn't get free. Then she heard a voice full of venom and danger.

"Where do you think you're going?" As Amari twisted

to escape, she found herself face-to-face with Clay Derby.

"Let me go!" Amari exploded, but Clay held her arm as firmly as the shackles she had once worn as he pulled her close to the trunk of the tree.

"I been looking for you and that white girl you run off with for a long time now," Clay drawled. "My father would have been proud of me, God rest his soul."

"How you find?" Amari asked in furious frustration.

"Wasn't hard. You leave footprints the size of a horse." He laughed with disdain, spat on the ground, and pulled a rope from his doublet. He first tied Amari's arms together, then tied her to the tree, pressing himself against her to keep her still.

"How you know where to look?" she wanted to know.

"Oh, the doctor made up that cock-and-bull story about highwaymen and seeing you all head north. But he is a poor excuse for a liar. Everybody went north looking for you, but I figured you might try something stupid like running south."

"Why you care?" Amari asked with quiet anger.

"You are mine, gal." His leer turned into a confused scowl. "I have missed you, Myna," he admitted. "Didn't you miss me a little? I thought you liked me." He touched her face gently.

In spite of her fury, Amari was amazed at the plaintive tone in his voice. "Why you not just let me be?" she asked angrily.

Clay leaned over very close to her face. "Because I aim to reclaim what's mine. You hear me, Myna?"

Amari took a deep breath, closed her eyes, and this time it was her turn to spit. She spat directly in his face. Clay roared and slapped her so hard that her head bounced back against the tree trunk. She felt herself fading into a faint, but she felt victorious. Clay slapped her again, bringing her back to full consciousness. Amari glared at him.

From the shadows, Amari heard Hushpuppy growl.

"Where is the child?" Clay asked Amari as he looked around.

Amari looked at him with narrowed eyes. "Dead," she said emphatically.

"I don't think so," Clay replied calmly. "That would save me the trouble of dashing his head against a tree. I followed your footprints, remember?"

Amari struggled against the ropes. She had never been so angry. If he hurt Tidbit, she would kill him, she vowed.

"And where is the white girl?" Clay asked as he watched her struggle. He seemed to be amused.

"She leave us—go north," Amari lied.

"You know, you're as poor a liar as the doctor," Clay told her as he ran his hand down her arm. "I shall enjoy punishing you when we return to Derbyshire Farms. I am master there now, you know. My father died suddenly—not long after you ran off."

"Massa Derby dead?" Amari asked with surprise. She wondered if Mrs. Derby had breathed a sigh of relief. Amari lowered her head. *Is it wrong to be glad that someone is dead?* she thought.

"Yes, the doctor said it was his heart, but I believe he was poisoned," Clay said ominously.

Amari peered into the darkness and prayed that Polly and Tidbit would not try to save her and get caught themselves. Again she heard Hushpuppy growl from the darkness of the woods, quietly but with menace.

"What happen when we go back?" Amari asked, trying to keep Clay talking.

"Oh, you'll be punished severely—perhaps a brand on your face or maybe the removal of a finger or toe. I have not yet decided."

Amari felt her heart quicken, but she refused to let Clay see that she was scared.

"I fully intend to teach you the folly of trying to run away from me. But tonight," he said, his voice dropping low, "I intend to make up for lost time. I really have missed you, gal." He stroked her leg, and Amari kicked at him.

Undeterred, Clay put his hand on Amari's other leg. A dusty blond shadow erupted from the woods at that moment, both hands shakily holding the musket. Polly closed her eyes and squeezed the trigger. The sound was deafening. Amari screamed. Clay sank to the ground with a moan.

"He be dead?" Amari asked fearfully as they crept close to him.

Polly, her face showing both terror and surprise, dropped the gun, then fell to her knees and turned Clay over. "No, he is not dead," she declared with relief. "It's a good thing I am such a poor shot. I didn't want to hurt him, just frighten him away!"

Clay's eyes fluttered and he groaned softly.

"The bullet barely grazed the side of his head. He will be fully conscious soon. We must hurry." She tore at the knots that held Amari.

Amari looked at Polly with gratitude, amazement, and new respect. "I not know you so wild!"

Polly grinned. "I didn't know it either. I just knew I had to do something quick and sudden." Then she got down to business. "It is *his* turn to be tied," she suggested.

"He get loose soon, yes?" Amari asked.

"Probably," Polly replied. "We don't have much rope. I suppose he will be able to undo the knots eventually. But at least we will have some time to get away."

"He should die," Amari declared, no regret in her voice.

"Maybe so, but it is not for us to do," Polly replied.

They pulled Clay over to the tree and bound him as tightly as they could. "We must get out of here quickly," Polly said. "Someone may have heard the gunfire."

As they backed away from him, he began to stir. "He be wakin' up," Amari whispered frantically.

Polly grabbed Clay's knapsack and tossed the gun inside it. "We must flee! If he gets loose, he will surely find us and kill us."

"Maybe not," Amari replied. She pointed to a spot just beyond Clay's thigh where a large rattlesnake slithered toward him.

"What should we do?" Polly whispered.

"Nothing," Amari replied quietly.

Clay opened his eyes and focused slowly on Amari, Polly, and Tidbit sitting a few feet away from him. A trickle of blood oozed from the wound on his head. He pulled at his restraints. "How dare you?" he roared as he became more aware of what they had done. He yanked at the ropes. "I'll kill you for this!"

"I don't think so," Polly replied.

"Mark my words, you'll pay for this!" he warned viciously as he tugged at the ropes some more. "When we get back, I'll throw that boy in his mother's cooking pot and make her watch him die!"

"We not go back," Amari told him clearly.

"Oh, yes, you are," Clay swore as he continued to struggle with the ropes. "You can't even tie a decent knot," he crowed triumphantly, freeing one arm. Even if you run, I will find you and catch you, and I plan to spend the rest of my life making you suffer."

"Rest of life might not be long," Amari observed quietly. The snake, unmoving, coiled tensed and ready only inches from Clay's leg.

Clay looked directly at Amari, his face a mask of rage and confusion. "I tried to be kind to you," he told her. "How can you repay me like this?"

She looked at him with pity. "You just not understand."

Angrily, Clay continued to wiggle and struggle with the ropes that held him. Then he turned his head and spotted the snake. He froze. The snake was motionless as well.

Amari looked at Polly. Polly looked at Tidbit. They all looked toward the woods. In silent agreement they hurried away from Clay.

PART EIGHT

POLLY

36. SHOULD WE TRUST HIM?

THEY RAN. FASTER THAN POLLY THOUGHT POSSIBLE, they jumped over logs and under low-hanging branches, the only thought being to put miles between them and Clay Derby. Her left side cramped and ached, but they dared not stop. With great urgency, they hurried through the darkness, Amari clutching one of Tidbit's arms, Polly the other. His little feet barely touched the ground. Sweat poured down Polly's face. Finally, after what seemed like miles of frantic running, they stopped by a shallow river to rest.

Amari was breathing so hard, she threw up. Tidbit collapsed by the stream and then crawled into the water to cool off. Slowly, her pounding heart slowed, but Polly knew they were probably still in grave danger.

"Do you think the snake got him?" Polly asked.

"Maybe snake not mad enough to bite," Amari said as she worked to catch her breath. "Maybe Massa Clay got loose and kill the snake," she added fearfully.

Tidbit emerged from the water, dripping wet. "If Massa Clay find us again, he gonna take me to my mama?"

Polly clasped her hand to her mouth, shocked and saddened at the child's question. Polly looked at Amari, then told Tidbit carefully, "Tidbit, if Clay comes back, he will try to hurt us. So we have to keep running and stay very quiet. Do you understand?"

Tidbit shifted from one foot to another, looking surprisingly mature. "I don't care if he beat me. I just wanna see my mama." He was blinking back tears.

Amari grabbed him then and pulled him to her. "I know, little one. I know."

Polly sat down with them, and the two girls tried their best to comfort the little boy. Through it all, she listened to the night sounds but could hear no approaching footsteps. "Do you think we did wrong to leave him like that?" she whispered to Amari.

"Massa Clay not in our hands no more," Amari replied.

Reluctantly, Polly picked up Clay's knapsack and looked through it. In it was a hunk of dried salt pork, a few apples, some wrapped cheese, and several hard biscuits. She gave one to Tidbit.

"My mama made this bread," he said, first sniffing it, then holding it close to his body. "I wanna go see my mama!" He began to cry.

Amari looked at the boy sadly. "We come too far to go back," she said. "'Sides, if I goes back, I be a slave again. And I ain't never bein' no slave ever no more." Polly nodded thoughtfully and stood back up. Amari picked up Tidbit, and they headed south once again.

They did not stop for two days, moving even during the day, staying well away from the roads as they did. They saw people only in the distance. Tidbit's little legs struggled to keep up. Many times he had to be carried or cajoled into continuing the journey. There was no sign of Clay, but they never stopped looking over their shoulders.

"We should have tried to find Clay's horse," Polly said wearily one evening.

"No," Amari replied. "Better this way."

One evening, bone-weary and dragging through the red-clay mud of still another shallow river they had to cross, they paused to search for crayfish or clams. "I found five!" Tidbit whispered excitedly. Even he knew to be ever vigilant and quiet.

Then Polly saw him: a boy about their age, sitting on a rock overlooking the river. He was hunched over a fishing pole and did not appear to notice them.

Polly motioned to Amari and Tidbit to get back into the darkness of the pine trees. Hushpuppy also silently disappeared. But just as Polly stepped backward, the boy looked up.

He had dirty reddish hair, a torn shirt, and wore no shoes. He gazed at Polly without much surprise. "Who are you?" he asked bluntly.

"I suppose I could ask you the same thing," she retorted, hands on her hips. She wanted to show him how bold and unafraid she was, but her heart quaked.

"What are you doing out here in the middle of the night?" he countered.

Polly raked her fingers through her hair and brushed a twig off her dress. She couldn't believe she was worrying about how she *looked*! "Getting some fresh air. And who goes fishing after dark?"

"I do."

"You catch anything?" she asked.

"No. Too dark," he admitted. He looked at her closely in the moonlight. "I never seen you round these parts before."

Polly replied saucily, "There's probably a lot you've never seen."

"What's your name?" the boy asked.

"Polly." She immediately gasped and put her hand to her mouth. She should have told him Sarah or Sally or anything other than her real name!

"So, Miss Polly, you look like you got a lot to hide. You're dirty, you look hungry, and you look lost."

"I know exactly where I am. I am speaking to a young man who does not have the good manners to be polite to a lady!" She tried to speak to him with dignity, but it was hard with muddy feet.

He laughed. "My name is Nathan. I live in that little house through those trees there. We ain't got much—just a house, a barn, some chickens, and a couple of skinny cows and pigs. But we got a little land, and it's ours, and we make do. My daddy drinks at night, so I go fishing. And you are probably right about my manners—my mama would have taught me, but she died." He tossed a stone into the water. "But I do know a pretty girl when I see one—even if she is muddy-footed and saucy-mouthed."

Polly was surprised to find herself blushing. Her whole face and neck felt like hot, stinging needles. She'd never felt like this before. She cleared her throat. "I must be on my way," she said as she tried to go around the rock on which he sat.

"Do you know where you are?" he asked.

"Of course," she replied.

"Where?" he challenged her.

"I don't have to tell you anything," she said with a boldness she did not feel. She glanced nervously in the direction of the forest where Amari and Tidbit hid.

He gazed at her curiously. "You're not far from Savannah, Georgia." He paused. "Is that where you want to be?"

"Exactly," Polly said with annoyance.

"What about the others?" he asked quietly.

"What others?" Polly said, trying to bluff. "I am alone."

"The slave girl. The little boy. The dog." He continued to gaze at her with a half smile. "I spotted you yesterday, and I been following you."

Polly's eyes went wide. "You've been . . . Why?" Polly asked nervously. "Do you work for Clay Derby?"

"Never heard of him," Nathan replied. "I just figure you must be runaways, but I never seen such a raggedy bunch before."

"We are on a mission of mercy," Polly began desperately. "I am mistress of—"

"Of mud?" The boy interrupted her and laughed out loud. "Y'all look like you need some mercy yourselves. You are obviously nobody's mistress—I figure an unhappy indenture. The two little Negroes are runaways for sure." He paused and gazed at Polly long enough to make her feel uncomfortable. Then he said slowly, "I figure that your little 'mission of mercy' is worth a bucket of reward money."

Polly backed away from him slowly. "You mustn't tell," she whispered, pleading. "We have come so far, and our journey has not been easy."

Nathan grinned. "I can see that." Then he pointed to the woods where the others were hiding. "Tell your friends to come out. Maybe I can help."

Polly hesitated, unsure of what to do. She knew Amari and Tidbit had heard everything.

"Go on, Polly-girl," Nathan said gently. "Call them. You can trust me."

Again her father's special name for her was spouting from the mouth of a cocky young man. This time, however, she almost liked the way Nathan said it, with just a hint of a Georgia twang. She opened her mouth to call the others, but before Polly could speak, Amari stepped quietly out of the darkness of the trees. She held Tidbit on her hip. Hushpuppy, hovering close, growled quietly.

Nathan looked at them for a moment, then asked, "Are you all hungry?"

Polly nodded stiffly, still uncertain.

Nathan jumped down from the rock and stood face-to-face with the dirty, tired group. "Look, I got to tell you, my daddy would turn y'all in, get the reward money, and have it drunk away by Sunday next. But me, I think slavery is stupid. I figure anybody ought to be free enough to go fishing at midnight if he wants to." He grinned again. "It is a big country, with room enough for the Indians, for black folk to find their own place, and for pretty little white girls with dirty feet!"

Polly was sure her furious blushes were evident even in the moonlight. She'd never met anyone who made her feel so fluttery.

Amari coughed. "You got food?" she asked quietly.

"Not much," Nathan replied. "Follow me." They trailed the boy through the forest, which thinned gradually to a clearing where a small garden and a larger field of crops could be seen. Two small buildings—a house and a barn made of rough wood and logs— stood nearby. "I'm going to hide y'all in the barn. I do most of the work around the place, so Daddy is not likely to find you if you stay quiet." He led them through a small door, pulled fresh hay for pallets for them, and told them he'd return in a moment.

Amari looked around nervously. "This be a trap?" she asked.

"I hope not," Polly replied. "He had an honest face."

Amari smiled at her. "I think his face make you happy."

Polly blushed again. "Nonsense," she said quietly. She didn't want to admit that Amari was right.

Nathan was back a few minutes later with bread, cheese, dried venison, and apples. "This is all I could find, and my daddy is going to wonder why I got so hungry, but I'll just tell him I been out all day hunting. Eat," he urged them.

The hungry group of travelers took the food gratefully. Tidbit even ate the apple cores and promptly fell asleep on the nearest pile of straw.

"Where y'all headed?" Nathan asked the girls.

"South," Amari replied.

Nathan looked confused. "Don't most runaways head north?"

Amari glanced at Polly, who lowered her voice and asked Nathan, "Have you ever heard of a place called Fort Mose?"

Nathan looked up in surprise. "That's down in Spanish territory. Far south."

"It be real?" Amari asked.

"Of course it's real. You been heading toward a place that you didn't even know for sure existed?" he asked, scratching his head.

"Amari always believed in it," Polly explained.

"My father does some trading—much of it illegal, I'm sure—and you'd be surprised who shows up here from time to time. I've met French beaver trappers, English gun sellers, and Dutchmen who sell indentures."

Polly tensed.

"Last month," Nathan continued, "a Spanish priest from this place called Fort Mose came through here, trying to teach my daddy the 'one true faith.' Daddy just laughed at the man and told him to get out. Unless a man has a plan where my daddy can make money, he's not interested."

"What man say 'bout Fort Mose?" Amari asked. "Streets of gold?"

"Streets of mud would be my guess," Nathan replied. "It is a small place but different from most. From what I could tell, it is run by Spanish soldiers and priests. Runaways are welcome and given their freedom, as long as they promise to swear allegiance to the Spanish king."

"Freedom to do what?" Polly asked.

"Freedom to stay there, I suppose," Nathan told her. "If you leave, you lose Spanish protection and are subject to the laws of the colonies."

Polly and Amari exchanged looks.

"No whippings?" Amari asked, unconsciously touching her scarred back.

"I would think not," Nathan said, sympathy showing on his face. "How far have you come from?"

"Charles Town. South Carolina Colony."

Nathan looked impressed. "That's an awfully long walk." He was quiet for a moment. "Can you tell me what you were running away from?"

Polly thought for a moment. "A very bad situation," was all she would say. "Do you know the woods around here quite well?"

"For sure," Nathan replied proudly. "I know every rock and holler and tree within a hundred miles. Squirrel and deer see me coming and tremble, 'cause they know they could be my dinner!" He laughed.

Polly felt relaxed with this pleasant young man. She had a feeling that her father would have liked Nathan—taking him fishing and telling him tall tales. She wished she could talk to her father just one more time—ask his advice or listen to him laugh uproariously at his own jokes after dinner. "It is so very kind of you to help us," she told Nathan. She felt herself reddening again.

Nathan looked directly into her eyes. She had to look away. "I will show you the safest path through the forest after you have rested," he said. "Remember to stay very quiet. My father is just plain mean."

The three travelers nodded and snuggled into the clean straw. Polly dreamed of her father for the first time since his death—his bawdy jokes, his weakness for ale, and the soft grin on his face whenever he looked at her. "My princess. My Polly-girl," he would say when he kissed her good night. She slept soundly for the first time in many days.

But the next morning she was awakened suddenly by a red-faced man who held a pitchfork in his hand. He towered over the three children. "What this we got here in my barn? Two niggers? And a dirty little white gal who must be poor white trash if she be sleepin' with 'em!"

Amari jumped back, pulling Tidbit behind her.

"Please, sir," Polly began to say.

Then Nathan appeared in the doorway, his face showing both agony and apology as he looked at Polly. "What you got here, Daddy?"

"You hear anything creeping around last night, boy?"

"No, sir," Nathan said. His voice cracked as he spoke.

"Didn't I tell you about locking the barn door to keep out animals? Never figured I'd have to lock out the likes of this here. 'Course, they ain't much better than animals." He laughed roughly.

"I'm sorry, sir. I thought it was locked." The look on Nathan's face pleaded with Polly to understand—or to forgive.

Polly wasn't sure if she should believe his looks of apology or not. She looked at Nathan with great disappointment. "Let me explain, sir," she began, trying to appease Nathan's father.

"Shut up, gal!" the man roared. He leaned in close to Polly's face. "Trespassers! I'll have the lot of you hanged, lessen there be a reward out for you. If that be the case, I will get my money, *then* see you hanged!"

Polly was terrified, but she continued. "There is a large reward, sir, for the return of these slaves," she said slowly. "I am in the process of bringing them to Savannah. My mother is sick, and we need the reward money." She managed to make a teardrop fall, although he could not know it came from fear rather than sorrow.

The man hesitated. He looked at her closely, tightening his grip on the pitchfork. "Do say, now."

"Sir, can you help me get home to my mother?" Polly begged. "You can have the reward money. I just want to get home to my family."

"You look to me like you be lying, gal. If I find you been lying to me, I swear I'll kill you all. Nathan!" he called suddenly. "Get in here, boy!"

"Yes, sir?"

"Lock the barn tight this time. You hear me, son?"

"Yes, sir."

"After I eat and you feed the animals, we'll take them down to Savannah. I'm going to make me some money on this motley lot one way or another." He strode out of the barn, tossing the key at Nathan.

Nathan turned to Polly as soon as his father was out of earshot. "You must believe me, I did not betray you."

Polly did not reply right away. She stared at him, then, realizing they didn't have much choice but to trust him, she shrugged her shoulders. "Can you get us out of here? We don't have much time!"

Nathan nodded. "If you head due west, you will run into a swamp. It's not pleasant, but he's not likely to pursue you there. Hide for a day or two, then head south."

Polly gave him a small smile.

"How we get out from here?" Amari asked, bringing the subject back to the immediate problem.

"Hit me," Nathan told them.

"What?" Polly and Amari said at the same time.

"Use the handle of the pitchfork. Knock me down. Hit me in the head. Then run for the swamp!"

"I cannot hit you!" Polly exclaimed.

"Give me it," Amari said, picking up the pitchfork. She looked at Nathan and smiled. "You be good person. I hit you not with hate, but with much thank."

Nathan nodded as Amari raised the handle of the pitchfork in her hand.

"Wait!" Polly cried.

Amari lowered her arm.

"Will we ever see you again?" she asked Nathan softly.

"Probably not. My father will beat me for sure when he figures out what has happened. But remember me, will you?" He grinned briefly, looked at Polly for a long moment, then said to Amari, "Do it! Hurry."

Amari swung firmly. The handle struck Nathan's head with a sickening thud, and he crumpled into the straw.

"Is he dead?" Tidbit asked. It was the first thing he had said all morning.

"No," Amari replied as she touched Nathan gently on the neck. "He be fine. Let us flee!" She grabbed Tidbit's hand and dashed out of the barn. Polly took one last glance at Nathan lying there, then followed them.

They hurried across the field, past the sharp edges of the palmetto palms, and deep into the darkness of the woods. Amari led them, as if by instinct, it seemed to Polly, due west, far away from their usual southern route. They dared not stop, but they slowed to catch their breath.

Exhaling with difficulty, Amari said softly, "Follow me." She led them quickly to an area where the ground they walked on was soft and squishy; water oozed between their toes as they walked. "Swamp," she told them.

"Snakes," Polly added, thinking of the slaves in the rice fields.

"Gators," Tidbit whispered fearfully.

"Safety," Amari told them all. "Nobody find us here." They held hands and slowly marched into the sucking ooze. The mud, covered by a shallow layer of liquid slime, seemed to try to grab them and pull them down with each step. Deeper and deeper they ventured into the swamp; soon the muck was to their knees. Thick mud covered their thighs, then their waists.

Amari had to lift Tidbit onto her hip as it became impossible for him to wade through it any longer. Finally, as deep into the swamp as they dared to go, under the shade of a huge mimosa tree with branches that were covered with hanging moss, they stopped. Birds called shrilly above. Something slithered past Polly's leg. She gasped but did not cry out.

They waited. The mud turned cold.

PART NINE

AMARI

37. LOST AND FOUND AND LOST

THEY STAYED IN THE SWAMP UNTIL WELL AFTER dark. No one pursued them. After listening carefully for the sound of dogs or hunters and hearing nothing but the burping of bullfrogs, Amari signaled that they should ease out of the mire. Slowly, the children made their way to the edge of the swamp and collapsed on the relatively solid ground. Thick, black mud covered them completely—it was even inside their ears.

"Nathan must have told his father we went in another direction," Polly whispered.

"He good man," Amari said in agreement.

"Amari, we gotta wash!" Tidbit piped up as he tried to scrape the mud off of his arms.

Amari smiled at the muddy boy. "You look like little dirt ball," she teased. "But rain be washin' you soon. Just wait."

The rain began about an hour later, gentle at first, then hard enough to rinse off the mud and chill the children as well. It rained all night.

"I be so tired," Amari said, shivering, as they stopped to eat some of the food Nathan had given them. She looked at her swollen feet and her insect-bitten legs. The others looked just as weary. "But we gotta use the dark to move."

No one spoke much. Amari walked slowly and without much energy. Just before dawn they reached the outskirts of Savannah, but they made a wide detour to avoid the populated areas. The rain finally stopped, and the warmth in the air felt wonderful.

"Do you think Nathan's father will look for us near Savannah?" Polly asked.

"You wonder about Nathan or his father?" Amari responded with a small smile.

"I don't think he betrayed us," Polly replied. "He is not like his father."

"He be son of evil man," Amari told her. But then she added, "Evil man be father of good man."

Polly looked thoughtful, then voiced the fear they all had been holding. "What about Clay?" she whispered.

No one had an answer.

As daylight approached, they looked for a place to rest for the day. Hushpuppy had a knack for finding huge overturned logs or shallow caves or even abandoned shacks for them each day. He led them this morning to a small wooden shack, not much bigger than an outhouse, hidden in a thicket of trees. Its door, dangling on one hinge, had blown open, so the earthen floor was covered with leaves and animal droppings.

"It looks like it might have been a hunter's shelter," Polly observed.

Amari looked carefully inside and outside the small building. It was clear that no one had been there for a long time. "Safe for now," she stated.

It was so small, the three could barely sit down together, but they were grateful for shelter and a place to sleep, even if they had to do it sitting up. They shared some of the nuts and berries and tried to sleep. Hushpuppy curled up under a tree not far away.

Amari dozed, then was startled awake by the rustling of leaves and the snapping of branches. Something or someone was approaching fast, and there was no time to hide.

A furious-sounding voice bellowed, "Patrick! I know you're in there, man. You can't hide from your responsibilities out here anymore! You're as useful as a lighthouse in a bog! If you don't get home and take care of your family, I swear I'll—"

Tidbit shrieked in alarm as the door flew open and a woman, dressed, amazingly, all in buckskin, stared openmouthed at the three children. Equally astonished, they stared right back. She was a large woman, with ruddy cheeks and stony blue eyes. Thick ringlets of dark hair escaped her bonnet, which also seemed to be made of buckskin.

"What is this? Who be ye? What you done with my Patrick?"

Polly spoke up. "We have not seen anyone, ma'am." She could not think of anything else to say. Amari and Tidbit cowered beneath the woman's gaze.

"Where y'all come from?" the woman asked suspiciously.

"Savannah, ma'am." Amari hoped the woman couldn't sense Polly's lie.

"What y'all doing in Patrick's shed?"

"Sleeping, ma'am," Polly answered, truthfully this time.

The woman stared at them with eyes of thunder for a moment or two, then she sat down heavily on the ground and doubled over with gales of laughter. "Well, I'll be gob-smacked," she said between laughs. "'Sleeping, ma'am,'" she said in a tiny little voice, mimicking

Polly. "Y'all must be on the ockie—runaways for sure—am I right?"

Amari could see that Polly was unsure of what to say.

"What we got here? Two slaves and a . . . What be ye, gal?"

"Indentured servant, ma'am," Polly said quietly.

"Hmmm," the woman replied. "You ever see a pothook, lass?"

"By the hearth?" Polly asked, confused.

"No, around your neck," the woman said. "That be the punishment round these parts for runaway indentured gals. An iron collar with hooks on it."

"Oh, please, no, ma'am," Polly pleaded. "Please, not that."

The woman laughed again. "You've no call to be askert of Fiona, child. I ain't going to turn y'all in. I'm just telling you what the punishment be for runaway indentures. Punishment for runaway slaves be a lot worse, now," she said, looking at Amari and Tidbit.

Amari spoke softly. "Who you be, ma'am?"

"Me? I am Fiona O'Reilly. My pa brought me to this place from Ireland when I was just a wee snip of a thing—'bout the age of that cub you be holdin' on to. He be yours?"

Amari started to say no but thought better of it. "Yes, ma'am. He be mine." She pulled Tidbit close.

"Well, you can't stay here, none of you. My Patrick is a good man but a hard man—a mite lazy, mind you, one who would rather be a-hunting than clearing the fields for harvest, which I guess explains my clothes. He brings me skins, and I make my clothes! I can sew a garment from anything!" She looked down and laughed at her buckskins.

Tidbit could not stop staring at the large, unusual woman. "Your man kill many deer to make that dress for you," he said solemnly.

Fiona erupted in laughter once more, smacking her large thighs with her hand as she chortled, "Little one speaks true, but there be no telling what my Patrick might do if he finds you here. For sure he won't be a-laughing."

"Well, we'll just be on our way, then, ma'am," Polly said as she motioned to the others to gather their belongings to leave. "We don't need any more trouble. It has been a long, hard journey."

"Savannah's only half a day's walk from here," Fiona said quietly. "Methinks you not speak true before."

Polly bowed her head and glanced at Amari. Her look seemed to say, *Trust her.*

"We could use some help, ma'am," Polly admitted. Amari hoped they were doing the right thing.

Fiona seemed to think for a minute, then said firmly, "You're coming with me. Be quick about you, now!" She picked up the edge of her heavy skirt and hurried through the woods.

Amari, Polly, and Tidbit had no choice but to follow the woman, who in spite of her size moved nimbly through the woods. Hushpuppy dashed after them.

Fiona's home, larger than the cabin that Nathan and his father shared, sat neatly between several rows of corn and beans. Amari noticed small shacks off to the right—slave quarters, she knew.

Fiona led them to the barn, which held two wagons, three horses, and numerous pieces of farm equipment. "Climb into the back of that one and hide," she commanded, pointing to the smaller of the two wagons, "until I think of what to do with you."

"You keep slaves here, Missus?" Amari asked meekly as Fiona bustled around the barn, muttering to herself.

"Of course, child. Everybody has slaves. How do you think we handle this land? But my Patrick is a good man and does not mistreat his property. Our slaves like it here." Amari couldn't understand how the woman could see no wrong in owning slaves as long as they were well treated.

"Then why are you helping us?" Polly asked.

Fiona looked at her carefully and thought a moment. "It's like this: If my Patrick brings home a new slave like he did last week, for example, that's his right as master and man of this house, and I dare not interfere. As a woman, I ain't got muckle to say about those kind of decisions. But when I got the chance to decide for myself, I find it gives me pleasure to choose to help you be free. That's the truth, and I did not know it until I spoke the words." Fiona looked immensely pleased with herself.

"Thank you," Amari murmured as she helped Tidbit climb into the back of the wagon.

"Wait here," Fiona told them. "I will send someone in here to hitch up the wagon." She hurried out of the barn.

Amari nervously looked around the barn. "She be good woman?" Amari whispered to Polly.

"Yes, but she is afraid," Polly replied. "I do not think she has ever made her own decision before. I hope her husband does not return soon."

The barn door opened then, and a thin, stooped black man limped over to them. "I'm to harness the wagon," he mumbled, not even glancing at Amari and Polly.

Amari jerked her head suddenly. She knew that voice! "What be your name?" she asked.

"Buck," he answered slowly as he led the large brown horse to the wagon. "They calls me Buck."

Amari knew the perfect modulation of that voice, the deep bass edged with gold. Her mind ran quickly back to the reddish dust of the road that led to Ziavi, the shrieking of the blue turaco birds at dawn, the taste of her mother's groundnut stew. She shook her head to hold back the tears. "Are you my Besa?" she asked in Ewe.

The man looked up quickly. On his face was a small, faded birthmark, shaped a little like a pineapple. "Amari?" he said softly.

"My Besa, my love, I have found you. It is I, Amari!" Her heart thudded as she allowed all her memories to come rushing back. She jumped from the wagon and ran to him.

But just as she reached him and was about to embrace him, he held his hand out and stopped her. "No, don't!" he pleaded.

"Besa!" she cried with urgency. But then she saw—the Besa she had known no longer existed. His right eye was missing. His face, deeply scarred on that side, looked like old leather. Half of his teeth seemed to be missing as well.

"Oh, Besa, what has happened to you?" she asked him, finally touching his arm softly.

"I have had five owners since I saw you last, Amari. Owners!" He spat on the ground in disgust. "To even say the word makes me hate them more!"

"We are alive," she said gently.

"I'd rather be dead!" Besa replied bitterly, glaring at her. "You have been treated well, then?"

She bowed her head. "No. I have not. I have been raped. I have been beaten. I have been made to feel like I am nothing. But I live."

"My spirit is dead," he said, his voice empty. "They beat it out of me with their whips, cut it out of me with their knives, shot it out of me with their guns. I can barely see, and every step causes me pain."

Her stomach churned as she listened to his ordeal. "Come with us!" Amari cried suddenly. "We have run away—all the way from Charles Town. We are heading to Fort Mose, a place where everyone can be free."

Besa looked at her as if she were crazed. "There is no such thing as freedom, Amari. I tried to escape several times. Each time I was caught by their dogs, beaten, and then sold. You will be caught as well."

"We will *not* be caught," Amari insisted. "We have already come this far. Give yourself a chance to believe once more," she pleaded. "Please come with us, Besa." Amari reached out to him again, but he jerked back. She felt her heart turn inside out.

"I no longer believe in anything," Besa told her harshly.

Amari inhaled sharply. *What have they done to you?*

Besa looked up at the faces of Polly and Tidbit, who were peering over the side of the wagon. "You travel with a white girl?" he asked with surprise. "First chance she gets, the white one will turn on you. Trust no one."

"She is my friend," Amari told him stiffly, realizing, as she said it, that it was true. She softened then. "Please, my Besa. You are my past. Come be my future as well."

"No," he said with finality. "I will take no more risks. I have found a woman here—a good woman. She keeps me warm at night, and she carries no dreams in her heart. She is safe." He turned slowly from Amari and finished harnessing the horse to the wagon.

She stood there in the dust, one hand reaching toward Besa,

but the distance between them had become so vast that she knew she could never touch him again.

Fiona returned to the barn then, full of orders. "Put fresh hay in the back of the wagon, Buck," she commanded.

"Yes'm," he said, lapsing back into lazy English.

"You're to say nothing of this to the master when he returns, you understand?" Fiona said to him.

"Oh, no, ma'am. I knows how to keep my mouf shut."

"Well, get on with you, then. I thank you for your help, Buck."

Besa turned and gazed at Amari, a mask of resignation on his face. He limped slowly out of the barn. He did not look back.

Polly touched Amari on her shoulder. Amari covered her face with her hands. Her shoulders heaved; she could barely contain her grief and her anger. *It's not fair!* she screamed to herself. *Look what they have done to him! I hate the whites! I hate them!*

"What is the problem, lass?" Fiona asked with concern. "You know that God prefers prayers to tears."

Amari glanced up at the large woman and shook her head ruefully. *Prayers? What good have they done?* Then she pulled herself back to the reality that faced her. It was hard to hate what the whites had done and be thankful to Polly and this white woman in the same moment. "I be grateful for your help, ma'am," Amari managed to say. "Your kindness make me much happy."

Visibly pleased, Fiona showed them the bundles she had brought from the house. The first was a pile of clothes. "My Peggy, God rest her soul, left this world one year past. She died of the fever. About the age of you gals, she was." She paused.

"I'm sorry, ma'am," Polly said. "You must miss her. We have all lost loved ones as well."

"Yes, I suppose you have," Fiona replied. "Well, you need fresh clothes—those you have on are filthy and torn. Put these on."

Fiona gave the girls two simple dresses, one of blue calico and the other of brown flannel. Each dress was well worn. She had also brought bonnets, aprons, and shoes. Polly changed quickly.

Amari took her time. She slowly peeled off the ragged shift she wore. Fiona gasped as she saw the ugly welts on Amari's back.

"Oh my goodness, child. What happened to your back?"

"Whip, ma'am," Amari said simply.

"You must have been extremely disobedient," Fiona exclaimed.

Amari looked up with daggers in her eyes, but she remembered the danger they were in and struggled to make her face emotionless. "My massa thought so, ma'am," she said quietly.

"Is that a *brand* on your back?" Fiona continued. She reached over and touched the raised and blackened letter on Amari's shoulder. Amari flinched. Full of shame, Amari wished the woman would drop the subject. "We brand our cattle, of course, but I've never bothered to check to see if any of our slaves carry brands. Is that a common practice, dearie?"

"Yes'm," Amari mumbled. It was hard not to explode.

"Well, there's nothing so bad that it couldn't be worse," Fiona said philosophically. She glanced one last time at Amari's back before she slipped on the brown dress, then hurried over to Tidbit. Fiona handed him a fresh shirt and a clean pair of breeches.

"What should we do now, Miss Fiona?" Polly asked.

"You running north?" Fiona asked.

"No, ma'am," Amari replied. "South."

"Why?" Fiona asked, looking perplexed.

"Freedom," Amari replied. "Place call Fort Mose."

"That's in Spanish territory," Fiona told them. "Your journey is one I would not take."

"All we know be dead and gone," Amari tried to explain. "Only left be hope and dreams." She thought sadly of Besa and angrily of their dreams.

Fiona nodded. "My father brought us to this country for freedom, but he died doing it. My Patrick works hard for our freedom, and still death found us. Hope and dreams are all any of us have." She wiped away a tear.

Again Amari wondered how a slave owner could speak so strongly about freedom.

"How far to Spanish territory?" Polly asked after a moment's silence.

"I do not rightly know. But it is too far to walk. I'm giving you all this wagon, lass," she said to Polly.

"What will your husband say?" Polly asked in alarm.

"I'll tell him thieves came in and took it while he was out a-hunting!" Fiona replied with a laugh. "Serves him right for staying away for so long. I'll tell him they took off heading north."

"I know the horse is valuable," Polly added. "We are very grateful." She reached into the sack that Dr. Hoskins had given them, looked briefly at Amari as if to make sure she agreed, then offered Fiona the coins.

"Thank you, ma'am. You be so kind," Amari added quietly.

Fiona quickly tucked the coins into one of her large pockets. "Big Brownie is old and 'bout to die. Better to die on a journey than in a barn, I say. He may get you where you need to go."

Tidbit ran to her and hugged her. "You nice like my mama. Soft like my mama."

Fiona nodded and her eyes welled up. "You children get going. May the good Lord take a liking to you, but not too soon! Here's a bit of food—oranges and biscuits and a little salt pork." She lifted the bundle and put it beneath the wagon seat.

"Thank you for everything, Miss Fiona," Polly said. "Should we travel on the main road?"

"You drive the wagon, lass. Can you pretend to be a mistress?"

Polly hesitated. "Yes, ma'am. I think I can do that."

"If anyone stops you, tell them these two are your slaves. If you think there is danger, hide them under the straw."

Polly nodded.

"Travel by night and follow the road south. I've never been that far, but I hear tell that it goes straight through Georgia Colony to the end of the world—Spanish territory."

They climbed into the small wagon—Polly holding the reins of the old horse, Amari sitting next to her on the seat. Tidbit sat in the back on the hay. Dusk was approaching.

"May your feet bring you to where your heart is. Godspeed," Fiona called as they waved. "Godspeed."

Amari looked back once for Besa, but he did not appear. She shed no tears. Besa was now a memory, tucked away with all the rest of the things she had lost.

Hushpuppy bounded into the back of the wagon into Tidbit's arms just as they pulled onto the road. The moon shone brightly that night, and Amari decided it was lighting a path to her future.

PART TEN

POLLY

38. THE SPANISH SOLDIER

WITH THE WAGON, THEY MADE REMARKABLE TIME.
What might have taken them three or four days walking, they
covered in one evening, rolling not exactly smoothly over the
bumpy, rutted road, but thankfully. Old Brownie seemed to have
regained a bit of his youthful energy, neighing and shaking his
mane at the start of each evening's travel.

Polly chuckled to herself as she remembered a horse her father
had once owned. Old Fart, he had called it because the horse had
had a terrible problem with flatulence. He eventually sold it to a
farmer he didn't like. "One fart deserves another!" her father
had joked, making up funny horse stories, complete with vividly
descriptive sound effects, all to amuse Polly. Her mother had
frowned with mild disapproval at first, but eventually, the three of
them ended up laughing uproariously in front of the hearth that
whole evening. Those were the times she missed—not the days
of hunger or rats or sickness, but the warmth of the fire when her
family laughed.

"What do you miss most about your mother, Amari?" she
asked as they rumbled down the road in the starlight.

Amari was silent for a moment, then she said, "Seem like no matter what I ask her, she always got the right answer. Sure be nice to talk to her one time."

Polly nodded in understanding. "My father wasn't perfect," she admitted, "but my mother truly loved him. She would light up like a lantern when he walked into a room." She paused. "At the end, she was in severe pain, but she was so brave, never complaining, only worrying about what would happen to me."

Amari pulled the reins so the horse would step around a branch on the road. "I never seen my mama scared, never seen her not know what to do." She breathed deeply of the night air. "Even the night she die, she fight like a lion."

"You know, you're brave as well, Amari. Your mother would be proud of you," Polly said honestly. "Your belief in Fort Mose, along with your strength and courage, is what has brought us this far."

Amari shook her head. "I be scared all the time," she admitted. "I never be brave as lion like my mama."

Polly looked up at the sparkling night. "I think of my mother at night as we travel," she told Amari. "It helps." Amari glanced at the sky and smiled as if the thought was comforting.

"What about *my* mama?" Tidbit asked then. "I wanna go back home."

Amari and Polly both hugged him. "We gotta find new home," Amari told him. "Your mama want you to be big boy. You know she love you, even if she can't be with you." Tidbit seemed unconvinced. He put his thumb in his mouth and leaned against Amari.

By day they still hid as best they could, sleeping under the wagon and praying they would not be discovered. There had been no sign of Clay.

Polly noticed that Amari seemed to be having trouble sleeping. One afternoon when Amari woke with a start, covered with sweat, Polly told her quietly, "You must think of your young man as dead, Amari. I am so sorry."

Amari nodded her head in agreement. "Maybe been better if I not see Besa like that."

"Maybe it was a good thing," Polly suggested quietly. "Perhaps it will give you strength to go on."

"Make me feel sick inside," Amari told her. "And angry, too."

Polly traced a pattern with her finger in the dirt. "You know, I never really knew any black people before I came to Mr. Derby's place. I mean, everybody had slaves, of course, but I never actually thought about them. And I certainly never had a black friend before," she admitted.

Amari looked away. "Sometime I hate white people," she admitted softly. "I never hate before I be a slave." She stretched her arms. "I never even see white person until they attack my village. It be hard to have hate feeling and like feeling at same time."

Polly said, "I understand, Amari."

Amari looked at Polly and said shyly, "I think now I have friend with pale skin."

Polly replied quietly, "For certain you do."

Amari looked into Polly's eyes. "If we gets to Fort Mose, you gonna stay?"

Polly didn't answer right away. "I don't know. I have not thought about it deeply. I truly have no place else to go."

Amari shrugged. "I never go back to my land," she said, her voice plaintive. "But this be land of white people. Maybe you find a place for you."

"Maybe," Polly replied thoughtfully.

Amari put her head in her hands and rocked. Finally, her voice full of anguish, she revealed her concerns. "Maybe nothing be there, Polly. Maybe it be no good place. Maybe Besa right and we be catched."

"And maybe he is wrong, and you and Tidbit will be forever free!" Polly said firmly. "You told Fiona that Tidbit is yours. He *is* your child now, Amari. He needs you to be strong."

"Maybe I not be strong enough to be a mother," Amari said doubtfully.

Polly smiled and looked at the sleeping child. "You would die for that child."

"Yes, for sure," Amari admitted. "In my village all women be mothers to all the children. Maybe Tidbit belong to both of us," Amari said.

Tidbit opened his eyes and grinned. "Tidbit belong to Tidbit!" he said cheerfully. Amari's sad mood seemed to lift as she and Polly tickled him. Even when they played and laughed, however, they did it quietly, always watchful of footsteps or danger, always fearful of the return of Clay.

The land in southern Georgia lay vastly undeveloped, with fewer and fewer settlements of farmers. Amari did see in the distance, however, occasional garrisons of soldiers the farther south they traveled.

"Those soldiers make me nervous," Polly whispered to Amari, not wanting Tidbit to hear.

"Soldiers carry guns," Amari said, remembering the men who had attacked her village. "That not be good."

"Let's be extra quiet tonight," Polly suggested.

The moon hid behind the clouds, and the night shadows played tricks on Amari's imagination. She kept looking behind her. Nevertheless, they drove their little wagon carefully and slowly down the deserted path that night. It seemed to shout their location as it managed to hit every bump and hollow in the road.

They'd traveled for several hours without saying a word, when, without warning, a shadowy body appeared about ten feet in front of them. "Halt, who goes there?" the male voice called out shakily.

Polly thought immediately of Clay—perhaps he had found them once more. Amari clutched Tidbit to her, and Polly grasped her arm. She was not sure if the man had seen them. To get so close and then be captured!

The voice spoke again. "*¡Pare!* Halt! I mean, stop, I mean *¡Pare!*" The footsteps moved unsteadily. "If you mean me harm or if you be *un fantasma*—a ghost—go away!" Whoever had been speaking fell silent.

"What should we do?" whispered Polly.

"Run!" Amari whispered back. "Leave the wagon!"

The two girls climbed down to the road, motioning to Tidbit to jump. But Tidbit, instead of silently slipping from the wagon, shouted, "Who be that, Amari?"

The shadowy voice on the road roared. Tidbit screamed. Polly's heart sank. She knew they were captured. But the person on the road didn't grab either of the girls—he reached out and snatched Tidbit from Amari.

Tidbit protested loudly and wriggled to get free. Then the voice yelped in pain, and suddenly Tidbit was back on the ground. Amari grabbed him back close to her.

"He bit me!" a man's voice whined. Polly relaxed a bit. It wasn't Clay's voice and, when she thought about it, not even a threatening voice.

Polly headed toward the man, then stopped. Hushpuppy barked hysterically. The silence of the night completely destroyed, they all stood there on the road like actors in a play, each waiting for the other's next move.

Polly spoke first. "Are you drunk?" she asked, trying to understand the man's unusual behavior.

"*No estoy borracho*—I am not drunk," the man responded. "I never partake of strong spirits, but it might help, however, in this insect-infested country." He belched. "What I am is afraid of things in the night—wolves and bears and such."

"And children?" Polly asked.

"Why not? It is dark and you surprised me."

"He is soldier," Amari said, her voice low.

"Now, that is a fact," the man replied in agreement as he

stumbled on the road. *"Soy un cabo en el ejército del rey*—I am a corporal in the army of His Majesty King Philip V. Of course, I have never met the king, but who am I to question kings and generals?" He burped again. "Greetings to you from *mi país de España*—my beloved home country of Spain."

"You are Spanish?" Polly asked suspiciously. She wished she could speak the language.

"And most proud of it, my dear. And missing my home mightily." He sighed. "I am Domingo Salvador, just another lonely soldier from Madrid."

"So why you grab the child?" Amari asked him angrily.

"The night frightens me. He could have been a bear. *Tuve miedo*—I was afraid," the soldier admitted, seeming to cower from Amari's words.

"I not no bear," Tidbit stated, sounding mildly insulted. Then he giggled.

"What are you children doing out here *a media*—in the middle of the night?" the soldier asked.

Polly replied with another question. "Where are the rest of the soldiers in your company, and why are you out here alone at night?"

"They are asleep, but we patrol the area for English troops and runaways. Me, I would rather be home with my Maria. We had just married when I was called to this service." He swatted at his arm. "All I have for company are *los mosquitos y las memorias.*" He belched once more.

"What do you do with runaways?" Polly asked carefully.

The soldier looked at Polly with bleary eyes. "Officially, runaways do not exist until they leave the colonies. But once they cross *El Río del Santa María*—the St. Marys River—we help them to St. Augustine. King Philip does not believe in slavery of any kind," he told them proudly.

"Which way to this river?" Amari asked warily.

"Just two days' journey down this road," the soldier replied. "Why do you ask? You be *fugitivos,* runaways?"

"Of course not," Polly said. "Maybe you are intoxicated after all. I am returning to my home from a visit to my grandfather's house."

The young soldier replied. "I am sorry to have frightened you."

"Go back to your company, Corporal Salvador," Polly told him, "and I will not tell my father that I saw you on the road."

"Oh, *gracias,* thank you, *señorita,*" the soldier replied as he smoothed out his uniform. "On the morrow I will believe you were all in *mi sueño*—my dream." He then looked at Polly seriously. "Be very careful, *señorita.* The soldiers of the English are cruel and dangerous. The river you need to cross is not far."

"Thank you, sir," Polly said, realizing he was not as simple as he looked.

The Spanish soldier looked at the three children and smiled. "The place you seek, my children, is called Gracia Real de Santa Teresa de Mose. The English call it Fort Mose. It is two miles north of St. Augustine."

Sounding suspicious, Amari spoke up. "What you know 'bout that place?"

Corporal Salvador sat down in the middle of the road. "It is *muy pequeño*—very small. Only about a hundred people live there—just a few families. But they own the land they work on, and *ellos son libres*—they are free—to do as they please," he added quietly.

"What are the people there like?" Polly asked.

"Mostly freed slaves. Some white folk—mostly Spaniards, *españoles*. Lots of Indians from different tribes—Creek, Seminole, Cherokee—all living together. There is nothing like it *en todo el mundo*—in all the world."

"White soldiers in charge?" Amari asked.

The Spanish soldier laughed. "Actually, no. *El capitán* of the fort is Francisco Menendez, a black man. He was once *un esclavo*—a slave."

Amari looked impressed.

"Of course, I know you are not interested in this place and simply returning home to your father," the soldier continued, "but if you should ever be in that location, you would find churches—Catholic, of course—shops, gardens, and simple homes. Lots of *niños*—children—as well." He looked at Tidbit, who scooted behind Amari.

"You are right, sir," Polly said, continuing the pretense that none of them knew what they were actually discussing. "My father must be worried by now. I must be on my way."

Corporal Salvador saluted the small group of travelers and told them gently, "*Buena suerte*—good luck, my children. *Vaya con Dios*—may you go with God." With that, he disappeared back off the road and in the direction of his camp.

"It be real!" Amari said with excitement in her voice. "We must hurry."

"No streets of gold, however," Polly warned. "Not that I believed Cato, anyway."

"Streets of free," Amari whispered. "Much more better." She was grinning.

PART ELEVEN

AMARI

39. CROSSING THE RIVER

THE NEXT MORNING BROUGHT THE SUN, brightly illuminating not only the road, but also Amari's spirits. She could barely contain her nervous anticipation, with images of neatly cobbled streets surrounded by safe stone walls dancing in her head.

"We must be very close to the river," Polly surmised. "I can't wait! Do you think we dare to travel during the day?"

"Yes, we find it now," Amari said as she stretched her arms up to the sun. They hadn't eaten since yesterday morning, and she felt drained and shaky. And in spite of her determination and excitement at being so close to their destination, she couldn't erase the reality that for now the three of them were hungry and thoroughly exhausted. She stumbled as she tried to walk a few paces, then she sat back down on the side of the road.

"Are you are all right, Amari?" Polly asked with concern. "Get back up on the wagon."

"Just tired," Amari replied, but she climbed up without protest, holding on to Polly's hand for support.

"We gotta find something to eat!" Tidbit reminded them.

Amari rummaged in the wagon to see if any food remained. She found one small pouch full of berries. She gave them all to Tidbit. So, when they came across a grove of wild apple trees, Amari could hardly keep herself from shouting with joy. All of them—even Hushpuppy—filled up on the sweet fruit as they crouched as far from the road as they could.

That evening they finally reached the banks of the St. Marys River. It lay dark and smooth ahead of them. The moon shone brightly, illuminating the scene. Cypress trees decorated the edges, their branches and roots leaning over as though welcoming them. Amari thrilled at the sight; it hardly seemed possible that they could be so close to freedom.

Tidbit looked at the river fearfully. "I scared of gators, Amari," he said, pulling away. "This water be real deep."

"You got good reason," Amari replied, remembering that awful day. "But I take care of you."

"I don't see any alligators," Polly said, "but that doesn't mean they're not there. Lots of snapping turtles, though. Look!" She pointed to the gray-black rocklike creatures that moved lazily in the sandy mud on the bank of the river.

"Too far to swim," Amari admitted.

"It's very wide," Polly agreed. "How will we cross it?"

Amari replied, "We come too far to stop now." She could see flickering lights in the distance, indicating settlements or garrisons of soldiers or, maybe, Fort Mose. Her heartbeat quickened.

"We need a boat," Polly replied.

The horse, which had been eating the soft greens that grew by the riverside, whinnied softly. He shook his thick mane and ventured into the shallows to drink.

"Can horse swim?" Amari asked with sudden inspiration.

Polly looked dubious. "Sure, but the river looks awfully wide."

"Maybe we just wish we be across," Amari countered. "We gotta try." She unharnessed the horse from the wagon.

"We gonna ride across the river on back of Brownie?" Tidbit asked, jumping up and down.

"Suppose we fall off?" Polly wanted to know.

"S'pose gator get me?" Tidbit added.

Amari took a deep breath. "We not gonna give up now," she said. She patted Brownie on his neck, grabbed his mane, and pulled herself slowly to his back. The horse didn't seem to mind.

So Amari then pulled Polly up, who reached down for Tidbit. Polly placed Tidbit snugly between them, hugging him tightly. Even though Amari had never ridden a horse before, she found she was not afraid. Slowly, she nudged the horse to the water's edge, all the while watching for alligators or other predators.

The horse clearly loved being in the water. He pulled with all of his might to get free of the shallows, then he seemed to relax as the water became deep enough for him to swim. Hushpuppy swam deftly beside them.

Amari noticed the horse was moving his legs as if he were galloping, heading confidently to the other side of the river. The three riders were wet up to their waists, but the horse was strong and steady, and they did not slip into the water.

"This be fun!" Tidbit cried exultantly as they moved silently on the dark water. He still peered to each side, however, checking for alligators.

Amari held her breath, the excitement almost more than she could bear. Freedom lay on the distant sandy bank of this river. No one spoke. The moon shone brightly, making everything seem to glow.

Hushpuppy reached the shore first and immediately began shaking water off his fur. When the horse pulled the children up onto the sandy beach, Tidbit jumped off right away and cheerfully ran on the wet sand.

Amari jumped off next, hugging Tidbit with joy. "We be free, little one. Free!" She danced around the beach area, swinging Tidbit in the air.

Polly joined in, and Tidbit giggled with glee. Hushpuppy, however, began whimpering. Then he gave a nervous growl.

Amari paused and looked with concern at the dog. Though she couldn't see what was upsetting Hushpuppy, she instinctively grabbed Tidbit's hand and led him away from the shore. Amari turned to warn Polly when she saw it. "Look out, Polly!" Amari yelled hoarsely. Polly turned her head. "Gator!"

The alligator, close to ten feet long, moved with unbelievable speed, but Polly was even faster. She shrieked and scrambled away up the riverbank. The sound of the alligator's jaws snapping together on nothing but air encouraged all three of them to run wildly into the edge of the woods.

Breathing heavily, Polly asked, "Is it gone?"

"It be gone," Amari said as she looked back to where they had run from and scanned the water's edge. "Gators not go far from water."

"I be so scared, I almost pee!" Tidbit admitted.

Safe and feeling truly free, the three travelers sat down on the ground and laughed and laughed and laughed.

THEY SLEPT THE REST OF THAT NIGHT UNDER a tangle of branches that might have been left by a storm. They woke to warblers singing, making melody with a red and black woodpecker that tapped a beat on the trunk of a tree.

Amari stretched, then announced, "Today we go to find Fort Mose. It is time."

"We gonna find food there?" Tidbit asked, rubbing his tummy.

Polly grinned happily. "I expect so! Time to meet the future," she said.

"How long this gonna take?" Tidbit asked.

"Not sure," Amari replied. She knew they were close, but she had no idea whether it would take two days or two weeks to arrive at Fort Mose. Overcome with the enormous thought of finally reaching their destination, Amari felt herself filling up with emotion. She wanted to shout, scream, jump—they had finally arrived!

The three of them climbed back up on the old horse, then headed due south. Amari felt comfortable as the horse ambled slowly through the thick stands of palm trees that shadowed them, for they reminded her of the palm trees in her homeland so far away.

She slid off the horse with Tidbit and walked for a few miles.

"What this place be like, Amari?" Tidbit asked. He alternated between running off to chase the dog and returning to hold her hand.

"Don't know for sure. People be kind, I hope," she replied.

"What if they don't like us?" Tidbit continued as he tossed a stick to Hushpuppy.

"Who not like you?" Amari said to him with a laugh. "You be such a clever little boy."

"Will my mama be there?" Tidbit asked seriously. He had never removed the pouch his mother had placed around his neck.

Amari stopped short. She knelt down on the ground so she was eye to eye with Tidbit. It seemed to Amari that he had grown taller and gained maturity while on this journey. He had seen so much in his few years. "Teenie love you very much, you know that?"

Tidbit nodded, biting his lip.

"She can't be here with you, but she knows you be safe, and that make her happy."

"Is she all right?" Tidbit asked.

"Your mama is glad because she know you be full of joy. That make her smile so big, that smile find you here in this far place." Amari paused, remembering Teenie's lessons and her sacrifice. "Why you think she give you that piece of kente cloth you wear round your neck?" Amari asked him gently.

"So she always be with me," the boy replied. He had begun to tremble.

"What did your mama keep a-tellin' you while you be with her?"

"She tell me stories about Africa and about her own mother, and she tell me, 'Long as you remember, ain't nothin' really gone.'"

Amari, blinking away tears, hugged him. "You gonna always remember?"

"I ain't never gonna forget nothin' she done tell me," the boy said with great seriousness. He squeezed the leather pouch.

Amari raised Tidbit's face so he would look around. "She be in every breeze and cloud, every leaf and flower. She smilin' at you right now."

Tidbit thought about that. Then he asked her solemnly, "Will you be my mama now, Amari?"

She hugged him tightly. "Oh, yes. Forever I will. You be my little boy. Always."

"Polly be there always too?"

"Always," Amari promised again, even though she knew that keeping promises was sometimes impossible in life.

He hugged her back, then asked quietly, "Is I still a slave, Amari?"

Amari looked at the boy with love. "No, Tidbit, you no slave. You free man, just like your mama dream. You never be slave again."

The boy grinned at that. "You be free too, Amari?"

Amari looked up at the vast, clear sky and exhaled. "Yes, I be free too. Never no slave no more."

Amari thought back, however, to what Polly had said at the start of this journey: "Freedom is a delicate idea, like a pretty leaf in the air: It's hard to catch and may not be what you thought when you get it." Amari wondered if this long and arduous journey would bring her the happiness she dreamed of. Maybe this place would turn out to be a terrible disappointment.

That afternoon they finally saw it—the place they had dreamed of for so long. For a moment they could only stop and stare. *Fort Mose. Fort Mose.* The fort itself was a tiny structure, actually— only about twenty yards square. Surrounded by a wall made of logs covered with earth, it carried no markings to indicate what it was, but Amari knew in an instant that this was the place. Surrounding the walls was a ditch filled with those prickly palmetto palms that had sliced them when they ran from Nathan's house. Soldiers, both black and white, patrolled outside the wall, and she assumed more stood watch inside in the watchtower, which stood higher than the walls.

Outside the walls of the fort, small houses with roofs of thatch dotted the landscape, huddled close together as if for protection. Small gardens grew near each house.

"It be much smaller place than I thought," Amari whispered.

"Nathan was right about the streets of mud," Polly said with a small laugh.

"Freedom not big. Freedom not pretty," Amari declared. "But freedom sure do feel good."

"WHAT WE DO NOW?" TIDBIT ASKED AS THEY peeked at the fort in the distance.

Amari could barely contain her eagerness. "We go in!" she said joyfully.

Tidbit jumped from one foot to the other, and Polly kept covering her mouth to hold back a case of nervous giggles. Then, as if they did this every day, they boldly headed down the road toward the tiny fort. The horse ambled behind them.

Amari grabbed Tidbit by the hand, then reached out to Polly with her other hand. Polly gripped it firmly. The two girls looked at each other and understood all that was not said.

And they began to walk. First slowly. Then faster. Finally, almost trotting in anticipation, they walked down the hill, past the first few houses clustered near the road, and directly to the gate of the fort, about a half mile ahead. One house in particular, a small rounded hut made of rough logs and covered with thatch, stood very close to the road.

"Where y'all goin'?" a woman's voice called out.

Amari tensed, then stopped. The woman, dressed in a simple

green calico dress and a bonnet to match, was standing in front of the house and waving to them. Her skin was dusty brown—the color of earth, Amari thought.

A fire burned in front of her house, and the smell of cooked rabbit filled the air.

"Uh, we be heading to the fort," Amari replied cautiously. She held Tidbit's hand tightly, but she released Polly's. Polly stepped back a little.

"Y'all be hungry?" the woman asked.

"Oh, yes'm," Amari replied.

Tidbit crept closer to the woman's woodsy fire. "We be *real* hungry, ma'am!" They all laughed at that, and the woman motioned for them to sit down. Polly tied the horse to a tree.

"How far y'all come?" the woman asked. She spooned three bowls of steaming food for them—corn pudding and roasted rabbit—acting as if greeting strangers was what she did every morning. Perhaps it was, Amari thought. The woman even tossed a bone to Hushpuppy.

"We come from Charles Town, South Carolina Colony," Amari admitted quietly.

The woman whistled through her teeth. "That be a far piece," she said. "You walk all this way, or you come by boat?"

"No boat," Amari replied, thinking how much quicker and easier their journey might have been if they had had a boat. "We walk."

"Hard journey?" the woman asked, glancing at their battered feet.

"Yes'm, very hard," Polly replied.

"Always is," the woman said with resignation.

"This be Fort Mose?" Amari asked, wanting to be absolutely sure they were in the right place.

"Sure is, chile. Gracia Real de Santa Teresa de Mose."

"I done dream of this place," Amari said softly, "for very long time."

"Dreams disappear when you wake up—ever notice that, chile?" the woman asked as she gave Tidbit more food.

Amari looked up in alarm. "Why you say that?"

"Relax, chile. You safe." The woman spooned a plate of food for herself. "My name is Inez. I was a slave in Georgia. Me and my man, Jasper, run away last year and come to this place. We figure we done made it to heaven, then the Spanish soldiers took him away."

"Why?" Amari asked with concern.

"It be like this," Inez said. "The English soldiers control the colonies. The Spanish ain't no saints who think everybody ought to be free. They free the slaves because it makes the English soldiers angry and because England be losin' lotsa money when they lose slaves."

"I don't understand," Polly said, looking confused.

Inez continued. "See, the Spanish own this Florida territory, and it be needin' protection from the English, who they is always fighting with. So they sometimes make the runaways serve in their army before they be truly free. That's where my Jasper is— down in Cuba someplace, serving in the Spanish army."

"But that's not fair!" Polly exclaimed.

"Everything that done happened to you been fair?" Inez asked her.

"No, ma'am," Polly answered quietly.

Amari thought about this, then asked, "You free, Inez?"

Inez smiled. "Yes, chile, I got my papers that says I be free. I be free to work hard, free to be hungry, and free to miss my man. But yes, chile, I be free. Now, tell me who you are and who this little one be," she asked, nodding her head toward Tidbit.

"My name be Amari, and this be Tidbit—he my son now," Amari said out loud for the first time.

"My real name Timothy," Tidbit said quietly.

Amari looked at him in surprise.

"Mama name me Timothy," the boy said, "but I was real little when I was borned, so everybody call me Tidbit. But Mama always told me when I get to be a man, my name be Timothy."

Amari smiled with pride at the child who would one day be the man named Timothy.

"Well, Mr. Timothy, let me be the first to call you by your free name," Inez said, lightly pinching the boy on his chin. To Polly she said, "So what be your story, chile?"

Polly shifted her weight and finished what she was chewing. "I'm Polly. I was an indentured girl. I ran off with Amari and Tidbit because . . ." She paused. "It was very bad when we left." She bowed her head, as if the memory was too much to recite.

"Troubles never be over, chile," Inez said gently. "But it be good to share them with friends."

Polly looked up. "We could not have made it without each other," she acknowledged, smiling at Amari.

Amari returned the smile as she finished eating.

"Food be good thing too!" Tidbit said, interrupting. "More, please?"

As Inez was refilling Tidbit's bowl, Amari asked, "Who live here in this place?"

"Only about a hundred folk. Mostly runaway slaves who now be free. Some Indians. Some whites—mostly Spanish soldiers. Two priests. Everybody gets along because nobody got much. Everybody know everybody else. Sometimes blacks marry up with Indians, sometimes with whites. It sure ain't like nothing else, I reckon."

"Cato be right—little bit," Amari murmured to Polly.

"A few months back," Inez told them, "we had 'bout twenty escaped slaves come here from Georgia Colony. Their massa traced 'em here."

Amari looked up in alarm and thought of Clay. "They had to go back?" she asked. She wondered if Clay could ever, would ever trace them here.

Inez laughed. "No, chile, them folks just stood there and laughed at him—right in his face. He had no power here, so he had to leave."

"So we're safe now?" Polly asked. "Even if someone from Carolina Colony should find his way here, he could not make us go back?" Amari knew that Polly was worried about Clay as well.

"'Bout as safe as you gonna be," Inez replied. "You say your name be Polly?" she asked as she looked at Polly closely.

"Yes, ma'am," Polly replied.

"A young feller come through here just a few days ago, lookin' for somebody name of Polly. A redheaded white boy. Could he be the one you worryin' about stealin' you back to Carolina?"

Polly covered her mouth in surprise. "Is he still here?"

"I thinks not. He might be down in St. Augustine, but I don't know for shure. He mighta said somethin' about comin' back this way. I don't rightly remember. He be a friend of yours or a foe?"

"A friend, I think," Polly replied. Her sunburned skin turned a little redder.

Amari turned to Polly and grinned at her. "So what we do next?" Amari asked Inez.

"Y'all need to meet Captain Menendez," Inez suggested. "He be the one who welcome y'all officially, find you place to stay, and get you registered down in St. Augustine."

"What does that mean?" Polly asked.

"Well, you gotta meet with the priests—everybody here be Catholic, you know. And you gotta promise to serve the Spanish king. Personally, I don't see much difference between a Spanish king and a English one. Both of 'em rich. Neither of 'em ever show up here." She chuckled. "But that be what they makes you do when they takes you down to St. Augustine. Everybody got paperwork, chile, but the difference here is it make you free."

Amari grinned at that, excited to start the process. "Free," she whispered.

At that moment Amari looked up as a tall, dark soldier with black and gray curly hair, deep-set dark eyes, and a spotless uniform walked purposefully from the fort toward them. *He reminds me of Father,* Amari thought with a pang.

The man nodded to Inez, looked over the tired and bedraggled new arrivals, and said in an officious tone, "Welcome to Fort

Mose. I am Francisco Menendez, captain of this fort and responsible for all who live here."

Amari wasn't sure what to do, so she stood up and bowed. Polly did the same and said, "Thank you, sir." Tidbit, copying the two girls, bowed as well, but he leaned too far and fell over in a heap.

The captain chuckled, picked up Tidbit, then sat him down carefully. "Feel free to sit, my children," he said to Amari and Polly with a pleasant smile. "Please introduce yourselves."

Amari made the introductions, telling him briefly of their adventures on the journey and their desire to stay there as a place of refuge. She was amazed at how easily she was able to convey her thoughts in English.

"You have just learned English since you have been in this country?" he asked.

Embarrassed, Amari was afraid she had said something incorrectly. "Yessir," she replied quietly.

"Then I must compliment you on a remarkable job—to learn so much so quickly. Are you ready to learn Spanish now as well?"

Relieved, Amari grinned at him and nodded.

"Life here is not easy," the captain warned.

"Oh, no, sir," Amari said quickly. "We knows hard work. Even Tidbit—I mean, Timothy—is willin' to work."

"I am an escaped slave as well," the captain told them. "I have been recaptured twice and taken back to slavery. But I escaped each time and finally made my way back here. This place is not heaven, but it is so much better than the hell of slavery."

"Yes, sir," Polly whispered.

"How many years left on your indenture?" he asked Polly.

"Fourteen years, sir," Polly told him.

"That's madness!" the captain replied. "This Derby fellow must be out of his mind."

"Yes, sir," Polly said with sorrow. "We saw him kill a slave and a newborn baby the night before we left."

"Well, you will be safe here as long as we have the protection of the Spanish. What skills do the three of you have to offer?" he asked.

Amari thought for a moment. "Before we leave, suh, I feel like I worth nothing. But I knows how to cook and hunt and find herbs. And my mother taught me how to make threads from cotton. My father be a skilled weaver in my village and I watch him as much as he let me. If women be 'lowed to weave here, I got lots abilities," she said proudly.

Inez interrupted quietly, "You got more than that, chile."

"What you mean?" Amari asked.

"Now is not the time," Inez answered cryptically. "Later."

The captain ignored Inez and said to Amari, "Women can do anything they have skills for in this place. Can you build a loom?"

Amari closed her eyes, thinking back to her father's sturdy brown hands and how deftly they had constructed his loom, how nimbly his fingers had danced as he wove, and how magically the designs seemed to appear on the fabric. She wished she had spent more time with her parents when she'd had the chance. "Yessir. I remembers well how my father made it."

He nodded his head with satisfaction. "Good. You can earn good money as a maker of cloth and clothes."

"Money?" Amari asked with surprise. "I be paid for my work?"

"Of course," the captain replied. "Only slaves work for no reward."

Amari looked at Polly and beamed.

To Polly the captain asked, "Now, what can you offer? We all work together here."

Polly, seemingly unsure of herself at first, glanced at Inez, who gave her a nod of encouragement. "I can cook and clean. And," she added as an afterthought, "I can read and write."

Captain Menendez looked up with instant interest. "You are educated?"

Polly looked surprised at the captain's reaction. "Yes, sir. My parents had their troubles, but they taught me to read and write and count."

"There is a profound need for education for the children here," the captain said, his brows furrowed as if he were deep in thought. "Freedom means very little if there is no knowledge to go with it."

"I'd be glad to teach the children, sir," Polly offered.

"We'll start a school!" the captain said with excitement. "Do you think you can do that?" he asked Polly.

"Of course, sir." Polly glanced at Amari and Tidbit, a broad smile on her face.

"Excellent!" the captain said, clapping his hands together. "We have much thirst for learning. I shall have Jesse, our carpenter, make plans to build a small school."

"Can you show me how to make Timothy on paper?" Tidbit asked, obviously impressed with Polly's hidden talent.

"Yes, I can, Timothy," Polly replied. "And much more."

"And you, little man," the captain said, turning to Tidbit, "your job here will be to learn to read and write, but I shall apprentice you to the carpenter, so that you can learn to be a builder as well. Would that suit you?"

"Yassuh," the boy replied. "I be likin' that just fine."

The captain turned to Inez. "Give them the dwelling that had been occupied by Felix and his wife. They have moved down to St. Augustine." Inez nodded.

The captain began to leave, but then he turned back to the new residents of his domain. "Tomorrow we will begin the formalization process. But for now rest, relax, meet the people here. Inez will take good care of you. You are indeed welcome—even your dog," he added with a smile. He saluted and walked away.

Amari was thrilled and her face showed it. It was the first time since she had been taken from her homeland that she had met a black man in a position of authority. "Close your mouth, chile," Inez said with a chuckle. "Round here it ain't unusual to see a black man in charge. He wear his uniform well and be using his power wisely. He been around for a long time. Even the Spanish soldiers don't be messin' with Captain Menendez."

"I like his uniform," Tidbit said as the captain disappeared down the road. "Can I be a soldier?"

"Perhaps one day, when you are all growed up," Amari told him.

"I be fightin' for my freedom," the boy said, pretending to hold a musket.

"All your life, little one," Amari told him. "Take your time."

"I feel good about this place," Polly said with contentment.

"I'm so tired of traveling, I could sleep for a week."

"You do that, chile," Inez told her. "Y'all still got a heap of healin' to do. You got family now—folks who will help take care of you. Go on and rest if you've a mind to."

Polly scooted close to the fire and held her hands out to its warmth. Amari knew that Polly had much to ponder as she gazed at the flames. She, too, had found a place of safety, at least for now.

Inez stood up and said to Amari, "Walk with me, chile. I wants to show you where the captain done give you to stay. It be on the far side of the cornfields."

"Timothy, you stay here and take care of Polly, you hear? I be right back," Amari called. Tidbit, who was busy chasing a chicken in Inez's yard, waved good-bye.

"Even the air here smell free," she said to Inez as they walked.

INEZ SHOWED AMARI THE BOUNDARIES OF THE little settlement—a river, a marsh, and the hills they had traversed earlier. The entire community would fit in one tiny corner of Mr. Derby's plantation, Amari observed, as she walked past the small gardens of the people who lived there. Several people waved. To Amari's amazement, Inez pointed out a blended family whose Spanish mother and Negro father sat in front of a fire with their two children, as well as a family of Seminoles, who lived in the house next to them.

"Everybody here come from someplace else—ain't nobody been here very long. Don't nobody know how long they gonna stay. It just be good for right now," Inez explained. Amari understood.

She thought of Cato, who had dreams of streets of gold. "How this place come to be?" Amari asked.

"Folks been livin' here for a long time, but Fort Mose got made official by the king earlier this year of our Lord, seventeen hundred and thirty-eight," Inez explained. "Fort Mose s'posed to be protection for the town of St. Augustine," Inez said. "The Spanish king ain't no fool."

"How this little spot o' land s'posed to do that?" Amari asked.

"When the soldiers come, it be from the way you come—from north of here. St. Augustine be real important to the Spanish, so we out here as the outpost. I 'spect that's what Fort Mose is all about," Inez replied.

As they reached the thatched cottage that would be her new home, Amari thrilled at the sight. Surrounded by a small garden where vegetables were already growing, the dwelling was much larger than the slave shack she had shared with Polly back at Derbyshire Farms. With a window, a back door as well as a front door, and a hearth for cooking, there would be plenty of room for the three of them. It was perfect! But then Amari had a terrible thought.

"You got fightin' here?" Amari asked with alarm.

"Not much yet, but when there do be fightin', our men gonna be the first to die," Inez told her.

"Seem to me it be better to die for freedom than live as a slave," Amari said with feeling. It was hard for her to absorb the fact that she was truly free.

"Yes, chile, it be hard for a woman to be a slave," Inez replied slowly. "I know—I lived it too. Massa be messin' with you in the night." She kept her eyes away from Amari.

Amari bowed her head and looked at the ground. "For me, it be the son. I was his birthday present."

Inez touched Amari's shoulder with understanding. "How long you been on the road, chile?" she asked.

"I think about two month—it be hard to say."

"You been feelin' poorly on your journey?" Inez asked.

"We always hungry," Amari told her. "Never enough to eat. Never enough rest. But, yes, I been feelin' sickly."

"You ain't sick."

"I ain't?" Amari asked hopefully. "But I feels real bad 'most every day."

Inez paused a moment. Then she said gently, "You be with chile, Amari."

Suddenly, it all made sense—the nausea, the dizziness, the feeling of being heavy and lethargic. "Oh no!" Amari cried. She slumped to the floor of the cottage.

Amari thought with revulsion of the hated nights she had been called to Clay's room. The smell of the lantern by his bed. The stench of his sweat. She thought she would vomit.

"This cannot be. Not now. Not when freedom be in my hand," she whispered.

Inez squatted beside her. "You all right, chile?" she implored.

"No, ma'am. I cannot do this. This child make me think about bein' slave." Amari wept.

"Babies don't know nothin' 'bout no slavery. They just knows 'bout love," Inez said gently.

"I hate it!" Amari cried, clutching at her stomach. She could not erase the image of Clay's hateful face from her mind.

"No, chile. You don't hate it. Already you be lovin' it. In your mind you already protectin' it from the bad memories you carry. I sees the struggle on your face."

"No!" Amari cried out.

"Yes," Inez whispered into her ear. "Your heart be sayin' yes."

Amari did not want to admit that Inez might be right. "I be so scared," she whispered to Inez.

"I know, chile, but you ain't the first. You got women here who will help you, women who done gone through the same thing. Like me," Inez offered.

"You?" Amari asked through her tears.

"I had a chile, my massa's chile for shure. She be as pretty as the dawn—blond hair, blue eyes, and skin the color of weak tea."

"What happen to her?" Amari asked.

"Massa's wife hated that chile. Had Massa sell her when she was not much older than your Tidbit—sold her down to New Orleans. Massa sold his own flesh and blood." Inez gave Amari a hug. "I never seen her ever again."

Amari hugged Inez and swallowed her own tears. "I be so sorry about your baby. You must for shure knows how Tidbit's mama must be feelin'. I hope your child be safe and happy like Tidbit is."

"Lord only knows," Inez said as she looked to the sky.

"I feels so stupid," Amari told her. "I shoulda figgered it out."

"You ain't had no mama to see the signs and take care of you," Inez told her softly. "And it probably was best that you didn't figger it out while you was on your journey. You had to focus on survivin'."

"What I do now?" Amari asked her in alarm.

"Relax, chile. Let nature take its course. You ain't got but a few months to wait."

"My chile be born free?" Amari asked.

"Oh, yes, Amari. Your chile be free."

"Free." The word felt like cool water on Amari's lips.

Inez looked around the cottage. "I'm gonna make y'all a broom for your new place. I'll get Tidbit to help me gather the branches. You stay here and think about your future, chile. It be a good day to spend some silent time. I'll be back directly." She turned and left, heading back to her own place.

Amari placed her hands on her belly, full of wonder and confusion. *I cannot do this!* she thought frantically. She felt like running away from herself, from this new reality. *But I'm so tired—I just can't run anymore. Not from the past. Not from my future.* She closed her eyes and leaned against the wall of the cottage. Distorted images of Clay Derby's face floated into her mind. The most disconcerting image was the look of genuine affection he occasionally showed her. Amari beat her hands on the dirt floor, tears of anger welling in her eyes.

What shall I do? Amari thought helplessly. She willed herself to imagine her mother, who would know what to say and how to comfort her. All of her mother's dreams of growing old and watching her grandchildren play had been brutally dashed into the dust. *This child carries the spirit of my mother,* Amari realized suddenly, as well as the essence of her father, little Kwasi, the murdered people of her village, and the spirits of all of her ancestors.

Amari opened her eyes and glanced out of the small door of the hut to the bright sky above. It was getting close to sunset. She lovingly visualized Afi, who had been the friend and mother she needed during that horrible journey to this land. Afi, who had told her that her destiny lay somewhere beyond those horrors. Amari had understood none of it at the time, but now, perhaps, it was beginning to make just a little sense.

Wiping away a tear, Amari thought painfully of Teenie. "Long as you remember, chile, nothin' ain't really ever gone," she'd said many times. Amari vowed never to forget. She wished with all her heart that Teenie could have come to this place with them. Teenie had also understood that Amari had been brought to this land for a reason, had sensed Amari's strength before Amari knew she had any, and had placed her own child in Amari's care for a chance at freedom.

She inhaled sharply as she thought of Mrs. Derby, of the infant who had been given no chance to live, and of all the other women, both black and white, who continued to suffer as property of others. Amari also said a prayer of thanks for Polly, who was, incredibly, her friend.

Amari refused to think of Clay any longer, for she knew his evil spirit could never touch the love she was already beginning to feel for the child within her. Inez had been right about that as well.

If this child is a boy, Amari thought, *I shall name him Freeman. He will stand tall and proud and be forever free. I shall teach him my native language and tell him of the beauties of my homeland. If it is a girl, I shall name her Afi, after the one who loved me and helped me find my destiny. I will tell this child of her ancestors and her grandparents and tell her the stories my father told me. My child shall never be enslaved,* Amari vowed fiercely.

Amari glanced toward the west and watched the sun set. It glowed a bright metallic copper—the same sun that set each evening upon her homeland. She knew that she had found a home once more.

AFTERWORD

ALTHOUGH THIS IS A WORK OF FICTION, THE FACTS OF the story are true. Fort Mose (pronounced Mo-ZAY) was a real place. As early as 1670, enslaved Africans began to escape and make their way south, rather than north, down the Atlantic coast to the Spanish settlement at St. Augustine, Florida, where they were offered liberty and religious sanctuary. These runaways eventually established Gracia Real de Santa Teresa de Mose, the first free black town within the present-day borders of the United States.

Located two miles north of St. Augustine, Fort Mose was a frontier community of homesteaders from diverse cultures—including Caribbean, West African, Native American, and European—creating a complex family network. Their skilled labor, technological ability, art, music, ideas, and traditions served as valuable resources to the area.

In 1738, when this story takes place, the United States did not yet exist. There were a series of loosely connected colonies, most of which were ruled by England. The area known as Florida, however, was controlled by Spain, which made for some lively clashes and political posturing between the two countries. For example, the Spanish promised freedom to any escaped slave who became Catholic and promised to fight with the Spanish against the English.

A West African Mandingo by birth, Francisco Menendez, formerly enslaved in Carolina, arrived in St. Augustine around 1724. He became captain of the black militia of St. Augustine and fought to ensure the promises of the king of Spain. The black militia was well known in the area for their bravery. Captain Menendez was well respected by people in both Fort Mose and in St. Augustine and had a reputation as a fierce fighter.

In 1740, although the black militia fought bravely against General James Oglethorpe of Georgia, who sought to return escaped slaves back to the colonies, Fort Mose was badly damaged. Most of the citizens of Fort Mose, however, had already been safely moved to the protection of St. Augustine. The fort was rebuilt a few years later, larger and stronger, but it was finally abandoned in 1763 when Florida became an English colony.

Designated a National Historic Landmark in 1994, Fort Mose is now an important designation on the Florida Black Heritage Trail. Although the actual site is now underwater off the coast of Florida, it remains a tangible reminder of the people who risked and often lost their lives in their struggle to attain freedom.

Note to teachers and students about resources: I did years of research to write this book, using hundreds of sources. It is impossible to include in the story all the information that I learned. If you'd like to learn more about this period in history, the list below contains not all, but some of the best sources that I found. Please do not let this list limit your research. There are many more books and Web sites on the subject of slavery and freedom. I offer this list as a service, just to get you started.

WEB SITES
Daily life of slaves: http://www.sciway.net/hist/chicora/slavery18-3.html

Housing: http://www.sciway.net/afam/slavery/houses.html

Hunger and hardships: http://www.sciway.net/afam/slavery/food.html

The work day: http://www.sciway.net/afam/slavery/work.html

Slavery time line: http://innercity.org/holt/slavechron.html

The Middle Passage—the journey of slaves from Africa to the New World:
http://www.juneteenth.com/mp2.htm

Runaway slave ads:
http://etext.lib.virginia.edu/etcbin/costa-browse?id=r38040013
http://etext.lib.virginia.edu/etcbin/costa-browse?id=r38040015

Maps of the slave trade:
http://www.uwec.edu/geography/Ivogeler/w111/slaves.htm
http://www.africanculturalcenter.org/4_5slavery.html
http://exploringafrica.matrix.msu.edu/curriculum/lm15/stu_actone.html

The African/Atlantic slave trade:
http://www.sciway.net/hist/chicora/slavery18-2.html

http://www.pbs.org/wgbh/aia/part1/1narr4.html
http://exploringafrica.matrix.msu.edu/curriculum/lm7/B/stu_7Bactivityone.html

Slavery:
http://www.pbs.org/wnet/slavery/timeline/1731.html
http://www.innercity.org/holt/slavechron.html
http://www.pbs.org/wnet/slavery/resources/index.html
http://hitchcock.itc.virginia.edu/Slavery
http://lcweb2.loc.gov/ammem/snhtml/
http://www.sciway.net/hist/chicora/slavery18-2.html

The Middle Passage:
http://exploringafrica.matrix.msu.edu/curriculum/lm7/B/stu_7Bactivityone.html
http://www.juneteenth.com/middlep.htm

Fort Mose:
http://library.thinkquest.org/CR0213580/fortmose1.html
http://www.pbs.org/wgbh/aia/part2/2h14.html
http://www.oldcity.com/sites/mose/
http://www.archaeology.org/9609/abstracts/ftmose.html
http://library.thinkquest.org/CR0213580/fortmose2.html
http://library.thinkquest.org/CR0213580/fortmose4.html
http://dhr.dos.state.fl.us/services/magazine/01winter/mose.cfm

Indentured servants:
http://odur.let.rug.nl/~usa/D/1601-1650/mittelberger/servan.htm
http://www.stratfordhall.org/ed-servants.html?EDUCATION

Underground Railroad map:
www.cr.nps.gov/nr/travel/underground/detailedroutes.htm

National Underground Freedom Center—Cincinnati, OH:
www.freedomcenter.org

Underground Railroad resource study:
www.historychannel.com/blackhistory/?page=exhibits2
www.nationalgeographic.com/railroad/
www.undergroundrr.com

Slave narratives:
http://afroamhistory.about.com/od/slavenarratives/
http://core.ecu.edu/hist/cecelskid/narrative.htm
http://docsouth.unc.edu/neh/texts.html
http://metalab.unc.edu/docsouth/neh/neh.html
http://lcweb2.loc.gov/ammem/snhtml/snhome.html
http://xroads.virginia.edu/~hyper/wpa/index.html

BOOKS

Blassingame, John W. *The Slave Community: Plantation Life in the Antebellum South.* Oxford: Oxford University Press, 1979.

Captive Passage: The Transatlantic Slave Trade and the Making of the Americas. Washington, D.C.: Smithsonian Institution Press, 2002.

Carney, Judith A. *Black Rice: The African Origins of Rice Cultivation in the Americas.* Cambridge, MA: Harvard University Press, 2001.

Clarke, Duncan. *Slaves and Slavery.* London: Grange Books, 1998.

Currie, Stephen. *Life of a Slave on a Southern Plantation.* San Diego: Lucent Books, 2000.

Deagan, Kathleen and Darcie MacMahon. *Fort Mose: Colonial America's Black Fortress of Freedom.* Gainesville, FL: University Press of Florida/Florida Museum of Natural History, 1995.

Dean, Ruth, and Melissa Thomson. *Life in the American Colonies.* San Diego: Lucent Books, 1999.

Everett, Susanne. *History of Slavery.* Edison, NJ: Chartwell Books, 1997.

Franklin, John Hope and Alfred A. Moss, Jr. *From Slavery to Freedom: A History of Negro Americans.* New York: McGraw-Hill, 1998.

Hagedorn, Ann. *Beyond the River: The Untold Story of the Heroes of the Underground Railroad.* New York: Simon & Schuster, 2002.

Harms, Robert. *The* Diligent: *A Voyage through the Worlds of the Slave Trade.* New York: Basic Books, 2002.

Haskins, Jim. *Get on Board: The Story of the Underground Railroad.* New York: Scholastic, 1993.

Hawke, David Freeman. *Everyday Life in Early America.* New York: Harper and Row, 1989.

Howell, Donna, ed. *I Was a Slave. Book 5: The Lives of Slave Children.* Washington, D.C.: American Legacy Books, 1998.

Johnson, Charles and Patricia Smith. *Africans in America: America's Journey Through Slavery.* New York: Harcourt Brace, 1998. (Also available on video)

Kelley, Robin D. G. and Earl Lewis. *To Make Our World Anew: A History of African Americans.* Oxford: Oxford University Press, 2000.

Kleinman, Joseph and Eileen Kurtis-Kleinman. *Life on an African Slave Ship.* San Diego: Lucent Books, 2001.

Landers, Jane. *Fort Mose. Gracia Real de Santa Teresa de Mose: A Free Black Town in Spanish Colonial Florida.* St. Augustine, FL: St. Augustine Historical Society, 1992.

Lester, Julius. *To Be a Slave.* New York: Scholastic, 1968.

Rappaport, Doreen. *Escape from Slavery: Five Journeys to Freedom.* New York: Harper Collins, 1991.

Thomas, Velma Maia. *Lest We Forget: The Passage from Africa to Slavery and Emancipation.* New York: Crown Publishers, 1997.